GONE
ARE THE
LEAVES

GONE
ARE THE
LEAVES

ANNE DONOVAN

ISIS
LARGE PRINT
Oxford

First published in Great Britain 2014
by
Canongate Books Ltd.

Published in Large Print 2014 by ISIS Publishing Ltd.,
7 Centremead, Osney Mead, Oxford OX2 0ES
by arrangement with
Canongate Books Ltd.

CIP data is available for this title from the British Library

ISBN 978–1–4450–9926–2 (hb)
ISBN 978–1–4450–9927–9 (pb)

Printed and bound in Great Britain by
T. J. International Ltd., Padstow, Cornwall

I

Feilamort: The colour of a dead leaf.

But dead leaves are of different hues. Cooried round the trunk of the mithertree, they shade frae rich gowd tae near-black with everything inatween; edges owerlapping like the fabric scraps I steek intae coverlets.
   Mibbe they are at different stages of death.

Froths of hair trail frae the cowl: grey-brown silk glisks in the weak November sun. The fabric of his cloak was rough and coorse: edges frayed, the warp and weft like tracks in a ploughed field. Bitter needles of cauld must have penetrated his soft skin on the journey; his airms prickled wi gooseflesh when I helped him doon frae the pony. "Merci," he whispered. I mind his een that day, feartness drownt in the brown, grummlin their beauty.
   They were all feart, the wee laddies, but the others hid it neath a shield of jokes and swagger, shoving their neighbour aff the bench, tugging hair, giggling and tickling each other. There was five of them that day, and we brocht them intae the hall, fed and warmed them in front of the great roaring fire. Waiting for the

mistress to arrive, the others jouked about; he stayed apart, crept close to the hearth and lay doon, curled on the harsh flagstones, his body tense, his eyes darting round the room like a whippet who fears he'll be kicked awa frae his place.

My Lady is douce: she smiles and strokes and pets all around her, her voice trills and gurls like a burn in full spate. But she skiffs surfaces, seeks fair weather. Jules, her page, followed her, hauding the train of her velvet frock while she walked the line of lads who stood, backs to the fire. Quiet now, they stared as she examined each in turn, patting this one on the heid, stroking that yin's cheek. Jules was expressionless, but nae doubt he'd be minding the time, three year syne, when he was in their place, and thinking on the months to come when one of them would take his.

They were pretty lads, all of them, the unsuitable already weeded out; boys with harelips, jug-ears, pocked skin, had nae place in My Lady's service. But even as she cooed and murmured to them, asked their names and whence they came, there was nae doubt in my mind which she'd favour. When she reached him she stared, as I'd seen her gaze intae her glass while she decided which necklace to place round her bonny white neck. His hair tummled tae his shooders, touslie grey and brown like the bark of a tree. His skin was clear, as though he'd been fed naught but milk and honey, and his lips curved like a lassie's, bramble-stained. The fear was still there in his een, but it lessened, and he gazed at her like a calf.

4

"Mon petit. Et vous est . . .?"
"Feilamort."

I was in my thirteenth year then, three-four year aulder than the laddies who had arrived. My family was neither ower-muckle nor poor, and we were all in the service of our Laird and His Lady one way or anither, our lives thirled to theirs. My faither assisted the steward and my auldest brother assisted him, while my mither supervised the care of fine linens and laundry. I sewed and mended, ran and fetched, up and doon the back stair, invisible except when needed.

At nicht I slept with the other maids, at the far end of the passage frae My Lady's chamber. The wee lads, the new pages to be, were in the room next to ours. Their noise and cairry-on soon subsided for they were wearied after a long day, and, in spite of their bravado, lonely for hame. As I lay in the neardark, just a glimmer of moon, I heard a snuffling sound, like a pup. I kent it was him and I slipped frae under the blanket I shared with my sister Catriona.

The others slept sound, in a row on their pallets. He was at the end, hauf-in hauf-out the covers that the boy next him had harled awa in the nicht. Een wide open, he gazed at me. I covered my lips with a finger to indicate silence, held out my haund and led him in beside me. His wee shivery body gradually warmed, and I lay, his back tucked intae my front, watching his breath rise and fall in the grey moonlicht.

★ ★ ★

I saw little of him or the others the next few days. Their training had begun, and they were the province of Douglas, whose job was to harden them, initiate them intae mysteries in which women had nae place. The days were short and the licht poor. I sat close by the slit of a windae in the chamber next My Lady's, fingers stiff wi cauld, stitching. I loved the feel of the needle pushing through the fine cambric, the near-invisible track of white on white, steeks tiny as a spider's footprint. My mither's daughter, I'd been an apt learner, progressing quickly frae baissing and ranter tae invisible seams. Noo I was trusted tae surfle a sleeve wi lace and work some of the brusery, patterns of twined leaves on a shawl. My mither still made the special garments: the priest's vestments, the gouns worn by my Laird and Lady for important occasions. But with the passing of time even the sharpest-eyed seamstress would find her gaze pearl ower like a misty morn. My grandam kept sewing till she was near-blind, working by feel alone, but she was rare. In time, my mither would let me tak ower mair of the delicate work while she supervised.

But in the poor licht there were only so many hours you could sew and I was needed for other tasks. I was glad tae fetch watter at the well, for it was warmer outside than in, and, best of all, gang doon tae the kitchen, where there was aye a bleezing fire. Scouring the big pans warmed ye up and you could blether while you worked. And Elinor was there.

Elinor was around my age but seemed far aulder. She was aye scripping at me, in jest.

"You're a richt babbie, you know nothing."

"Time enough you'll know too much," my mither would answer when I asked her about something Elinor said.

The day her talk was of the young laird who was visiting the castle with his family.

"Look at all this food. Louis is beeling that we've tae use so much of the salt cod — he says we'll have naething left tae see us through the winter — but My Lady insisted."

"Why is he so important?"

"He's going tae marry Lady Alicia."

"Lady Alicia's just a wee lassie."

"She's auld enough tae be betrothed. And the Laird is desperate tae unite their families."

"Though," she whispered in my ear, "Jules says he's already united their families, the way he looks at the boy's mither."

"How d'you mean?"

"Oh Deirdre. Jules seen him ficherin wi the lady at the top of the back stair. He doesna know if that was all he done, though Louis says the Laird prefers the back road tae the front and that's how he's only got the one lassie, though he and My Lady have been married lang enough tae faither a whole brood of boys."

"I dinna ken what you're talking about."

"Ach, you'll learn soon enough."

The silvery wab sclints in the low sun. Shining draps strung atween the branches of the rowan. Here and there a tiny beastie, like a French knot embroidered on it. Nae sign of the wyver who spun the wab; mibbe he's awa, working on anither already.

I was sent tae gather firewood frae the big pile in the corner of the yard, but I seized the chance tae pause for a minute, watch the beauty. When I see a wab or a leaf glaizie wi licht or the remnants of the rain clinging tae a branch, I long to haud on tae that moment. I wish I could embroider something this fair but, nae matter how I try, I ne'er succeed. Even when my mither let me stitch some of the wee pearly draps on My Lady's collar — warning me within an inch of my life what would happen if I lost one, they're that valuable — it wasna as bonny as a raindrap in the sun.

The priest says that nothing can compare to the creation of the Lord and he's richt, nae doubt. But I yearn to mak something with which I could feel satisfied.

A feathery sky seemed as if t'were about tae float doon upon our heids. Inatween the clouds was cleaner than any blue you see in summer: autumn blue against a tree gowden wi leafs ready tae fall at the least whisper of breeze. Azure like Our Lady's robe.

"Bleu," he says, "but the Italians say azzurro."

I've escaped frae the hoose this morn, collecting chestons for the kitchen. The lad tagged alang; he's taen tae following me like a wee dug when I gang outside. My mither encourages this. She doesna like my being out alane, no since my bleeding started; she willna speak of it but I ken fine the reason. Last year Margaret, the cooper's lass, was got with child when she was barely ages wi me. Some tinker's lad passing through at harvest time and ne'er seen again. She'd nae idea whit happened, said she thought the laddie was playing a game. "Knowing Margaret, it would be the truth," says Elinor.

I love tae run by mysel through the woods or lie on the brae, gazing at the clouds or the trees, and it's no the same if I have tae go wi one of the ither maids. But this laddie is different. He's that quiet it's like having a wee deer or a squirrel follow ye, peaceful like. He and I exchange the words for colours and trees as we go, nae mair.

"This yin is still green."

"Vert."

"And this is yella."

"Jaune."

We stood aneath an oak, and the wind blew a scour of leaves ower us, broidered his grey-brown hair wi gowd.

He laughed. "What call you when . . ." he waved his airm downwards through the air.

"When they come doon, you mean . . . they tummle."

"Tomber."

"Like tomb."

Autumn is the season of death yet tae me it is mair alive than any. Leaf fall, tomber, is death, but whit a bleeze of glory precedes it: brichtness like a pain through the heart.

My mither, who has looked on many deathbeds, says it is so for those about to souch awa; the soul, ready to leave its earthly hame, becomes mair true, and you see the person clothed in their real self, no the worn-out auld rags they bore in the everyday. I mind my grandam in her last days; though her een were filmed like lace, it was as if she could see beyond everything. In life she was a busy wee body, blethering and footering intae all things, but at the end, calm like a pointed star, she made me understaund the priest's tales of saints. Afore my grandam's passing I thocht naebody was like these folk, eyes raised tae heaven, seeing beyond the earth, but Grandam truly saw intae anither world.

Of course, they're no all like Grandam. Many a time when I was wee, I'd be sent out tae play, far frae the screams that would thicken your blood. Auld Jock the Miller fought his way out of life, kicking his legs as if he were on a march. I think I understaund him better; I dinna ken whit Heaven could be if it's no like the leaves in autumn, especially on a morn like this, when the frost draws every vein with silver. Me and the laddie scuff our way through the fallen ones, as wee birds follow each ither frae branch tae branch. Sheltered under a tree I see a brichtness and bend tae look mair closely.

"Feilamort," I say. "Look."

We bend, our heids close. It's a pink rose, frosted, but still alive and in bloom.

November is the month of the dead, when we remember those who have gone afore us and pray for their souls. My grandams, my grandfaither I never kenned, the twa sisters and one brother who died as babes: our family is fortunate, our losses no so great as many ithers'. Helena, who scours the pots in the kitchen, lost every bairn she's ever conceived, some afore birth, some while they still suckled. One, a wee lass wi gowden curls, lived till she was three. "A faery child," my mither said, shaking her heid as she sewed. My minnie isna one for greeting — she sheds her few tears in private — but her een mist when she speaks of this bairn and her voice is aye saft wi Helena.

"Tae loss a bairn is the hardest thing for a woman to bear, but to loss them all ... some day you will understaund, Deirdre." She looked at me. "Sometimes I wonder if you would be better never to bear them at all. What would you say to the convent?"

"I hae no mind to the convent, Mither."

This isna entirely true. Twa Sisters come tae the castle for provisions each month. Sister Felicity is auld with a face like a cloutie dumpling and breath like rotting kale. But Sister Agnes has skin like parchment and lang white fingers. Elinor's sister went intae the convent and she tells tales of clean white sheets and bells for prayer ringing through the nicht. Sometimes I think it would be grand tae have your life laid out like a track: nae mud, nae doubts, just a path to God, simple and straight and paved; all you'd need to dae is to thole it. But then I think on the leaves, and I want the mud and the stour and the guddle of another life, and surely the mess of a baby is preferable to the cleanness of a cauld bed.

★   ★   ★

The trees long for us. Their branches dance in the wind and the dry leaves send a shower of notes across the sky. The birk spreads itsel across a coverlet of leaves, shelters us. My grandam tellt me of the aulden days when the forests streetched for miles and you could loss yoursel in them, ne'er be found. Wolves and wullcats skulked in the darkness, bogles and bodachs made it their hame. But they cut them doon, the nobles, for boats and weapons and fancy furnishings. These few trees we hae left are all the mair precious.

We sit in silence. Only when I'm wi him can I stop and contemplate the trees. My sister and Elinor think I'm daft; if there's any time on a fine day they'll lie and sleep under a tree, no look at it. The laddie feels the longing too: his silence is restful to the heart.

Last nicht he sang and the sound of angels rang through the great hall, like a flocht of siller birds swooping and diving. Lintie and throstle, feltie and laverock, cheetle and chirm and chirple. He seemed transparent, as though you could see through his skin: he and the voice as one. Silence was the only fit response.

My Lady clapped and gushed ower him, petted him as she does the whippet who lies at her feet. My Lady is a fine singer hersel and loves the voices of boys. Each year a page is chosen for his voice, but never have I heard one like this.

My voice is like the craik of a craw; I mouth the words of the hymns in chapel. But there is nothing I love mair than beauty, be it a leaf, or a cloud or a clear note. Some year syne I tellt my mither how I see God in

12

the trees and the flowers and the sky and she made me confess to the priest. He said it was a deep sin — thou shalt not have false gods before me — though not mortal as I wasna auld enough to have full knowledge or consent of what I did. I dinna understaund what is wrang with finding God in His works; surely that which is sublime is the best path to Him.

There is a bleezing fire and great sconces line the walls, throwing shadows. My Lady's jewels glint in their licht. The tables have been cleared and the room made ready for dancing. Each year up till now I have danced with the ither maids and wee lads, loving to birl till my cheeks were pink and my heart gowpin. This year I sit in a quiet corner, watching. I canna jump and skip wi the wee ones, my body has grown in ways that mak me uncomfortable and feart that I will be looked at. I am different frae my sister. Catriona is only twa year aulder but she is a young lady; my mither and faither are already planning a husband for her. She dances with grace, she smiles at her partner and I can see the heids turn tae look at her in her new goun, made by my mither frae one of My Lady's castoffs.

Naebody looks at me. I dinna ken whether to be glad or no; the priest says it is a blessing to be plain, a woman shouldna attract the attention of men. In front of me are the mairried women, blethering of their babes and men. Further ower the auld men congregate round the ale. A rustle behind me and I turn my heid to see Feilamort creep frae his place wi the pages and settle hissel on the hem of my cloak, coorying in. I turn and

13

wrap an end ower him. He looks up wi they big broon een and smiles afore he closes them.

The next day Elinor tellt me that the Lady Alicia isna going to marry the young laird after all.

"They're all leaving in the morn, at first licht."

"But whit has happened?"

She paused frae scrubbing the big table.

"Naebody's saying. Louis thinks My Lady found out about Her Laird's dalliance wi the mither of the lad but I dinna think she cares a wheen for his cairry-on. Mair like it's her fancy for the lad that's put a stop to it."

She pushed a lank of hair awa frae her face; her brow was drint wi sweat.

"I dinna ken whit you mean, Elinor."

She laughed.

"Ask your mither tae spare you frae the sewing a day or twa and help oot in the kitchen. You're needing these innocent wee een opened." She gied my breist a squeeze through my gounie. "You're coming alang. It disna dae tae be too innocent at your age."

I felt my face flush hot. "I ken whit happens atween a man and a wumman, I ken it's like the kye and the sheep. But I dinna ken whit you mean about My Lady."

"You must be the only one, Deirdre. My Lady is much younger than Her Laird."

"Aye. The Laird's an auld man."

"And she was bare your age when she became a bride." Elinor continued scrubbing, makking lang strokes across the wood. "When the twa of them sit thegether it's like a sweet young berry next an auld

14

wrinkly russet laid up for winter. Imagine that on a pillow. Or under a coverlet."

I said nothing. I kent I shouldna be speaking like this — if my mither heard us she'd thrash me — but I couldna help mysel. I wanted tae hear mair.

Elinor looked round tae see if aabody was near, then said in a low voice, "She loves the lads."

"Whit lads?"

"Deirdre, ye ken that only Marie is permitted tae serve My Lady in her bed-chamber?"

I nodded. Marie is the maid My Lady brocht frae her hame; she speaks French with her and she is the one who combs her hair and helps her wi her dressing.

"Mind last year when Marie was taen ill, real bad wi the gripping pains in her guts and had tae tak to her bed for twa days?"

I dinna, but I nod, wanting to hear the story.

"My sister Frances had tae serve My Lady in her stead. I had hoped it would be me, I am the elder after all, but then, mibbe she kenned I'd be too observant."

Frances doesna see much and says less.

"But even Frances noticed. At that time it was the young esquire — Fraser, I think — but she's fickle, changes with the wind. She likes tae tak her pick of the lads when they get tae fourteen or fifteen."

"Whit aboot the Laird. Does he no ken?"

"He kens richt enough but turns a blind eye. He's danced the reel o bogie plenty times hissel. But mibbe it was too close tae hame when she picked on the lad intended for her ain dochter."

My Lady spends hours on her knees in the chapel, attends Mass each day and pores ower holy books. Many a time as I sat stitching in a corner of the hall, I have seen her walk up and doon, conversing with the priest on points of doctrine.

"But she'll go tae Hell."

"Mibbe she'd rather have her Heaven in the here and noo."

They left the next morn, and made their adieus with all the fyke you'd expect, nae sign that there was any ill feeling atween them. I observed the young laird kiss My Lady's haund, and it did seem tae me that there was a look of longing, of hesitancy in his bearing. But then he was a daft loon, gangly as a colt, legs too lang for his body. My Lady showed nae sign of disturbance, she was as elegant and gracious as ever. And Her Laird bade them fareweel wi his usual heartiness.

Elinor's words had been running through my heid last night afore I went tae sleep. How would it be for a lovely young woman tae lie wi a man like the Laird? He was what my mither called a fine man; he had a barrel of a chist and sturdy legs, a red and wrinklit face and muckle haunds. His laugh rang out rough and ready and he was happiest out of doors wi the men, riding or hunting. My Lady's music and manuscripts meant nothing tae him. The widow lady who was the mither of the intended was fleshy and bightsom, ate weel and laughed hearty at the table. The twa of them were surely a better fit. I could imagine the Laird's haund on her rump as she ascended the narrow staircase afore

16

him, while My Lady's faery beauty was mair suited tae the slender youth.

My cheeks flushed again. I must turn my mind frae sich things or I will need tae confess tae impure thochts and I couldna bear that.

We processed frae the castle: my mither and faither aheid wi my wee brithers; Elinor, Catriona and I following. On Good Friday the church had been bare, the statues covered, the tabernacle empty, Our Lord crucified. On the third day He is resurrected: bells ring out and the chapel is a bleeze of licht, flooers everywhere, mair lovely than any Easter I had kenned. This year the Archbishop was to say Mass and a special choir had come a distance. Their choirmaster had studied ower the sea wi a famous musician, and was counted the greatest in the land. The Laird had paid for everything.

"The prayers and masses will tak the rest of this year tae get through," said Catriona.

Elinor laughed. "They say the Laird's indulgences would streetch frae here tae Rome and back. But mibbe he is mair afeart of death than in the past, and thinks to mend his ways."

"Surely he's no ill?" I asked. The Laird strode at the heid of the procession, My Lady on his airm; nane could look as freck as he.

"There's mair quarrels among the nobles; thus far we have kept out of them, but if it gets worse, the Laird may no be able tae avoid trouble."

"There's aye skirmishing and bickering," said Catriona, as we entered the pew behind my mither, who turned and quieted us with a look.

The Easter service is the loveliest of the year, wi bells ringing and much incense; we light the Easter candle, reciting the promises made at baptism. Though the readings are ower-lang, ye can sit and look round at the flooers and candles, at all the folk dressed up in their best. I love to gaze at the statue of Our Lady, with the stars round her crown and the babe in her airms. The Archbishop's vestments were white for Easter but with gold broidery; it would be fine indeed to mak vestments like those.

At Communion, I knelt at the altar and Father Graham placed the host on my tongue. The breid melted tae nothing and I returned tae my place, filled with the wonder of it, the body and blood of Our Lord. The church was full; folk were restless and the bairns footered and whispered, but when the choir sang, all was stillness. It was that different frae our usual Sunday Mass, where all sing thegether, whether craws or linties. The choir, come frae Stirling way, was famed for its harmonies. Their choirmaster composes settings for the Mass hymns and each section of the choir had its part; some were high and some lower, but they blended thegether with sich perfection. They sang a hymn I hadna heard afore, one which lifted the heart to Heaven. I listened, lost in its loveliness, then, efter the first twa verses, I heard something even mair beautiful, as though an angel had joined the earthly voices. Feilamort had begun to sing. I watched him in the pew across frae me; the laddie was oblivious to the effect of his voice, it was as though he sang to hissel and there was no one around him.

After Mass there was much feasting at the castle where the high heid yins and the choir were entertained in lavish fashion; I was needed in the kitchen and kept busy the rest of the day. When the guests were served and we paused for food, there was a jolious time as we listened tae the news of Stirling frae Andrew, the groom, and his lads who accompanied the retinue.

"What is the speak of the toun, Andrew?" asked Louis, pouring him some ale.

"Weel," answered Andrew. "Did ye no hear about the Abbot, who thocht he could fly?"

Douglas pointed to his cup. "I hae thocht I could fly mony a time mysel, but only when I had a bittie too much of this."

Andrew grinned. "I dinna think ye can blame the ale in this case," he said. "He's a gloustering wee bauchle, aye strushing about the place. Nae doubt he thocht he was going tae flee up tae Heaven."

"Whit happened?" Archie, one of the wee laddies, knelt at Andrew's feet, gazing up, desperate tae hear the tale.

"A set of wings were made for him. Bonny they were too, constructed frae the fedders of eagles."

Archie's een shone.

"He climbed up on the battlements, where he strutted back and fore for all tae admire. The gentry was up there wi him and us common folk stood underneath, watching. Then he spread his wings . . ."

Andrew streetched out his airms, mimed the flapping of a bird. "And took a heider ower the battlements."

"And did he fly?" asked Archie.

"Did he get killt?" asked Douglas.

We all waited as Andrew took a sup of his ale.

"Did he peuch! He fell in the midden ablow."

We were all laughing, and wee Archie chuckled that much he near fell ower.

Andrew went on. "He got up, his fine claes clarted frae heid tae fit in keech, and started blaming the mannie who made the wings. It was all his fault, announced the wee gamphrell. He must have used the fedders of hens insteid of the plumage of eagles, and since the hens covet the midden and no the skies, the wings wouldna tak him upward."

While we were having a merry time in the kitchen, much had happened upstair and, in bed that nicht, Catriona tellt me about it.

"Efter the Archbishop left there was a great row between the Laird and My Lady. The choirmaster had asked My Lady to send Feilamort tae the sangschool and be trained up to join the choir. My Lady doesna want to let him go but My Laird says it will pit them in good stead with the Archbishop and thus with the King."

"Shush," said a voice frae the ither side of the room. Catriona moved closer to my ear and lowered her voice.

"She refuses and My Laird says she is a selfish — I will not repeat the word — who thinks only of her ain pleasure and what use is a singing lad to her, she can get a dozen of them. And she says not one with a voice like this and he says that is why he should be singing for the glory of God and she says much you think of the glory of God, you are only thinking of your ain skin."

The arguments atween My Lady and the Laird continued and, while they rarely sparred in public, it was obvious frae their demeanour that things werena douce. My faither seemed trauchled too, no about their fechting but about the land.

Catriona was now betrothed to Robert, a steady lad who worked alangside our faither, and she took great pleasure in explaining all he had tellt her about the matter.

"It's all about the feu-ferming, Robert says."

"Whit's that?"

"The tenants of the King's lands, the lairds and the gentry, will now be renting them in perpetuity insteid of a fixed term."

"Is that no a good thing?"

"The new feu is thrice the auld one and the lairds have tae pay it all in advance. They dinna ken how they will mak any siller. Robert says the King is trying to raise a heap of money so he can have all his fancy palaces and pictures and boats."

Catriona shook her heid. "But whit can they dae? At least the Laird has the prospect of keeping the land. There is talk that some of the nobles, men who have farmed their land for a hunner year, have had it taken awa and given to those who are friends of the King. It is wise to remain on his side."

The time when trees turn gowden and rid is the bonniest of the year. One misty morn, Feilamort and I jouked out without being seen, walked in the forest. Dampness sparkled, specks of watter dreeping doon like pearls on a lady's ballgoun. The wind had been strong the nicht afore and our path atween the huddled trees was strewn wi leaves. Further on, in a place exposed tae the scourge of the weather, a young birkie had been uprooted and lay on its side like a wounded fawn, severed frae the earth that nourished it. I turned awa, unable to look at it.

When we returned, my mither called me.

"Lady Alicia is to have a new dress, a special one. And I want you to embroider it."

"Oh thank you, Mither."

She smiled. "I ken you are ready tae tak on something like this. And if it pleases Her Ladyship, she may let you work some of her ain dresses."

Lady Alicia is a bonny wee thing wi skin white and soft as snaw. Her hair is bricht copper and glinting in the sun; it curls and ripples like a bush in autumn, sparkles like the gossamer. The dress is of emerald velvet and I am tae broider a panel on the bodice. I look at the threids my mither has laid out on the table. We are fortunate for My Lady brocht fine fabrics and twines frae her hame in France and she has mair sent ower whenever she can. Usually the pattern is laid out and I fill it in, mibbe choosing atween red or deep blue. But the day I am tae tak whitever I wish under my mither's supervision.

I choose gowden yellow, crimpson and ochre.

My mither watches carefully, says nothing. I ken she is thinking that young girls usually wear lighter colours.

"Vert, jaune, wald, vermeloun. This is a dress of autumn. These colours will make Lady Alicia's pale skin glow and her rid hair sing."

"Aye," says my mither.

I sit with my minnie and the other women. The act of sewing pleases me, maks me calm and contentit: the rhythm of the needle pushing in and out, tiny stitches forming a line and a pattern. And now I am permitted my ain flichts of fancy: berries and leaves intertwine, and a bird keeks frae under a tangle of leaves.

We dinna talk as much as the folk who work in the kitchen. We are up the stair, close to the chaumers of the Lady and the Laird (no that he is often tae be seen indoors during the daytime) and too much mirth and chatter isna seemly. The women speak a little of the betrothal and the fine party which is to tak place but my mither keeps a sharp eye out for any talk which would be frowned upon or anything she thinks I shouldna hear. I dinna mind, I ken Elinor will report the claik of the kitchen. And, in any case, I am happy here in the clear light of the morn.

Feilamort lurks in the shadows. He has been excused the usual duties and training in case he catches cauld and is unable to sing for the party. My Lady suspects his chest is weak; she feeds him dried fruits and wraps a cloak round him. Certainly he has never looked strong. The other lads are filling out under the regime of fresh air, riding and archery practice. They are big and bonny, skin coarsening frae being outside. But his skin is like the vellum in My Lady's books, with a creamy transparency.

They've been running up and doon stairs since early morn. Louis is grumbling and clattering pots while the rest of the servants scuddle like mice to dae his bidding. The castle rings wi licht and laughter, voices blether in different languages. We ken the sound of French frae My Lady but Jules says there are some Spanish and Italian too. The guests' voices ripple and trill; ours are rough and burr-like in comparison. Their servants are housed in all the best places while we are stuffed intae cauld corners.

Lady Alicia is to be bethrothed again, this time to Monsieur Jacques, a young French lord whose faither is cousin to My Lady. It is perceived wise for them to mak their alliance with this family frae ower the watter, rather than within Scotland, since naebody kens how the wind will blaw and who will fall in or out of favour.

Louis has befriended their cook, Alphonse, and I hear the speak of the kitchen frae Elinor. According to Alphonse, the young lad's parents are charmed by My Laird and Lady.

"Mercifully, no as charmed as the last lot," laughs Elinor. "Her Ladyship has mair sense than tae start her haivers this time."

"So the betrothal will go aheid?"

"It has all been sorted by thon Monsieur Garnet," says Elinor.

"Who's he?"

"The French lord and lady's adviser. He's aye sniffing round the place, kens aabody's business. Alphonse says young Jacques and Lady Alicia are baith related tae some auld man who has nae heir and if they make a match, they will inherit a castle and a fortune."

They all seem guy happy wi the arrangement. The French lord rides wi the Laird, the ladies discuss their children and the French fashions, and at nicht they all come thegether to dine and dance and listen to the music. Lady Alicia and the young French lad lead the dancing. He is lighter on his feet than the last suitor, capers and gigs with grace. Lady Alicia is stiff but no awkward, aye a solemn lass. The colours of the dress tak fire in the licht frae the torches, bleeze in harmony wi her hair till she looks like an autumn tree hersel, douce and graceful. My Lady speaks to my mither, who in turn beckons me. I cross to My Lady, clumsy and embarrassed at her attention. I curtsy, barely daring to look at her. She holds out her haund tae me, its emerald ring clawed ower her bonny white finger.

"Ma petite, you have done well indeed. What a pretty sempstress you are turning into. You follow your bonne maman. I will ask for you to embroider one of my gowns too."

"Thank you, My Lady."

The dance ended and Feilamort came tae stand in front of the ladies. I looked round, feart I wouldna be able tae return to my place. My mither motioned me behind her, close by where I could see everything but stay out the road.

It is usual for merry tunes to be sung on these occasions; all must be licht and joyful. But Feilamort sang a doleful melody that tore at the heart, his throat rounding and clinging to the notes as though he couldna bear tae let them go. Listening tae him you felt as if you were fleeing with the notes, cupped inside them. I had ne'er heard this song afore and didna understaund the words, but the feeling of longing, of being left and lost, choked my heart. All around I could feel the silence; even the servants attending to their masters stood reverent.

"Mon petit, mon petit," My Lady cried. "Even more beautiful than usual, but why so sad?"

Feilamort looked at her with big brown een.

"La vie est triste, Madame," said the French lord.

"No, no, not at a betrothal. Now sing something heureuse."

And Feilamort sang again, this time a merry tune, but his voice so plaintive that its joyousness was tinged like a November sunrise, when it is hard tae ken if the sun is coming or going.

Monsieur Garnet was the only one no enraptured by the singing. Sleekit and weaselly he seemed, his face thin and dark, the bones jutting out; he looked at

Feilamort in a way that made me feel unricht. He saw
the beauty of his voice, but it seemed that he stood
apart, weighing it.

When the singing was ower, My Lady took Feilamort
to sit on a low stool at her knee. She fed him pieces of
apple and gave him sips of water and wine, stroked his
curls.

"L'enfant chante comme un ange."

"Beautiful, indeed, Madame." Monsieur Garnet
twisted his lips intae a smile.

"Every year I have a new page who sings for me, but
there has never been one like this."

"I have heard many fine singers but never one of
such quality."

"You have travelled much, Monsieur?"

"Indeed."

"I should love to hear of it; in this country one is
somewhat . . . limited."

Monsieur Garnet glanced at My Laird, deep in
conversation about hounds.

"The boy's voice has a particularly plaintive quality."

"Oh," she sighed. "If only one could keep them like
this. It is sad that the voices of boys must change."

"Some say that is what gives the voice its beauty, the
poignancy of knowing that, at the time of greatest
perfection, it could be lost at any moment. I recall in
the court of . . . I must not name him, you understand,
but at a great court we were being entertained by a
young boy with a beautiful voice and as he reached the
top note, the crescendo of the song, out came a croak
that would have shamed a frog."

27

My Lady put her haund to her mouth. "Oh Monsieur, how embarrassing."

"But amusing too, though not for the boy. I believe he never sang again, though of course the first break is not the end of the singing. But he could not bear the thought it might happen again."

Monsieur Garnet drew closer to My Lady.

"I have heard, though, Madame, of ways in which the voice may be preserved."

"Indeed."

"Rather extreme measures, of course, not to be undertaken lightly, but . . ."

He looked at Feilamort.

"Is he destined for an esquire?"

"That was, of course, why he came but he seems of a delicate constitution. The training does not suit him and to protect his voice he has been kept more indoors."

"And who trains his voice?"

"Our choirmaster, Father Graham, oversees all the singing. But Feilamort does not need to be trained; it comes naturally to him."

"A good Italian singing master could do wonders with your little lark; with proper training he would be able to delay the difficulty of the changing voice and allow you to enjoy his singing for longer. And, of course, he could also give lessons to Lady Alicia."

"Ah, but where would we find such a person? It would need to be a man of the highest ability and delicacy of feeling. Surely someone of that nature would be able to find a position far more attractive than this one."

"My Lady, no position could be more attractive than this."

"Monsieur, I am flattered of course, but this is a cold, rough country and our home is without polish, other than the little I try to introduce."

"I have someone in mind."

"We will discuss this further. But now, the dancing is about to recommence."

Snaw fell for my sister's wedding at the Yule time. The cranreuch had been upon us for days and a haze of frosty air rose frae the fields. Our toes nipped wi cauld on waking and steamclouds chuffed frae our mouths. But though auld Maggie blethered on about how the moonbroch foretellt a storm, the weather held and we tripped alang tae the chapel tae see her and her lad joined thegether.

Bonny she looked in the blue frock that suited her fairness, and happy too; Robert was a suitable match but there was true hert-liking atween them, and when they turnt tae us efter the words were said, their faces shone. We followed them outside and, as they stood at the door of the chapel, a wauff of snaw skirled around them; the blue skimmered wi white, Catriona shrouded for a moment, then revealed again, laughing and turning tae her man.

A fine party there was; the Laird is generous to his loyal servants and there was much feasting and merriment afore the bedding of the bride. I kept out the road as much as I could, avoiding the glaiber of the auldwives about who would be the next. When Catriona gied me a piece of her cake, one said, "Put it unner your pillow, lass, and you'll dream of the one you will marry." Feilamort wasna singing that nicht, as he had a glisk o cauld. I took the cake and shared it wi him, as we sat in a corner awa frae the festivities.

I felt strange and hingy; I was happy for my sister, but sad too in a way, for things wouldna be the same now she was wed. That nicht we werena cooried thegether unner the blankets, whispering. As I lay wi the ither maids, my mind was filled wi wondering of Catriona and her first nicht wi her man.

Signor Carlo arrived the week after Easter, in the midst of a thunderplump. It had been a bonny morn and I was fair scunnered at having to stay indoors. The blossom was white agin a blue sky as we sewed, and my heart felt full tae bursting with longing to escape intae the air and licht. Sometimes in the summer we tak our work outside but my mither thocht it still too cauld, since a kene wind bewaved the branches on the edge of the river.

Suddenly a shadow covered my work; I looked up tae see blackness fill the sky. A brattle of thunder, a flaff of lightning and the rain blattering doon.

It didna last, but the carriage clattered intae the yerd at the storm's height. My mither continued her sewing as if naught had happened. Then she nodded

30

tae me and said, "Run doon and ask whether any threids have arrived in the carriage alang wi the singing mannie." She kenned fine there were nane but she wanted tae let me gang doon and see him.

The hall was filled wi fowk. Aabody frae kitchen tae yerd who had a reason tae be there and hauf those who had nane were gathered tae watch. It is aye this way when the carriage arrives as it happens seldom. And a singing teacher, frae Italy.

He was wee, the mannie, like a droukit corbie in his thin black cloak and velvet shoon that were made for dancing, no travelling. He held a silken handkerchief tae his face as though feart of contamination. Even frae my position, I could smell the cloves and garlic, and some unfamiliar herbs.

My Lady held out her haund and he bowed low. "Signor Carlo, we are honoured. My husband is attending to his duties on the land, but he will be delighted to meet you at dinner. Please, come to my chamber, where you can warm yourself."

I almost forgot tae ask for the threid, but as I was about tae ascend the back stair it occurred tae me I had better pretend tae have done my mither's errand.

Donald, a shrivelled auld man who was bringing in boxes frae the carriage, said, "Naa, lass, I have nae threids for your mither, but there is something a gentie lass like yoursel will be interested in."

He held out a velvet pouch, steeked in silk. I oped it and out fell twa ribbons, one red and one blue. "Tie that round your bonny white neck, or use it tae tame these curls." He tugged at my fanklit brown locks.

I fingered the ribbons, saft in my haunds, their brichtness contrasting wi the darkness of my frock.

"But do they no belang tae Signor Carlo?"

"He'll no miss them. He has that mony parcels. And whit does an auld stick like him want wi triffles like these. Keep them, lassie."

"Thank you," I whispered, and rushed up the stair. I kenned that I would be able tae hear what went on atween the Lady and the Signor while we worked.

We sewed in silence. I caught glimpses of the next room and could hear the rise and fall of voices, mak out maist of what My Lady was saying. The Signor sat at the fire, his feet streetched out in front of him, steam rising frae his claes and his shoon; he held a cup of warm wine, infused wi cloves and spices. At his side was a plate of bannocks, no the kind we have for breakfast but thin delicate ones Louis maks for My Lady and her guests. One time when they were left ower after a party I sat in the kitchen wi Elinor and we ate them, nibbling like wee birds. The Laird canna abide sich dainties; if they are served he taks four or five and eats them thegether. He prefers the bannocks that we all eat, muckle slabs of oats that fill yer belly.

"You had a difficult journey, Signor?" My Lady asked.

"Not too difficile, Signora." His voice was wavery and thin. "But," he shivered. "Freddo, froid."

"It is a cold country," My Lady replied. "In many ways."

"I am used to travelling, I accept it."

"You have travelled to many countries?"

"When I was young I sang for the courts of Europe, now I train young voices. Music is my mistress. I follow her."

My Lady nodded.

"Do you wish to rest now, Signor? Dinner is at two o'clock. I am unable to prevail upon my husband to change the savage habits of this country and eat our main meal later, as I was brought up to do. He says that we must fit round the needs of the farm and the land. Only for large parties, at Christmas and on special occasions, do we dine at a civilised hour."

"I prefer to meet with my young pupils now, Signora, if it pleases you. I understand there are two?"

"I should like you to attend to the musical training of my daughter, Lady Alicia. This will be a part of her education as a young lady, and in keeping with her status."

Signor Carlo bowed his heid and placed his haund on his breast. "I am honoured, Signora."

"But I also have a young boy, with a very special voice. He came to us with the pages, but I do not think the training of an esquire is suitable for him. I wish you to take complete charge of him, and work with him as you see fit. His voice is paramount. Everything else takes second place and whatever you need for him will be provided."

"I understand, Signora."

Feilamort, a slight figure, like a wee speug wi his faughie claes and skinny legs, appeared at the door. He looked at me wi his huge broon een and I nodded towards the entrance to My Lady's room. He stood in the arch of the doorway, his back tae me. I could see he'd streetched, was takkin on the gangly look that the loons get afore they turn frae bairns tae lads.

My Lady's voice rang oot. "Mon petit, may I present Signor Carlo, your new master. Signor, your pupil, Feilamort."

Signor Carlo

The boy has a voice like an angel.

If I had a ducat for every time I heard this, I would be a rich man and not have to drag myself round the courts and castles of noblemen, attempting to coax some semblance of sweetness from unpromising voices. For once, however, the report is not exaggerated: the boy's voice is exceptional.

I have known children with greater range or more polish, but these are things which can be developed. The quality of plaintive beauty, however, comes from within and is the gift of the Lord, a gift given to only one in every ten thousand singers. To move an audience to silence or tears, to transform a space, whether a splendid cathedral or rough barn, into Heaven on earth — this is the gift, this is the reward for the years of drudgery.

Ah, but I digress. The country, as I expected from Monsieur Garnet's description, is dark and grey, the inhabitants, My Lady excepted, are equally rough and earthy. Though they claim the season is moving towards summer, I see little sign of it. The castle is cold; I suffer from chilblains and find it hard to play my lute. But to leave the castle is intolerable; the so-called carriage is a cart, the roads barely tracks and the surrounding countryside hardly worth seeing.

Each morning a vision of the sunshine and warmth of my homeland casts itself on my mind's eye, only to be dispelled by the incomprehensible tongue of the serving maid who brings a pitcher of water to my chamber.

Enough of my woes. The boy's voice, as I have said, is exceptional and I take my pleasure and satisfaction in teaching him. He is of a sweet and yielding disposition and My Lady has given me free reign over him. Already his voice has improved in timbre and his lung capacity is expanding. He is excused the duties of a page and the training required of an esquire. We spend the morning together, then, weather permitting, he runs out with one of the serving girls to get fresh air. There is no lack of air in these parts, though they lack most other things. Were I a young man I do not think I could bear it, but I have managed to establish a daily routine which brings me satisfaction enough. I teach the boy every morning, spend a quiet hour with my own music before dinner (which they take at an uncivilised early hour) then have a siesta before giving a lesson to Lady Alicia. My Lady enjoys my company during the later afternoon and on some evenings there is music and dancing. At the present time, though, there is precious little of anything resembling recreation, since all the servants are engaged in working in the fields.

Meals are less indigestible than I had been led to believe, though I dread what the long winter months may bring. Fish is plentiful in these parts and, though simple, the food is fresh. I remain in good health apart from the chilblains. The serving girl assures me that her grandmother's salve will soothe them.

I hope that my complaints do not suggest any lack of ardour for my task. I regard it as a vocation in its highest sense and devote myself to it with all the skills in my possession. My Lady determines to do all she can to preserve and protect the boy's voice. I trust I shall be of service to her.

Summer was at its best: bonny blue sky sprackled wi white, a hushle of wind fresh in the warm sun, but Feilamort was kept indoors, practising hour on hour, in the chamber next where we sat and sewed. I chafed for the sky, the air on my skin, but the brichtness of the days made them good for stitching and my mither kept us at work. My Lady was to have a party of grand visitors and there was much reworking and fancifying of gounies, as well as letting doon of dresses for Lady Alicia, who had taen a big streetch in her height the last months.

My Lady and and the Laird had argued lang and hard about these visitors, according tae Elinor.

"His birse was fair up — he tellt her that she should ken by noo that this was the busiest time on the land and till the crops were gaithered there should be nae visitors, diverting the servants frae their work tae wait upon them. Autumn was the time tae have guests, afore the winter set in and travel was dangerous."

Elinor was stirring a big pot of parritch. She paused at each cair of the spurtle tae tell me the next part of the story.

"So she tellt him that he only wanted guests in autumn so he could spend all day lang out hunting."

Anither stir.

"And he said it was the place of a gentleman tae hunt, and hunt weel."

Anither stir; wee bubbles rising.

"And she said that was about all he kenned of being a gentleman."

The parritch was ower-bummelling noo and I helped Elinor draw the heavy pot awa frae the heat.

"And did that engrave him worse?"

"Ach, My Laird is no sae easily fashed. He laughed and bowed low, said, 'It's as weel you are sich a lady, tae keep me in order.' "

It is pleasant tae sit and sew, while listening tae Feilamort's singing. Maist of the time Signor Carlo keeps him on exercises, hoitering up and doon scales, or learning the strange marks that mean the notes of music. But every noo and then he sings a piece all the way through, and, lost in the beauty, I forget to keep my needle moving.

The Signor believes that Feilamort needs exercise and fresh air so, except when the weather is snell or may draw to rain, he is allowed a walk afore dinner time. Signor Carlo doesna permit him tae gang by hissel so My Lady has gien me his charge; this suits the twa of us, as I am ettling for the outside world. The trees are in glory noo, and we rin towards them as if to sanctuary. Amidst the fankle of sauch and birkies, we wander till we reach a clearing, a hiddle where we find peace, as the birdies wheetle and wheep in the treetops.

I asked him aboot Signor Carlo and his lessons.

"I love to sing and if he helps me to sing better, I am happy."

"Is he a kind master?"

Feilamort chewed on a lachter of grass. "Kind enough. I no longer seek kindness."

I didna ken whit tae say. He sounded like a wee auld mannie. Whit had happened tae mak him so unlike a bairn?

"What songs do you like singing best?"

He smiled. "'Ave Maria', all songs which honour the Virgin Mary. I am . . ." He hesitated, seeking the word. ". . . devoted to Our Lady. She is my maman. I have no other." He took a holy medal frae under his sark; on it was an image of the Virgin, eyes turned tae Heaven.

I think on my mither, stitching, quietly ordering the maids' work, takkin fabric frae a lass tae sort her errors. I mind her face the times my brithers were sick and she tended them, watching ower as they fought their way through a fever.

"Let us go further," I said, jumping up. "They'll no miss us for a whiles."

It was fine tae feel the freshness on my cheeks and glimpse the brichtness of blue above the ceiling of leaves. At the far end of the forest we came upon the place where, last autumntime, the tree had been uprooted by the wind and lay flat on its side by a great jaggy hole. The wood torn asunder was splintered, grey and dry, and there was nae visible join wi the earth; the soil stuck on the roots was dry and crumblit awa tae the touch. Yet its branches had put out shoots which were growing in the sun; some tiny, others starting tae open. The buds on other trees were pink and green but these were greeny-grey, like sage leaves, ghostly and unhealthy looking, drab and straggly as if unlike tae live, but living. By some miracle, a deid tree deprived of roots and water, had put forth shoots and, in its dying breath, desired tae pour out life.

Elinor brocht mair blethers frae the kitchen. "Monsieur Jacques, the betrothed of Lady Alicia, and his parents are coming frae France. And there is another important guest, naebody is quite sure, some bishop or someone like that, and his servants. Nae wonder the Laird is angered."

"Why must they come the noo?"

"Naebody kens whit's going on. Best keep out the road of their politicking. You ken whit it's like, this yin is fechting with this other and then they become friends again. They're worse than the wee laddies that keep the fire gaun in the kitchen, bickering and falling out and in again."

Feilamort was to have new claes for the occasion and I was entrusted tae mak them. My Lady had received a parcel of fine fabric in preparation for the visitors, anither cause of argument atween her and the Laird, who thocht it extravagance.

"But then," whispered Elinor to me, in the licht of the fire one nicht, "she's the one wi the siller so there's little he can say."

"Surely her siller is his?"

"That isna the way with the nobles; her family is powerful and have sleekit lawyers tae mak sure she keeps charge of her inheritance."

My Lady unpacked her parcel in the presence of my mither and mysel. Feilamort stood in the corner, quiet, but watching intently.

"The colours are so beautiful," she cried. "But which to choose for my little songbird?"

My Lady looked at him. "Mon petit, you should be in scarlet and gold but somehow I feel it will not suit. Yet you cannot dress like this."

Feilamort aye wore browns and greys, failzit colours that meant he was barely noticed.

My mither gied a slight nod towards me. My Lady, as if she hadna seen this, exclaimed. "Deirdre, you have an eye, you chose beautiful colours for my little daughter. What do you suggest?"

I picked a velvet between grey and cream. "This is doo-colourit and I think t'will brighten his skin." I held it up and its soft and gentle tone suited him weel. "And I can broider the tunic with blue and green and flashes of crimpson, so it will mak it vieve."

I curtsied. "If My Lady approves."

She nodded and turned to my mither. "I do."

Ne'er had I taen sich pleasure in my work; the velvet cloth was saft and rich, the jewel colours of the threids sparked in the licht. All my time was spent on the tunic for Feilamort and, since the days had lengthened, I could loss mysel in the rhythm of sewing for hours. My mither made sure tae stop me every noo and again, pit her haund on my airm and gied me a gentle look. "You munna steek for too lang at a time, Deirdre. Especially on a garment like this, you need tae pause and draw breath."

Feilamort and I still went out after his lesson, and I was glad of the chance tae streetch my limbs. Concentrating on my work, I lost the sense of my body and it was only when I stopped that I realised my back was stiff or my legs cramped. My faither said I was like a colt, growing legs and airms and naething else. Auld Donald, who has travelled across the sea, tellt me I was like to the windmills they had there, muckle airms flailing round and round.

It was true my limbs felt lang and out of control. Only when I ran freely through the woods could I enjoy their power, insteid of trying tae control them in the cramped spaces of the castle, keep them ladylike and douce. The priest tellt us that our bodies are to be watched constantly lest they become instruments of sin, but surely if the Lord made them they must be good. I ken that the priest is a holy man; my mither says I must attend tae his words as he is wise, but my faither shakes his heid and says, "Dinna cross him, lass, but dinna fash yersel aboot him either. He is God's man, but he is also human."

The suit was finished and Feilamort came in for his final fitting. Shy, as if we'd ne'er run aboot the woods thegether, he stood, awkward, shufting frae one foot tae anither, eyes doon. I stroked the velvet, tugged the garments this way and that tae see if there were any improvements tae be made, but the suit was perfect. It made him look aulder too, less like a wee laddie.

My Lady clapped her haunds with pleasure at the sicht of him.

"Beautiful. The colour is perfect and the embroidery . . ." She stroked the top of the tunic, where I had broidered a garland of leaves, shining in crimpson and gold and green.

She turned to my mither. "You have taught your daughter well, Mistress. I am most pleased with you." My mither curtsied. My Lady turned tae me.

"And little Deirde, your work satisfies me greatly."

I curtsied.

She swept out, her airm round Feilamort's shoulders.

I'd barely seen Elinor during the preparations for the banquet as I had been kept busy wi Feilamort's suit, then set to work on makking ower some dresses of Lady Alicia. So I was glad when Elinor sat next tae me on the nicht. The food was the grandest I'd ever seen, with sauces for the roast, tasting of fruit and herbs.

"These are the ones Louis was no sae sythed wi," said Elinor, sooking a piece of meat slathered in sauce. "You should see what they're having." She nodded at the top table where the nobles sat. "Stuffed burds that tiny you could barely stick yer pinkie in. Louis showed me and thon wee laddie who turns the spit how tae stuff them — his haunds are too muckle. And the vegetables all roasted in some wine that Louis has been saving specially. I've ne'er seen aathing like it."

"Who are these folk who are so special?"

"Some of them are My Lady's kin and there are French and Spaniards too. There's some politicking gaun on."

"Ach, it's naught to us."

"I'm no sae sure, Deirdre."

She put doon her piece of meat and looked towards the big table. Elinor was rarely serious, aye joking and makking light of things.

She lowered her voice.

"There's talk that we may be leaving the castle."

"No."

"Aye. There is trouble brewing, and it's mibbe that the Laird's family could be on the wrang side this time."

"The Laird will never leave his lands."

"You are richt. But My Lady isna going to stay and die for a piece of Scots land. She may be gaithering allies so that she and Lady Alicia can go tae France or some far-awa place, out the road of trouble. With or without her Laird."

"And what would happen tae us?"

"There's a question. Some would go wi them. But who? And the rest, well, they'd be left tae fend for theirsels."

She pit her haund on my airm. "But, Deirdre, dinna speak a word, no even tae your mither. It may be havers. If I find out something I believe to be true, I will tell you."

I watched My Lady. Outwardly she was as usual; she smiled and laughed, nodded and charmed all. She had a way of looking round the table and watching to see whether anyone wasna engaged and drawing them intae the conversation. There was an elegance about her, like a swan wi its lang white neck, a grace lacking in almost everyone else. Whitever happened, My Lady would avoid trouble.

Efter the food was cleared awa, it was time for Feilamort to sing. When others performed there was loud applause and cheering, but when Feilamort finished his song there was aye that moment of silence, like the blue space that keeks atween the clouds after a rainstorm or the moment when a leaf falls frae the tree. Even the wee dug that lay at My Lady's feet seemed tae prick its ears as if it minded something lang forgotten. However oft I heard Feilamort I was awed, upliftit and yet misslie, longing for something; I dinna ken whit.

He sang three songs: one skipped and trilled, one ranged and soared, and the last tore the heart richt out of ye. I forgot my pride in the tunic that looked sae bonny on him, forgot the times we ran and played in the woods, and sat, tears running richt doon my cheeks, no caring wha seen them. His singing made you become the notes and the music, become the longing that he put into it. I wondered what it was that could affect us so. Had something happened tae the laddie, scarred him inside so that when he sang we felt his melancholy? Was he a messenger sent frae God, an angel? My grandam, my faither's mither, would have called him a faery child, one stolen frae the faeries and brocht up as a human.

"Sometimes when a barren woman wants a bairn sae badly she will get one frae the faeries put in her womb so naebody kens it is stolen," she tellt me. "But as it grows there is nae hiding it, at some time it will revert. A faery canna live happy in this world."

"Stop filling the lassie's heid wi trattles," my faither would say.

Grandam was a midwyfe and saw many a bairn brocht intae the world. She kenned when a bairn was lusty and fechting for life and when it was like as no tae pass awa early. I wondered what she would say about Feilamort.

My Lady called Feilamort tae her side and showed him tae the company. He was stroked and passed round frae one tae anither as if he were a kitten, then permitted tae sit nearby and watch the dancing. Signor Carlo was deep in conversation with Monsieur Garnet. I observed them. Monsieur Garnet stole glances at Feilamort, like a fox watching a chick. He stroked the straggly beard on his chin, and smiled. He was handsome in a way, but his upper lip quivered like one who has had the palsy. Signor Carlo ne'er gied awa his feelings. Aye calm and douce, his fingers smooth as a babe's. Helena says he slathers them in lard and pits them in gloves every nicht, tae keep them saft for his instrument.

Feilamort came ower tae where I sat wi the other maids. He made a mock bow. "May I have the pleasure of this dance, Deirdre?"

Mibbe My Lady had gien him too much of the wine. "I canna dance."

He took me by the haund and birled me ontae the flair. For a whiles I forgot that my body has grown in ways that mak me feel cumbersome and embarrassed; it was as if we were skipping through the woods where nane see us but the birds.

I love tae dance. I forget mysel and become one wi the music, dance till I'm hechling wi the exertion, my hert gowping. But tae dance wi Feilamort is different. He is musical in his dancing and, nae matter how fast and furious the dance, there is an underlying elegance and grace; it is like being close tae the river, you never loss the sound of it even when you arena listening.

Next day my mither and I sat alone as the maids were needed tae help tend to the guests. I was weary in my bones efter last nicht and my needle felt thick and blunt as it dragged through the fabric.

My mither spoke. "You fair enjoyed yoursel at the dancing last nicht, Deirdre."

"Aye, Mither, it was a fine party."

"You are growing up. I saw some of the young men watching you as you danced wi the wee laddie."

"I didna seek their attention. I only danced because Feilamort asked me, and he is but a bairn still."

"You are auld enough tae dance wi the bigger lads. Your faither says young William is turning out a fine young man, and his family is weel set up. We maun think on your future."

48

I stopped, my needle haufway through its stitch. William was a tall lad wi a rush of fairish hair and a birstle starting on his chin; I couldna have tellt the colour of his een.

"I am not ready for sich things."

"Your sister Catriona is marriet now and she is only a few year aheid of you."

"But she and I are different, Minnie."

"Aye." She smiled tae hersel. "I have kenned you a lang time."

I flushed. "I meant nae disrespect to Catriona. I love my sister, but she is a young lady and I am still . . ."

"You are no still a child."

"But I feel like one inside. I am happier in the woods with Feilamort or dancing wi him than I am with some loon."

I stopped. I ne'er speak tae my mither like this. I love her but there is something about her which doesna invite confidences; she is a woman of dignity who keeps her counsel, and I am of a similar nature. When my grandams were alive — baith bletherwives who could tell tales till the coos came hame — I sometimes let fall a secret, but, since they passed awa, I say little to anyone.

She touched my airm, then returned to her work. "My faither, your grandfaither who died when you were a babe, kenned plants. And because he observed them, he kenned folk. Some need tae be close by others all the time; they intertwine like the ivy, grow where they touch. And some, like the clow that grows on the rocks above the sea, need space, they maun be in the open and feel the wind and rain and sun on them. And that is like you, Deirdre."

We worked in silence for a few minutes.

"Women who marry must live close by folk whether they like it or no." She paused in her stitching. "Have you thocht mair about the convent?"

My hert flichtered in my breist.

"The Mother Superior was at the dinner last nicht. She was fair taen by the tunic you made. My Lady asked whether you might like to go into the convent as an embroideress."

Lang hours spent sewing fine linens for the altar, the priests' vestments in greens and purples and even crimpsons for martyrs' feasts. Quiet days, bells tae call to prayer: Matins, Lauds, Prime. Bright straight paths to God. Terce, Sext, Nones, Vespers. Compline. Bed. Alone in a cell.

"It would be a good life for you. You would be safe there."

"I dinna ken, Mither. I dinna ken."

Nae babes.

There are plans afoot for Feilamort. When we met in the forest that efternoon he was quiet and didna wish tae run about. I thocht it was because of the late hour, the wine, the exertion of the singing, but his skin was still like churned cream and his een clear.

"I think they wish to take me away."

"But My Lady willna let ye gang."

"She will be coming too. There is talk, I do not understand but I overhear much. Signor Carlo and

Monsieur Garnet have some plan about my singing. Signor Carlo tells me of his travels round Europe and the courts where a voice like mine is prized. He talks of comfort and beauty which is unlike anything in this poor land."

I looked at the trees, at the break in the forest where could be seen the fields gowden in the sunlicht, splashed wi rid poppies and blue cornflower.

"How could aathing be mair beautiful than this?"

"He says it is, he says there is sun most months of the year, that food is plentiful and fruit does not need to be dried and preserved in the winter. He tells of lemons as big as my fist fallen under trees, so plentiful that no one troubles to collect them, and sweet grapes for the tasting."

"Do you want to go with him?"

"I do not know." He picked a clump of grass, let it fall again. "I do not want to leave you. If My Lady comes, maybe she will take you with her as her sempstress."

"She will not. There is talk of my going to the convent as an embroideress."

"Do you wish it?"

"I dinna ken. I love tae sew and in the convent there is aye enough tae eat and drink, and I love tae pray too and mibbe it is easier there where your whole life is dedicated and there are nae distractions. But . . ."

I couldna have said it tae anyone else.

"I want a bairn."

I had ne'er sighed and gushed ower babes, no like some lassies, aye cuddling them, takkin them aff their mithers tae haud them. But lately, I have felt a burning in my wame, a restlessness and longing that pits me richt out of sorts. I may be sewing or running an errand for my mither when all of a sudden I am filled so full tae the brim with it I have tae stop and haud mysel.

Feilamort looked at me, his heid tae one side like a wee bird.

"You should have a child, Deirdre."

I burst out laughing.

"You sound like a wee auld grandfaither."

Nae mair was said about the convent ower the next few days, but I felt my mither was watching me closer than usual. My faither too, though trauchled wi the harvest and crops, was especially saft wi me when I saw him. He made sure tae sit by me sometimes at supper and, though it's lang syne since I was kissed goodnicht, he stroked my hair gently when we parted.

It was a confusing time. At this season the days are lang and it was usual for everyone tae be intent on harvest, working nicht and day, even the youngest bairns. This year, attention was divided atween the harvest and the guests. My Laird was up and out early, while My Lady stayed abed tae compensate for the late hours. The folk that worked the fields went on as usual, but there were quarrels about how the rest of us should be employed, My Lady wanting fine foods and serving maids for the visitors and My Laird wanting everyone who could be out in the fields tae be there. He was civil enough tae the guests and caroused at nicht wi the company. My Laird is a big man wi a big appetite who can work and play wi the best of them, never needing much sleep.

I barely saw Elinor. Our paths crossed when I was sent tae the kitchen or she brocht something to My Lady, but she would just roll her een and say, "God grant us the strength tae thole this." My times outdoors were curtailed too; my mither needed me as the ither maids were required to help elsewhere.

The day afore the visitors left, Feilamort and I went tae the woods for the first time in a week. He was quiet — tired out, I supposed, by the guests who regarded him as a plaything — and his face looked different, its lines stronger, less bairn-like. He had aye had a look of the itherworld about him and he made me think on the auld songs of my grandam, of the boy who went awa tae live wi the faeries and returned unfit for this world.

"The visitors leave on the morrow," he said. "We follow in a few months when arrangements have been made."

"Who's we?"

"My Lady, Lady Alicia, Signor Carlo and I. Also some others."

"No the Laird?"

"He will not go. But My Lady wishes to go to France with Lady Alicia. They will repay the visit that her betrothed made. And I will sing."

"When will you return?"

"I do not know. Maybe never."

"Never? My Lady willna let you leave her service, surely? I have seen her fond of lads afore but none like you."

"At first I thought so, but it is not true. She loves my voice."

"It isna only your voice. It is you."

He shook his heid. "My voice will not remain like this, Deirdre."

I flushed. "I ken."

"When it changes they will no longer want me. Signor Carlo has told me this very clearly. He says it is important to preserve and maintain the voice as long as is possible."

"He kens how tae train your voice; this is why My Lady sent for him. All these exercises and scales."

Feilamort looked at the ground. "There is something more he can do."

"I dinna understaund."

He never replied, but walked on slowly, looking up towards the trees.

Signor Carlo

I do not know the exact age of the boy, though, in these circumstances, precise age is not necessarily of help since physical development varies greatly. I have known boys who were still in the treble range at sixteen while others could no longer reach the higher notes at ten. That is, of course, very rare.

The circumstances of his birth are unknown; again, this is not uncommon. In nature he is gentle and keen to please; he works with diligence at his singing and, though uninterested in playing an instrument, attends to such aspects of it as will help his voice. He is small and slight but has shown some signs of physical development of late. His voice is still of the utmost purity and beauty and it is probably safe to proceed with the arrangements.

My Lady has reasons for wishing to visit the houses of relatives and renew connections. Lady Alicia has been somewhat sheltered in the environment of the castle and, while a lovely and pleasing maiden, would benefit from the experience of, let us say, warmer climes. This journey provides an ideal opportunity for the boy to be heard by those who can truly appreciate him. I am unsure, as yet, with how large a retinue My Lady intends to travel. The countryside here is rough and hard, and there are some dangers from brigands, but My Lady's husband is a man well versed in the ways of his compatriots. I am certain we shall pass through the kingdom safely and, once in France, we will be well protected by My Lady's kin.

My Lady made arrangements for me to enter the convent, where I would be trained in embroidery as a lay helper. If I proved acceptable to the Sisters, after a period I might become a postulant. My mither sewed the plain garb wi her ain haund, her lips as ticht as the stitches. Though rough compared tae My Lady's gowns, they were safter than the sirks and hempen cloaks I was accustomed to wear, except on special occasions. There would be nae mair special occasions though, nae dancing and merrymaking.

The visitors had gone and my mither was lax with me; perhaps she thocht I should mak the best of the last few weeks of freedom. Feilamort crept in efter his lesson, waited till I finished my work then we ran out tae the woods. Twas a day when all the world was grey, shading frae the palest grey of the sky next the horizon, tae the near-black of the tree trunk. And the carpet of earth and leaf upon which we sat was grey on grey.

"Signor Carlo says my voice has deepened."

He sooked a straw of grass.

"Likely it is the cauld."

"No, Deirdre." He paused, touched my airm. "Look."

And he pulled up his tunic and showed me his ba'cod.

Had it been any ither lad I would have turnt and run aff. My mither has aye been strict and we were brocht up tae be pure in word and deed, avoid any daffin and ladry. Feilamort, too, seemed set apart frae sich things, and no just because he was too young — I had seen many a lad of ten graip at a lass. I've kenned lads wheech up their claes and show theirsels tae lasses, joukin aboot. But this wasna like that; he handled it as if it were a bird's egg he'd found.

When you see a bairn pee, their wee mannie's that bonny and sweet, like a bud, you almost want tae kiss it, but there is something ugly about a man's graith. I have aye thocht on Feilamort as a bairn and — had I e'er thocht on it at all — would have expected tae see a wee doodly thing hingin frae his bit, but naw, it was big and lumpen. He held it in his haund, examined it as if it were no part of him.

"When this," he said, pointing at the baws, "drops in here, the voice descends. Signor Carlo says it will not happen all at once, that there is still probably some time, but no one can be sure. And the process has started."

He covered hissel.

I couldna meet his een. "But surely you are too young."

"I know not what my age is exactly — it may be that I am small, or it may be that I have started sooner. In any case . . . can you keep a secret, Deirdre?"

"Of course."

"Signor Carlo wants to do something which will preserve my voice."

"I dinna understaund."

"There is a way."

"Is it herbs?"

I ken that Signor Carlo has had potions frae auld Maggie, who bides at the far end of the woods, and kens sich things. Mint and angelica ease his wind, chives and yarrow cool the blood.

"Herbs will help for a while but he seeks a more permanent way."

He lifted a nut, dried and withered, frae the ground, placed it in his fist and squeezed.

"When this is not permitted to follow its natural course, then the voice will not be lost."

I shuddered.

"But it's horrible — it's like a horse."

He smiled. "I never knew horses could sing."

"But, do you want this?"

"I want to sing, it is all I know. And it is all that keeps my life as it is. Signor Carlo says there are places all over Europe where I will be welcomed and well treated. I will sing and they will look after me."

He placed his haund on my airm. "Look at me, Deirdre. I am not strong, I could never have managed the life of an esquire. I have no family, I was living on charity, sleeping on straw with other boys when they brought me here. I have no choice."

Signor Carlo

There are several methods of proceeding, though only one of which I have personal experience. A warm bath is taken, which causes both a somewhat anaesthetic effect and also enables the practitioner to feel more easily. Then it is a simple matter of squeezing. I say simple but of course it requires considerable skill and experience to do it well. I have seen the results of those who have not possessed such skill and, let us say, it is not a desirable outcome. If done with care, the boy is unharmed in any respect and there is no significant pain. If he is prepared for what is ahead, there is little distress. Many boys have a sense of relief; they know that their voice will be preserved and likewise their livelihood. For those boys who love God deeply there is the knowledge that they are sacrificing something of little worth in order to make the best of a precious gift of the Lord. For while the voice may be used to entertain ladies and gentlemen, its true end is to glorify its maker and to bring human beings to a knowledge of God. Where can we be closer to Heaven, where can we have a greater realisation of His glory and power than when listening to a most beautiful voice? I have urged the boy to think of the parable of the talents.

It seems a simple case. He has little contact with other boys and has, as yet, developed no interest in women which might make him troubled about what he would lose. It is, in fact, possible for an evirato to perform with a woman to some extent, though not, of course, to father a child. As I have said, he is dolce, gentle in nature; a pliable child. Moreover, his gift is remarkable. I am content, at first, to travel with My Lady to the homes of her relations, but after that, who knows where his gifts may take us.

My Lady is a fine woman; her subtlety and delicacy of manner are matched only by her shrewdness.

In the days that followed, I kept thinking of Feilamort and what he had tellt me. It made shivers run doon my back at the thocht of the cruel thing they were going to do to him, of the wee baws crushed like nuts in a nutcracker. If it was me, I think I would run awa, but he said he had nae choice, and that was true enough. Even the rich folk had precious little choice, so what chance was there for folk like us.

When I minded that time in the woods, my face flushed red. I kenned weel that you can be impure in thocht as well as deed, and that we shouldna have spoken of such matters thegether, a lad and a lass. But he was my friend and had naebody else he could tell. At nicht, afore I fell asleep, I kept thinking on the things that pass atween a man and a woman and how strange they were. When Feilamort had shown me his bits, they were that ugly and that much bigger than I had imagined. Yet it was God who made our bodies; in the Bible it said "and it was good".

Surely that was another reason why they shouldna touch him.

★   ★   ★

The sun cast lang shadows and the earth was damp underfoot after rain the nicht afore. We wandered deeper in than usual; the dampness and rotting leaves scented the air and it felt heavy and clinging. I longed for brichtness.

He broke the silence.

"It will take place soon."

My body tensed as if I could feel what he would undergo.

His voice was calm. "Before it happens, I want to know you. As a man knows a woman."

He looked that young, surely he wasna capable yet of knowing a woman. Yet Johnnie, the son of the smith, was said tae have got a lass wi child when aged ten, and surely Feilamort was aulder. I could see the line of his jaw, no longer rounded and saft like a bairn's but mair defined, the delicate bone curved intae his neck. Even though I kenned he had grown, I still thocht of him as much younger than mysel, but, for the first time, I saw he was nae langer knave-bairn, but haspan, and it confused me.

"There are plenty hures and trallops would pleasure ye." I couldna meet his een.

"I do not wish it."

"I ken what you wish, but it is wrang."

"Deirdre, you are the one I love. You are the one who is always kind, who has shown love to me. Soon I must leave and you will go into the convent."

Though he spake in a steady voice, his lower lip tremmled slightly. He looked at me and I felt my insides turn tae watter.

"It is a sin, we arena marriet."

"Let us handfast, pledge ourselves to one another."

The flame was up in my cheeks. I had ne'er felt like this, I had nae idea it was possible to feel like this. One minute this was a wee lad who played wi me in the woods, the next it was as though the world had gone tummle ower arse.

"No."

I gaithered up my skirts and ran; I didna ken if I was running towards hame or awa frae him.

But I couldna run awa frae the feelings. At dinner time, in the courtyard, when he passed through the room where we sewed, all the times we saw each other in a day, were the same and yet different. I tried no tae look at him, but when he was near I was feerich; my heart gowped and I fumbled ower my work. I wondered that no one noticed the difference in us, no even my mither. Sharp-eyed as she was, she was preoccupied with the arrangements for My Lady's departure and my leaving for the convent, and perhaps if she did notice, she thought it a summer storm that would flare and die almost in one.

But inside me, a fire had started. I felt it when he was near, a flare in my belly, a choking in my throat. And at nicht, lying in my bed, pictures in my mind, pictures I tried tae keep out, but couldna.

Mibbe if he had tried tae persuade me, by word or deed, I wouldna have done it. I knelt in front of the statue of Our Lady in the chapel and asked for her help but I couldna stop thinking of how it would be if they done the deed on him afore we lay thegether. I was feart tae go back to the woods with Feilamort, but mair fearful of no going. And though I had heard the priest speak out against handfasting, there were folk who thocht it as good as any other wedding.

We sat side by side, backs resting on the tree trunk. The wee birds chirruped as if their hearts would burst and I felt like greeting. Then, we stood and faced each ither.

He held out his haunds and I took them in mines: right to right, left to left in eternal union.

"Deirdre, I love you and take you as my bride."

"Feilamort, I love thee and tak thee as my man."

"And naught shall sever us."

At the word sever, a cauld shiver climbed up my back.

I canna say the things that happened atween us: an unknown journey, but with landscape so familiar I felt I must have travelled it a hunner times oer.

He wasna a wee laddie, he done what a man does. There was pain and tears but something else too: kissing and tenderness and the feeling of perfect stillness.

In the darkness of the forest we were hidden frae view and we clasped each ither close, like bairns but no like bairns. The licht startit tae fade tae an even darker grey and I said, "We had better gang inside, but separately."

"I always accompany you."

"They will ken if they see us."

It seemed impossible that they wouldna see on our faces the difference, the shining.

"We go in together."

We stood and he brushed the leaves and twigs frae my dress. He looked in my een with tenderness and squeezed my haund.

Three days efter we had first lain thegether, I set aff for the convent.

France

Six months earlier

A long weary journey. The hills steep, the path rough and inhospitable. The convent was situated in a lonely place, far from its nearest neighbours, the better for the nuns to contemplate, to send up supplication to the Blessed Virgin, to pray continually for those too idle, too ignorant, too mired in sin to pray for themselves.

Glad to reach sanctuary before night had completely darkened the sky, Father Anthony expected to sit down to broth and bread, enjoy a little conversation with Mother Superior before peaceful rest under clean white sheets such as only a French convent ever provided. Then a brief sojourn, saying Mass, tending to the spiritual needs of the Sisters before continuing on his journey. The letters he carried, from the head of his order to his brothers in Scotland, were not of import to anyone except the other friars, yet Father Anthony was happy to travel across land and sea, acting as a messenger, since it permitted him to do what he felt was his vocation: to spread the peace and love of God wherever he went. Even as a child he knew that he had been given this task. People felt better in his presence; his gentleness came easily, was not strained like that of many of his fellow priests. He did not have to suppress impatience or chafe against lust or pride; he felt no disgust at the sins confessed to him, but took delight in the redemption of lost souls.

He was met by Mother Superior, a woman with a shrewd eye and a calm face, as white as the headdress she wore. Young for the position she held, she had been there only a few years.

"I am sorry, Father. I know your journey was long and you are in need of sustenance, but I must ask you to perform the sacraments immediately. One of our Sisters is dying."

A younger nun offered the priest a cup of water, and, after drinking, he followed Mother Superior down a passageway. She paused at a door.

"She will pass away within the next day or so — it could be very quick or she could linger. But she is in sore distress. It sometimes comes on them at this time, though there is little enough which can trouble the conscience of an old faithful servant of the Lord."

He heard her confession, gave her absolution and comfort. But she was not comforted.

"Father, there is something which troubles me. It is not a sin, I did no wrong in the matter, but I feel uneasy and I do not wish to pass away without speaking of it to one whom I can trust."

The priest assured the woman that she could unburden her mind to him. In a high voice which cracked at times, she told him the story: sad, but commonplace enough.

There was a beautiful, virtuous and learned young woman who travelled far across the water to be betrothed to a young man. Though many were charged with protecting the young woman, the young man seduced her. On her journey back through France, she discovered that she was with child. She stopped at the convent, where word came to her that the father of her child had died and the shock caused her to go into labour. The child was not of full term but perfectly formed and lusty nevertheless; the young mother died a few days afterwards of a fever brought on by childbirth.

"I nursed her, Father," said the nun. "She loved the child with all her heart, but she was deeply distressed. She had been so pure that she could not bear to have been sullied. She knew she was like to pass away, and, with her dying breath, begged that her child should be looked after. The Mother Superior sat by her and held her hand, while I was close by.

"'Please, look after the babe,' she said, though she could hardly ope her lips. 'But do not tell my father. Do not ever tell him.'"

The Sister's eyes filled up as she spoke of the young woman and her child. She herself had laid her out and looked after the infant with the help of a wet nurse. But the Mother Superior decided to honour the young woman's wishes. The girl's father was informed of her death but not of the birth of the child. And in due course the child was placed with a noble family nearby and raised among other foundlings. The only keepsake he had of his mother was a holy medal.

"I do not know why she did this, Father," said the nun. "The Mother Superior, God rest her soul, was a wise woman, and had her reasons. And I am a lowly Sister. But all these years I have never stopped praying for the soul of that lovely girl and for her poor babe."

* * *

Father Anthony had taken vows of poverty, chastity and obedience. The first two caused him little difficulty, but the bounds of obedience were blurred at times. Outwardly he did as he was told, but a deeper sense of obedience moved him: obedience to the spirit of Christ, rather than to the instructions of his superiors.

It was unlike Father Anthony to take heed of a dream. He rarely dreamed and those dreams he remembered were usually of Heaven, of angels singing like birds in the softness of pearly light. But the night after hearing the nun's confession, he had a dream which so disturbed him that, in spite of his tiredness after the long journey, he could not sleep for the rest of the night. The dream was of the young woman's face, staring up from her deathbed, pleading, as the nun had told him she had pleaded.

"Please, look after the babe."

The vividness of this dream was unlike anything he had previously experienced. Sweat stood out on her brow — he could taste its saltiness on his tongue — and her hair, once golden, was lank and matted. He could see the whiteness of the rough skin flaking from her lips, and those eyes, melting in love for her poor infant.

Father Anthony had always had a devotion to the Blessed Virgin, but his devotion was to a lovely woman, dressed in blue, a crown on her head and a wistful look on her face. Her sorrow had been weathered, like a smooth old bench, worn to a sheen through usage. That night he saw the rawness of anguish she must have suffered at the knowledge that her child was born to pain and torture.

Next morning, after an early breakfast, Father Anthony set out to discover what had happened to the child.

Cool clean stane flairs, cool clean stane walls. Lang, lang corridors lighted wi high pointy windaes. Nuns' feet mak nae sound but those of the young women, who, like me, clean or sew or work in the kitchen, slap and ring through the air. A finger ower the lips, a shake of the heid, rebuke us for our lack of attention tae the detail of our lives. That is what my life had become, attention tae detail. In the silence every movement is magnified, every whispered word becomes an echoing cry, the stroke of a brush on the flair is a lightning crack. The priest tellt me convent life was a reflective one, but he was wrang. Every moment is taken up with duties, no like at hame, where you could let your mind wander as you sewed, or run out tae the woods and hear the wind and see the trees; we are thirled to the call of the bells. As we sew a Sister reads frae the Holy Gospels and it is hard tae think of aught else. And there is the body's exhaustion. I thocht I worked hard in the castle but here we are waked in the middle of the nicht to pray and have bare three hours' sleep at once. When I sit doon tae sew I start tae nod, but darena mak a mistake. If I dinna work weel Sister Agnes will mak me tak it all out again and mibbe even send me back. And while I miss my mither sair, and wish I could go hame tae my auld life, I ken it is impossible.

Every morn, Grainne and I sewed under the supervision of Sister Agnes with twa ither lasses destined for the Sisterhood. Grainne is a wild-eyed lass with a leg twisted and awkward, but she sews wi graceful ease. The postulants, Mary and Rose, had been in the convent for six month and were prone tae fits of giggles. Grainne and I were too feart frae Sister Agnes, who is cool and smooth as marble outside but sparks flint when crossed. We steek priests' vestments and altar cloths. Twa local women attend tae the mending of sheets and linens, but we have been chosen tae learn the finest work. Sister Agnes tellt us on the first day, and oft repeats, that we must be humble, that only by the grace of the Lord have we been sent here, and that we must use our talents solely for the glory of God, no for human vanity.

We pray afore we begin our work, then are set our task. At first Sister Agnes watched almost every steek but gradually she relaxed her hawk-like gaze. She let me work on simple filling in of colours till she was satisfied at my proficiency, then gied me a stole tae decorate by mysel. I asked her if I could work a cross with leaves entwined round it and she let me. I wanted tae add a wee robin; its red breist is the sign of Our Lord's blood shed for us, but she looked at what I had done and said, "I think that will be fine as it is, Deirdre."

I longed tae dae the work of Sister Agnes: she was broidering a picture of Adam and Eve in the Garden of Eden, a rich pattern of trees and leaves all outlined in

74

gold chainsteek. Birds were perched in the trees — ones sich as micht be found in Paradise, bricht green and blue and yella feathers spread out — and the ground was carpeted wi fruits in orange and purpoir and green. Sister Agnes stitched as she done everything: her white haunds stroked the needle through the linen that fast you could hardly see it, yet her work was perfect.

E'en so, I thocht I could mak something, mibbe no better, but different. In my bed at nicht, in the moments afore I fell intae sleep, the forest spread itsel afore my een, the forest where Feilamort and I had run, the carpets of leaves where we'd lain, the spring flooers in lilac and pink that specklet the leaves, even the grey and green and broon leaves crumbling intae the mud. And maist of all, the blue and pink sky wi the white clouds birling that you see when you lie on your back and stare upward. Though I was well-fed and well treated, I nae longer had the freedom tae be outside in the air and I missed it sair.

I missed Feilamort too, and the feeling grew as the weeks passed. When I first entered the convent I was too tired, too entangled in the newness of it, tae think on much else, but noo the thocht of him was oft in mind. No in the way of the body's hunger, but in the remembrance of his kindness and gentleness.

Signor Carlo

At last we have reached France and some measure of civilisation. I draw a veil over the journey: the crossing was not the worst I, seasoned traveller as I am, have experienced, but it was far from comfortable. We are now in the chateau of the cousin of My Lady, the parents of Monsieur Jacques, Lady Alicia's betrothed; our hosts are well set and everything is arranged for our comfort. Until he was sent to My Lady in Scotland, the boy lived here on the estate, but he seems to have little memory of the chateau itself; no doubt he was housed with other unfortunate orphans nearby.

The weather is pleasantly warm and our lives proceed with a graceful rhythm. The boy has resumed his studies in earnest after the disruption of our voyage, but, to my surprise, he has proved a redoubtable traveller. Though he appears frail and delicate, he seems to have a robust constitution and has borne with equanimity the trials of sea and horseback journeys. He is not prone to sickness and even the poor victuals along our route have not caused him great distress. This bodes well for his future.

My Lady's kinsmen are delighted by him. They keep a pleasant and social court and there is music and dancing almost every night. It is all I can do to prevent overuse of his voice, such is the delight our hosts show at his talent. And I have to keep the ladies from making too much of a pet of him; too much rich food and titbits are not good for the voice, and late hours mean that he is unable to study the next day. And, in the end, it is the study which is important. Mastery of the voice is what sustains a singer through years of work and there is no point in flowering too quickly; the plant which is not hardy enough cannot sustain the spells of frost. Allow this little one to gradually develop and his voice will last for many, many years.

My Lady is an excellent champion: a formidable lady whose protection is invaluable. She leaves his training to my expertise and is firm with those who beg for one last song or want to keep the lad by their side for a few more minutes, yet she does it with such charm and grace that they are never disappointed. Only the boy seems less than enthralled by her; while polite, he maintains that quiet detachment which characterises his intercourse with others.

Feilamort works, if anything, harder than he did before. Not that there is any straining or apparent effort; I have rarely met a singer who showed such ease, even in practice, even when having to repeat exercises, scales, breathing. It is rather that I detect a greater solidity of purpose; perhaps now that his path is absolutely clear and there are no alternatives, now that this sacrifice has been made, his will is set. In the few weeks preceding the operazione, I sensed a degree of equivocation on his part and wondered whether we should proceed; while it is clearly the best option, I am not in the business of forcing such a delicate matter upon anyone, and I made it clear to Monsieur Garnet that it must be the boy's free choice. I am aware that his choices are, of necessity, rather limited; nonetheless it is important that he is permitted to make them.

I recall the day, some weeks after the idea had been suggested, when he came to me and said he was prepared. His calmness of demeanour impressed me greatly. Paradoxically, I have felt more sadness in this case than I have done in those of other boys who approached the business in a less thoughtful way, a strange inconsistency on my part; given the sublime quality of his voice, the sacrifice should seem more justified. Yet I found myself caring for him afterwards with even greater than usual tenderness, soothing his physical pain with arnica and cool cloths, and offering succour to the anguish of spirit which necessarily follows such an undertaking; the former lasted only a few weeks, while he has borne the latter with considerable endurance.

I have observed numerous singers and they all possess a particular spirit, like a river running through them, from which they draw their strength and ability to pour out their music. In many cases this river takes a meandering course; some days it shines and on some it is sluggish. Others have a constant wellspring of energy but it is random and uncontrolled, going off like cannon; there is much show and noise but little substance. Neither type can sustain. This child's river is pure and sparkling but also straight and sure and strong; it seems to arise from the elemental rocks of the earth, to draw its strength from something deeper and truer than we can imagine. With God's grace, and my God-given skills of teaching, Feilamort could be great indeed.

Four weeks efter I entered the convent the first signs came. My bleeding had not arrived but that didna warrant notice. Even girls who bleed every moontime can have their rhythm disrupted by the different food and work. Grainne whispered that the nuns bleed at exactly the same time each month and that our time of bleeding would change to fit in with their cycle.

Twa weeks later, I felt the dry boke on waking. At first I thocht that it was just the early hour, having tae rise at three in the morn and mak my way tae the chapel through the freezing corridor. But a gripping pain writhed inside me for hours; I couldna bear tae touch the dry breid put afore us at breakfast and I was ravenous with hunger at dinner time, wolfing the broth and bannocks, hoping for fish, leaving the table feeling empty, even though the nuns' meals are generous.

I recognised the signs — my mither had suffered in exactly the same way — yet I was loath tae accept the truth of my condition. What the cat does under cover of darkness, what the dug does in full daylicht, and the result which comes frae their actions, have been nae mystery tae me since I was a bairn. But the yearning and the gentleness had owerwhelmed me, blinded me to what might ensue.

Signor Carlo

Monsieur Garnet has returned to the chateau; he has been visiting the surrounding lands, attending to the business of the estate. His position in the establishment is difficult to name; clearly he is of the greatest importance, yet he is not kin, which is unusual in these parts. The old crone who sweeps the floor needs no encouragement to talk on the subject of the household, having been here for a hundred years by the look of her. Monsieur Garnet was the son of a local farmer who made himself indispensable about the place and rose to his present position; according to her, he was always shrewd and calculating. Expert in the training of hunting dogs, he tolerated no insurrection and when one disobeyed him, punishment was swift.

"She was his favourite dog, Princess, a silky coat she had and a lovely face," said the ancient dame. "I was in the kitchen when he brought her in. Jumping about, she was, thought she was for some titbits. I was busy at my work and never realised what he was up to, as he warmed himself at the fire. Then suddenly he pulled out the poker he had heated up and thrust it into her eye. I'll never forget the noise she made, Sir, it made your blood run cold. A strange fish, I have always thought him, though he has risen so high and mighty."

He is certainly trusted by his master. My Lady's cousin, preferring the role of genial host, leaves the running of the estate to him; furthermore Monsieur Garnet seems to advise on matters other than business and was apparently instrumental in arranging the betrothal between Lady Alicia and Monsieur Jacques. Of course there are close connections between them, which makes the match eminently suitable, but, according to the gossip of the servants, their union will also seal their fortune, since it will ensure that the estate of a rich, childless old relative will pass to them.

At dinner I observe Monsieur Garnet. I feel it is important to have some measure of him, since it is he who will influence the direction of Feilamort's path, and therefore that of mine. Yet, in spite of my long experience of observation, I find him extremely difficult to comprehend. I have managed a little conversation with him on the topic of the boy's future, not as easy an undertaking as it might appear. Though Monsieur is a man of the utmost refinement of manner, and his outward demeanour is gracious, he has the ability to turn a conversation away from any topic he does not choose to discuss. On previous occasions when I attempted to broach the subject, he almost vanished into the air, while leaving me with the sensation of being at fault.

Today, he entered the room where we work each morning, having arranged that he might hear Feilamort. I had been somewhat surprised by his request, since the boy sings almost every evening; he does not seem a man so enamoured of music that he would wish to listen to scales and exercises. Still, he listened with attention, then said, "Are you content with your pupil's progress, Signor?"

"Content is perhaps not the right word. We aim to perfect, yet perfection is unattainable, for with each step achieved it seems we are more aware of how we have fallen short."

"I see you are a philosopher, Signor."

I shrugged. "A simple music teacher, Monsieur."

"You are too modest. You must agree that, under your tutelage, your pupil has made great progress."

"I thank you for your kindness."

I paused, waiting for him to take up the thread. He nodded at Feilamort. "You allow your pupil a few minutes to take the air?"

The boy left us and I seized my opportunity.

"Monsieur Garnet, I am most content with my position in My Lady's household and I know that you were instrumental in obtaining it for me."

He gave a slight bow. "Your references were excellent."

"Naturally I am only too happy to continue in the service of Her Ladyship and to teach my pupil, but I must admit to feeling some little doubt as to the future. Since Lady Alicia is to be married . . . perhaps My Lady will take up residence with her daughter?"

I did not fear Monsieur Garnet but in that moment I think I knew what it would be to feel afraid of him; he stood, appraising me as though I were a sack of grain or a partridge which some peasant had offered in lieu of taxes.

"It is true that Lady Alicia will be married soon, and it is entirely possible that My Lady will make her home here with her daughter and son-in-law. I cannot speak for her, of course. And it is true, as you may have heard, that at a future date Lady Alicia and her husband will inherit a substantial property. But My Lady maintains a keen interest in the boy's development as a singer, and his welfare. As do I. As a child he was brought up here on the estate so he is, you may say, a responsibility of mine.

"I am not expert in the voice as you are, but I understand that the art of singing and music is valued in Europe. If I may speak frankly, we both know that this chateau, while delightful, is no place for a talent like his. I believe that by travelling to the right places with the boy, continuing to develop his voice and to ensure that he is recognised and remunerated in a fitting manner, you will receive your just deserts."

He paused.

"I assume such an arrangement would be pleasing to you?"

For a week or twa I feigned to mysel that I was imagining it, that it was the food or the tiredness, but when another moon passed and there was still nae sign, I kenned that it must be true.

The first day of Advent. I lay in my bed on the Sabbath nicht. This was a day of rest and, though we spent much of it in prayer and listening tae scripture readings, there was some time tae think. And I was seized wi fear, a panic that gripped my throat and made me want tae cry out. If what I kenned was true, what would happen tae me and the bairn? The Sisters wouldna want a lass wi a bairn. Would they send me hame? Or would they, as I had heard tell, let me have the bairn then tak it frae me and send it awa somewhere. The cauld face of Sister Agnes rose in front of me.

I couldna bear it. I needed my mither.

Father Anthony

Father Anthony had an unswerving faith in God's plan. He saw evidence of it all around him: in the birds whose wings so perfectly fitted them for flight, in the bees and plants and flowers who inhabited the earth in such abundance. He was well aware that earthly life was far from perfect, that it was tainted by war and famine and disease, but he believed, with all his heart and soul, that these existed for reasons which human beings could not, in their ignorance, understand.

Though Father Anthony acknowledged the presence of evil, he did not, like many priests, believe that human suffering was always a punishment for wrongdoing, nor that it was necessary to suffer in order to be good. He himself was conscious of having suffered very little during his life. His health was robust, his vocation rewarding, and, though his parents had died, he had been too young to know them. The little he had suffered was through his empathy with the distress of others and this was tempered by the knowledge that many were visibly comforted by his presence.

People found it natural to confide in Father Anthony so he was unsurprised that it proved easy to discover where the child had been taken. The previous Mother Superior, who was responsible, had passed away, but a gardener remembered the incident well.

"I drove the cart myself, Father, and the wet nurse carried the babe in her arms. Not far the place is, less than a day's travel. The Mother Superior had a brother there, a steward or some such — shifty-looking creature — and he arranged it. It seemed good fortune, landing up in a fine chateau like that. Even though the child would have a humble position, better to be a nobody with a full belly and a roof over your head."

Father Anthony travelled to the chateau and made discreet enquiries in a village nearby. He discovered that the child had left the place some years before, sent across the water to Scotland in the company of other boys from the estate; they were pledged to the service of a Lady, the cousin to the Lord of the chateau.

Sister Elizabeth is the auldest of the nuns, and spends her days in front of the Holy Eucharist. When she was young she was beautiful and rich but refused every suitor; all she desired was tae be on her knees, praying. She said she would live a life of poverty and chastity. Her faither was sair angered by her and said, "Weel, lass, that's what thou shalt hae", and he sent her tae the convent.

They say that in the past the convent was full of Sisters like her. Many year syne, a holy woman lived in a wee hut near the castle; folk would leave food for her and ask her tae pray for them. She prayed day and nicht and Our Blessed Lady visited her. Mair women joined her, and that's how the convent came tae be. The Sisters here are holy women but they arena like Sister Elizabeth; as well as those who mak vestments, some tend the sick and ithers grow vegetables and herbs.

I had ne'er been close by Sister Elizabeth, only seen her at chapel in her place near the altar. Then one day Sister Agnes asked me tae tak a veil to her. Sister Agnes aye mends Sister Elizabeth's claes hersel, even though they are as plain as plain can be and need nae fancy steeking.

"Knock on her door, Deirdre, and say who you are and what you have brocht. If she doesna answer, leave this outside the door. She may be deep in prayer."

I was feart frae Sister Elizabeth. I tapped as lightly as I could on the door, hoping she wouldna hear and I could leave the veil without speaking tae her. But the second I put my haund agin the door, it sprang open and there she was, a big lanky wumman wi a neb on her that took up maist of her face. I'd only seen her at a distance in chapel afore; close up she looked just like an eagle, her beak curving doon so you could bare see her thin lips and her een, hooded, but so bricht and glittery like the gold threid Sister Agnes worked through the priest's vestments.

I offered the veil tae her but she never took it, just stood, looking intently at me.

"Enter, lass."

I hovered, hauf in, hauf out the door. It was forbidden tae enter a Sister's cell, unless tending to a sick nun. But she took my airm and pulled me in. Her grip was fierce; sharp and pointy fingers clutched my airm.

She pushed me to my knees. The cauld hard stane struck agin them. On the wall was a crucifix with a silver Jesus, airms outstreetched, hinging frae the dark widden cross.

"Do you see him, lass?"

"Who, Sister?"

"Our Blessed Lord."

"He is on the cross."

"Love Him with all your heart."

We knelt thegether, no speaking. Her breathing was loud, and she sighed, and then I heard what sounded like a chuckle.

She turned tae me, her een shining, a big smile across her face.

"Oh lass, we are so blessed." Then she looked straight at me.

It was like looking too close at a flame.

"Do you see baby Jesus? Does He come to you?"

I shook my heid.

"He is here in the room." She looked at me again, stroked my airm.

"What dae they cry you, lass?"

"Deirdre."

"Love the precious baby."

I drapped the veil and ran.

In the chapel, dim candlelicht casting shadows across the altar, I knelt and prayed for help. Sooner or later I would show. In a big wumman who had already borne bairns, it wasna obvious, but a young lass, who, like me, hadna much flesh on her, couldna hide it lang, even under the thick shapeless robes. And Sister Agnes was as sharp as the pins she kept in the pouch that hung frae her waist. If she had been different in nature, mibbe I could have tellt her, begged for mercy and kindness. But her charity was cauld, her kindness measured out for your ain good.

I tried tae speak tae her earlier in the day, asked if I could go hame at Yule tae see my mither. She gied me sich a look, as if she saw mair in me than I kenned mysel.

"Efter a few month in the convent, these feelings are common. At the start lasses are occupied with their new life, and forget tae be hamesick, then there comes a time when they start tae miss what they have kenned. You are a fortunate lass, Deirdre — you have a good mither and faither so it is natural you should miss them. You maun understaund that this will pass.

"If you see your mither noo it will only owerset ye. You maun wait till you are weel settled and you can bear a visit with cheerfulness. That will likely be nearer six month than three."

I hadna taen vows, so they couldna keep me agin my will, but we were forbidden tae disobey the nuns and I was feart that if I argued, she would be even mair opposed tae my going.

Her mouth turned up at the corners slightly in a hauf-smile as she looked at me. "I was once a lass like you, Deirdre. Trust me when I say that it will pass. Pray to the good Lord."

Father Anthony

Father Anthony arranged that, on reaching Scotland, he would serve the Sisters at a convent close to the castle where the child had been taken. It was natural for him to stop in the village, make a few enquiries of the gossiping wife who gave him a cup of milk and a bannock to break his fast on the journey. Here he found that once again he was too late, since the child had left a few months previously in the company of My Lady.

"A wee skelf o a lad," said the woman. "Bonny, but like a lass, no a lad. And with the voice of an angel."

There are those who can sense that a plant is poisonous; something about it, unnoticed by others, is repellent to them. In such a way, Father Anthony could discern the presence of evil. It was palpable; a cloying sensation attacked his nostrils, his head ached and his brain throbbed. In the presence of ordinary sin — the daily habits of sloth, greed, anger or spiritual carelessness — he remained unchanged; but from time to time he was plagued by this altered state, coming as if from nowhere.

But though Father Anthony was keenly aware of the proximity of Satan, he could rarely ascertain his location. On one occasion his instinct assailed him in the middle of High Mass in a cathedral filled with holy men, causing him to believe that his gift was actually a temptation from the Devil. He had spoken with his confessor about it but as yet had felt no confidence in his answers. Thus he was left in the position of being intensely aware of the presence of evil without fully trusting his feelings.

He had never seen the child yet he was conscious of great discomfort, emanating, not from the child, but from something around him. He was unable to rid himself of the sense that he must find out more in order to protect him from greater harm.

The sky was strippit in pale blue and pink, faded as though much washed. The birds were cheetlin sweet and bricht and I longed tae be outside. I had been happy to be chosen as an embroiderer, no having tae dae the roughest work in the rain and snaw, but noo I sorely missed the fresh air. At hame I had spent lang hours sewing but my tasks had been varied; I was oft sent a message tae the kitchen and I was free tae run outside. Now there was barely a day when I felt the air on my cheek, could tell whether it were warm or chill. The convent was dry and cool; dampness didna seep in like it done in the castle, but neither was there the big fire which warmed ye through tae yer banes. And at nicht it was lonely.

It was the custom that we lay by oursels, and I missed the warmth of the ither maids when I went tae my bed.

I tried tae pray to the good Lord and the Virgin Mary, but they seemed far awa. When I was wee they were all around me — Jesus played wi me outside in the grass or among the trees, and Mary watched by me at nicht — but here, where you would think they'd be closer, I felt them fade intae the distance. In the chapel

94

when I knelt and prayed at the Virgin's statue, the blue of her robe seemed tae melt like the edges of the sky close to the horizon. I kenned it was my shame and fear that kept me frae them; if I believed Feilamort and I were truly bound by the handfast I wouldna feel this guilt. I knelt in the dark chapel and asked for help, but nane came.

Then, a week later, God sent an angel.

Even if I hadna prayed, I'd have kenned Father Anthony was an angel. His een were on fire, glowing like the candles on the altar at Mass. I'd seen folk look like that afore but only for a short time — a woman wi her new bairn, a man efter a grand day's hunt. Father Anthony looked at you softly but as though his een were burning you clean.

Father Graham's sickness meant he was relieved of his duties for a lang whiles. Mother Superior had chosen Father Anthony, newly arrived frae the continent, as our confessor. Had I been at hame, I would have kenned all the blethers about him but here we were sheltered frae sich things. Of course there was gossip among the women who came in tae help wi the cleaning and kitchen and mending, but we were always under the watch of Sister Agnes and none dared speak out of turn. Grainne wasna like Elinor either, she was not given tae owermuch talk. But one day when the sunshine was bricht and the air fresh I was sent tae help one of the auld wifies fold blankets after a big wash. And Agatha would talk till kingdom cam.

"There was a wheen of blethers about this Father Anthony. The bishop was fair fashed about it."

"Why is that?"

"They say it's because the Archbishop isna keen on these Franciscan ways, but if you ask me — no that aabody does — he is too young tae be the confessor tae a pack o women and the Archbishop kens it's asking for trouble. But of course her lady high and michty Mother Superior, she kens everything best. No that I'm being disrespectful ye ken, she is a holy lady, but she hasna her feet on the grund like the last yin. The auld mother, God rest her soul, made fine sure any priest was weel ower eighty afore he set fit in the place. But this Father Anthony, his reputation goes afore him, he is everything holy and spiritual, he sees visions and walks haund in haund wi the Virgin Mary."

She gied the blanket a great tug that near pulled me aff my feet.

"Weel let's hope that's the only virgin he walks haund in haund wi. For in my experience — and I have had plenty of experience, borne ten bairns and buried six o them and twa husbands too — when a man walks haund in haund wi a virgin, she's no like tae remain one for lang."

Father Anthony held the host as if it were the last drap of watter in the desert. He pronounced the words of the Mass as if they were the last he would e'er speak. I had ne'er experienced sich as this in my life. Time seemed suspended, like the dew that clings tae the branch efter rain.

In a few days it would be the feast of the Purification and we would all be shriven afore it. Word soon spread

96

round the convent about confessing to Father Anthony. Nuns covered their faces wi their haunds so nane could see the smiles on their faces, young girls came out the confessional looking as though they had been wi their lover. Grainne, whose turn it was afore mine, took my haund and squeezed it, said, "It's like being with Jesus."

I entered the confessional, knelt doon. A sweet smell, like cedar and cinnamon mixed, filled the box.

"Bless me, Father, for I have sinned."

His voice was saft, no like the folk round here.

"Jesus loves you, your sins are forgiven."

"I havena tellt ye them yet, Father."

Auld Father Graham used tae get mixed up and absolved ye as soon as ye went in.

"Trust in the love of Jesus. Tell Him anything that troubles you, do not mind me, I am merely His servant and His vessel."

I couldna speak, I felt as if my heart constricted.

"Do not be afraid. You are His child, He knows we are little children who sometimes get troubled and in need of His love."

"Surely God doesna forgive us if we dinna feel truly sorry?"

"Let God decide what is true contrition."

"I lay wi a lad, Father."

"Tell Jesus."

"We handfasted, but I dinna think we can be truly marriet. Father, there is something else."

"Jesus, it is Jesus who hears you."

"Jesus, I am with child. Is it a mortal sin, Father?"

"Bless you and the child within. The Lord has already forgiven your sin. He loves you and your child."

"I am feart."

"The father of your child, where is he?"

"Far awa." The tears had started tae run doon my cheeks. "My Lady took him across the sea. And afore that, they did something tae him."

"Because he lay with you?"

"No one kenned that — they thocht he was too young. He is a singer, and to keep his beautiful voice, they . . ."

There was an intake of breath frae the ither side of the confessional and I realised I was speaking, no tae Jesus, but to a man.

"I have heard of such things."

"I am feart and I want my mither but Sister Agnes willna let me see her."

"Does anyone know of your condition?"

"No, Father."

"Let me speak to you further of this — I will do all I can to help your situation. And do not worry. God looks after you."

He said the words of absolution, and a feeling of peace descended on my soul.

Father Anthony

Father Anthony knew that his vocation came closest to its purest form in the confessional. Though he prayed daily for the humility that was demanded of a Franciscan, he could not resist a sense of satisfaction when he heard the secrets of hearts and souls and was able, by his gentle words of absolution, to make sinners aware of the grace of God. To hear the confessions of nuns was particularly rewarding. Young women struggling with their calling, older nuns who had developed a painful and acute awareness of recurring faults: his ministrations refreshed and renewed them all.

And he was no stranger to hearing sins of the flesh. At first Deirdre's confession had seemed an opportunity for reassurance and help. Then he realised her connection to the boy. The revelation pierced him like a wound: God had led him here and wanted great things from him.

Nae corner of castle or convent is safe frae prying een or ear. Even in My Lady's chamber or the Mother Superior's room there may be an eavesdropper at the door, a servant sweeping leaves outside a windae.

Father Anthony took me intae the woods tae meet my mither. There we sat under a tree, while he guarded us at a slight distance. I still dinna ken how he persuaded them tae let me see her but he seemed tae be able tae work magic.

Blinded by tears, I barely saw her face as she enwrapped me in her cloak. I cooried close, enfolded in her airms. Sobs shuddered through my body. I wept out all the misery that had been held inside me: missing my hame, my family, Feilamort and the fears about my bairn. I wanted tae stay safe inside that cloak forever, breathing my mither's scent like a new calf.

She stroked my hair till I calmed a little. My een were downcast. Now that the torrent of tears had subsided I felt ashamed. My mither had brocht me up in fear of the Lord, in understaunding richt and wrang. She had nae coorseness aboot her, as fine as the finest silks and velvets in her ways. I couldna bear she'd think her child coorse and low.

She lifted my chin, wiping awa a tear frae my cheek so saftlike I near started greeting again.

"My lass, you've got yoursel in a fine state."

I nodded.

"Father Anthony tells me that Feilamort is the faither of this bairn."

I couldna even nod.

"But how can this be? He's but a bairn hissel. Deirdre, please, lass, tell the truth. If you are trying tae shield some ither man . . ."

"No, Mither."

"Did anyone else touch ye?"

"No."

"Whoever it was, dinna be feared tae tell your mither. I must ken the truth if I am tae help ye."

"Truly, it was only he. It was because they were going to . . ."

"I ken what they did."

"We handfasted."

"Lass, these marriages are no a sacrament in the een of the holy Church. In the auld days, in wild places, where nae priest came for years on end, they tolerated them until they could be sanctified by the proper rites, but they're no for the likes of us. Your faither has a position. Your marriage maun be a true one."

"Minnie, I want tae come hame, I want tae be with you."

"I ken, lass, but it isna that simple."

She looked at me straight, serious. "Have you tellt anyone else?"

"Only Father Anthony."

"You must be brave and pray for God's help. Say nothing. You dinna show yet but it willna be lang and we must have our plan in place by then. Let me speak with Father Anthony."

"Minnie, can I no come hame?"

"And have your bairn brocht up in shame? Or have it taen frae you and gien tae some barren wife?"

She pit her airm round my shoulder. "Deirdre, trust me and Father Anthony. We will dae the best that we can."

The narrow bed seemed caulder and harder efter my minnie's saft cheek and warm embrace. At nicht I'd lay awake, imagine how it would be if, one day, Sister Agnes tellt me I could go hame. And there would be my mither and I'd fall intae her airms. Efter that the rest of the story would be vague, like a fog. It was easy tae imagine being rescued by her, but what then?

What did happen tae lasses who had babes out of wedlock? Usually they were marriet fast enough, afore the bairn came. Sometimes, likes of Margaret, when the faither was gone and nae husband could be found, the child was just brung up in the house. It barely kenned Margaret was its mither, there were that many bairns around. But this would be different. My mither and faither had a position and I would be disgraced. My Lady wouldna let a faitherless bairn be brocht up in the castle and, unless a husband could be found for me richt quick, there would be deep trouble. The likes of William wouldna marry a shamed lass — what man of any position would want me noo? Only the kind of man my parents would never have considered.

I had heard speak of women whose babes had been taen aff them at birth and gien tae some lady who had nane. My heart twisted inside at the thocht of it; I could feel the quickening of the bairn noo, wee secret jumps and kicks inside. I couldna gie it up.

A few days later, as I entered the sewing room, Sister Agnes spake. "Deirdre, you are to go to Mother Superior."

As I walked alang the corridor, my mind was filled with confusion. Mother Superior sometimes came tae see us as we worked, but rarely sent for one of the girls. Surely she hadna observed my condition.

Mother Superior was alone, seated in a wooden chair with angels carved on its back. The walls of her chamber were bare except for a crucifix on the wall.

"Deirdre, you may sit as I have some hard news for you."

We never sat doon in her presence. I placed mysel on the edge of the chair, waited. Mother Superior's face was unmovit, but her voice was saft.

"You must prepare yourself for a journey. Your mother is ill."

"No, no my minnie."

"You must be brave, lass. There is a growth and it has been recommended that she go on a pilgrimage to a healing shrine. Naturally she wants to take one of her daughters with her and since it is impossible for your sister to travel at this time, she wishes that you

103

accompany her. Your brother is waiting to take you back to the castle."

I rose, but my legs felt weak, and I held on to the back of the chair.

"Our prayers are with your mother."

Outside the room, I leaned on the wall. I felt sure that this was the plan, a way to get me awa, but I couldna be sure till I saw my mither. What if she were truly sick?

Thomas was doleful.

"I dinna ken aught about it," he said. "Our mither keeps close counsel. She hasna spake of this to a soul. She's no like these women who are aye bleating about their troubles and travails. Some would mak mair fyke about a skelf on their finger than she does about this." I kenned he found his wife Lizbeth a trial, for she trattles the day lang.

The journey was only a few miles but I ached tae see my mither. I was sure that I'd ken the truth when I saw her face.

"She is sewing," said Thomas. "Nothing maks her neglect her duties."

I entered the room and there she was, as usual, a fine piece of broidery on the frame in front of her. One of the aulder women sat close by, darning a shirt.

Mither turned tae me. "Dochter," she said.

I went tae her and she embraced me, speaking quietly in my ear. "Dinna be feart, lass, I am weel."

She said tae the wumman, "Gang doon tae the kitchen," then turnt to me.

104

"Sit ye doon, lass."

I searched her face but it gied awa naething. She kept stitching as she spake. She glanced round as if to check that there was naebody who might overhear us.

"Father Anthony has arranged all the permissions. You and I will go thegether, attended by himself. We will join another group of pilgrims as it is safer to pass through the land in this manner. I have arranged your clothes for you. We set aff the morn early. Father Anthony kens places for us to stay; we must be very grateful to him. And pray, child, that all may be well and healing take place. If it be the Lord's will."

My een glistered.

She drew me to her and I kenned she could feel the place where the bairn was coming. She whispered in my ear. "Your faither and your sister will wish to see you at dinner time. Show not too much affection to your sister or the bairns lest they realise. They will put it down to your shyness after being in the convent."

Then she drew apart from me, studied my face, and spake aloud. "Whatever happens, it is the good Lord's will and we maun submit ourselves to it."

Father Anthony

"My Dear Sir,

I beg your indulgence in reading and considering the matters contained in this letter . . ."

Father Anthony stopped, thought deeply before continuing his missive. He knew little of the man who was Feilamort's grandfather, other than that he was rich and learned. His daughter had been afraid to tell him of her condition but that meant little; often women hesitated to tell their parents of such things.

Though a scholarly man, well versed in the scriptures, skilled in the arts of composition, Father Anthony mistrusted the written word. He had spent many hours indoors, in silent stone rooms where monks transcribed sacred texts, but was drawn to the image of Christ preaching out of doors. His Christ was weather-beaten like the farmers and fishermen he met, and spoke to his people directly. Father Anthony's eloquence on the subject of love and forgiveness was matchless; he had no doubt of persuading the man to accept his grandson into his household if he could speak to him directly. Furthermore, a certain delicacy and circumspection prevented Father Anthony from narrating the entire story at this time.

Father Anthony's mind was filled with a vision of the joyful reunion of grandfather and grandson. He would finish the business to which he had committed himself, then proceed in the hope that his powers of persuasion would not fail him.

Blessed by Father Anthony, happed up in our wide-brimmed hats and gounies, we set aff next morn when it was barely licht, each cairrying a staff and scrip. Thus would folk ken we were pilgrims and we would be safe on the roads. Following Father Anthony, my mither and I walked side by side, linking airms. I was slower than I would have been a few month ago, but naebody expected my mither to be fast on her feet, so any weariness would be excused on the grounds of her illness. After the first hauf-hour, though, as dawn started tae show pink and orange above the treetops, I found mysel with energy renewed. I was in the fresh air again, hearing the chitter of the birds, seeing shoots start tae form on bare branches; I breathed freedom intae my lungs. My mither's airm, firm and strong, gied me strength, and the sight of Father Anthony, his brown robes merging intae the flair of leaves we trod, removed my fear. We walked in silence for a whiles, then Father Anthony began a rosary and we prayed to Our Lady as we journeyed. The rhythm of the prayer kept our weariness at bay. As I repeated the words I minded that Mary was a mither; she must have felt this heaviness as she walked too, maybe even the nausea. I kenned auld Father Graham would say this was disrespectful tae compare the Blessed Virgin with a lowly sinner like me but surely she must have special feeling for those who were with child?

As pilgrims, we should fast all day, but Father Anthony had excused me from it, on account of my condition. We stopped at noon and I ate twa bannocks, and drank frae a burn, cupping the crystal watter in my haund. It was cauld and fresh, fair set me up for the next part of the journey. Close to day's end we arrived at a house where they shared their meal with us. Efter a day on the road nothing could have tasted better than fresh fish frae the river, cooked ower the fire. They were an auld couple, the wumman kind and douce. She let me and my mither sleep close by the fire. Laying warm beside my minnie, I watched the embers flichter, feeling weariness seep through my banes afore I fell intae a dreamless sleep; I was as near tae Heaven as I'd ever been.

The next twa days passed in similar fashion. Father Anthony kent the road and had arranged for us tae stay at houses each nicht. We were still close by our ain lands, and twa women pilgrims and a priest were safe enaugh frae robbers. I mind those days as a blissful time. The weather was lithesome — dry with only a few skirps of douce rain — and our journey was ower easy ways. My mither's presence and the comfort of Father Anthony, the steady, prayerful walking of the days and the sweet sleep at the end. Nae thochts tae trouble me. And for the first time, the feeling of the bairn inside me. I'd felt it afore, the flichter of the wee birdie's presence, but ne'er had I enjoyed it. Aye too feart, wondering whether it had been noticed. But here in the open, my worries had been laid on the shoulders of my minnie and Father Anthony. They had a plan and I didna have to think. I had ne'er understood the words in the Holy Book afore, that the Lord looks after us, that we should trust in Him. But those days that was what I did, trust in the Lord, and for me the Lord's representatives on earth were my minnie and the good Father.

But it couldna last. In a few days we would join a group of pilgrims and travel with them. My mither had warned me, "Deirdre, keep thy counsel. I'll say that we have vowed tae keep silent other than is strictly necessary for the journey. We dinna wish tae attract attention."

Father Anthony added, "Most folk are serious and devout, but they do not leave their everyday selves behind when they set out on a pilgrimage. There are those who will gossip and poke about for scandal. The group we are with is from furth of this area so it is unlikely that they will know you or your mother, but we cannot be sure. So speak only when necessary."

"Here, lass." My mither slipped something cauld and hard into my haund: a ring, a plain band.

"You canna hide your condition for much longer. Better folk think you are wed. And if we keep silence, we dinna need tae answer any questions as to the name of thy husband. A dutiful daughter, assisting her mother on a holy pilgrimage. That is all you need to be."

Our stop that nicht was at a monastery. The monks kept a guest house for pilgrims, separate from their ain quarters, and by the time we arrived it was near full tae bursting with folk frae all airts and pairts. Strange voices we heard, hard tae mak out their tongues; even when they used the same words as we did, they didna pronounce them in the same way. Efter our peaceful journey, I found it hard tae thole the blethers and bustle of this company. As Father Anthony had said, folk brocht their ain selves on pilgrimage wi them and some of those selves were merry and wanton. It was as if I had been woken suddenly frae sound sleep by a trumpet blasting in my ear.

We found a place at the end of a lang table. There was silence while the monk said grace; this silence should have been kept during the meal but hardly anyone seemed tae tak note. I kept my een doon and ate my breid and brose without speak. My mither did likewise. Father Anthony didna sit near us — the priests were invited to the monks' table and it would have called attention had he remained in our company. I missed his presence and, as I ate, fear started tae rise in my throat, fear like a slow burning, that had nae reason to it but fear.

That nicht we lay thegether in the women's quarters on a hard pallet. It was much caulder than any of the houses we'd stayed in, nae bricht embers tae lull us intae sleep. My mither rubbed my haunds tae warm them. "Courage, lass. All shall be as God wills."

Signor Carlo

We have moved on to another chateau, this time in a less pleasant situation. The air is damp and close here and the boy's voice seems muddy, lacking the clarity and purity which have always been its hallmarks. The castle belongs to yet another of My Lady's relatives, a more distant connection, and our hosts are less congenial. I keep my eyes and ears open while maintaining the impression of being blind and deaf to all except music. Other than when required to perform, he and I remain in our own chambers.

I have seen my Lady only on the most public occasions and I know not what her intentions are. Monsieur Garnet did not travel here with us; apart from ourselves, the guests consist of an aged duke with a taste for obscure historical artefacts and the widow of a neighbouring landowner who brings her three young daughters — a welcome diversion and company for the Lady Alicia no doubt. The priest of the local church sometimes comes to dinner but he is a silent, forbidding character, more like a ghost at the feast than a guest.

I believe it is not My Lady's intention to stay here longer than necessary; it is a convenient stopping point on our journey and, knowing My Lady, there will be some reason of diplomacy involved too. I, being a simple teacher of music, know nothing about matters of state, but I understand that relations between England, Scotland and France have always been of the utmost complexity. And My Lady is the type of diplomat I admire and wish to be on the side of. Her mission is to ensure that her nest is feathered with elegance and comfort and those around her have a life of beauty and grace. Not that she is unaware of the more enduring type of grace — My Lady is as religious as the next — but I would wager that she could sweet-talk the Lord Himself if need be.

However, even she seems to have been infested by the heavy air of the chateau. She has received a missive which has disturbed her; I came upon her the other day as she perused it, and there was a tiny wrinkle on her forehead. I doubt not that our departure will take place soon.

It was a brave sight next morn when our group of pilgrims set out. Blessed by the Abbot, led by a priest with a crucifix held high, the trail of us lasted a goodly length. All happed up in the pilgrim's cloak and hat, hauding staff and scrip, but we differed in size and shape and age. Some were cairried on biers, and there was an auld man in a cartie pulled by his serving men. Mither and I concealed oursels among the crowd, like the deer who mizzles awa, at one wi the forest. We kept to our story of the vow of silence, but this became harder as the miles wore on. Beside us on the road was a wee wifie whose een were filmed ower, and she tellt us that she was hoping the Blessed Virgin would heal her affliction. But her ears seemed made even sharper by her lack of sight.

"So, dear, you're frae the west, I can hear it in your voice. I kenned a wumman spake just like you."

"We are bound by silence, auldwife," said my mither. "I'll thank you to help us keep it."

"Och aye," she said. "It's hard to keep silence on a lang journey like this and, unlike you, I am no fortunate enough to have a dochter with me. Mine were all taken in the last plague but I still bless the Lord. If Job could bear his afflictions I can bear mine. Now where did you say you came from, dear? And what malady are you hoping to be cured frae?"

The auld wifie's blethers were a vexation, like the rubbing of my shoon, but I was mair troubled by a man who seemed to keep looking ower at us. When Father Anthony came to speak to us I saw him watch us closely. He was smooth and weel fed, wi swarthy skin, oily and smooth as if he'd been weel basted, and under his cloak his robe was velvet, not showy, but expensive. I tried tae fix my een on the ground but once again I could feel fear rising. I wisht we hadna joined this group, had been able tae gang by oursels, but Father Anthony said it would draw attention, the three of us travelling thegether, and there was safety in numbers. Safety frae attack and robbery mibbe, but I didna feel safe frae discovery.

At nicht, afore I slept, I wondered what was to happen after we got to the place of pilgrimage. Would they tak me to a safe place where I could have the bairn? But what then? My mither would ne'er agree to the bairn's being taken frae me. I felt the fluttery wee movements and imagined what my wee birdie would look like. All I could see was the big broon een of Feilamort.

A lichtsome dissle of rain when we started out, then afore we'd gone a hauf-mile it was plowterin doon, thicht and grey so ye could bare see yer neb in front of ye. Had we been closer tae the woods we micht have had some shelter, but the skail started when we were

115

richt in the open. Soon we were droukit; the cloaks couldna keep out the wetness and we skleutered through mud, water spleitering ower wur faces.

Efter a while the rain stopped and the sun grew warm, but I was still chittering. My mither let me lean on her airm or I would have stumbled. I was feart we wouldna reach the next night's lodgings but somehow I fauchled my way on, one foot efter the ither. We prayed as we went; my haunds were nirlie with the cauld and it was hard to move the beads one by one as we prayed the mysteries: Joyful, Sorrowful and Glorious. It was the prayers that kept me going, the rhythm of the voices around me, the rhythm of my mither's feet and mines, wandling close by her, shaky-tremlie.

By the time we reached the pilgrim house, I could barely stand and was only half aware of my mither asking for blankets to enwrap me. Swaddled, laid on a bed, I could feel my minnie stroke my brow, hear her voice but didna ken what she said, just the feel of a warm liquid at my lips and oblivion.

I dinna ken what I said in my sleep but I am sure I must have called out, for my dreams were terrifying. Goblins seized my fingers and toes, nipping and biting and running their evil nails all ower my body. Their faces danced afore my een, black devils with coalred een, green bile escaping frae their lugs. Tails like whips. And their voices the most terrifying: they echoed as if they were far awa in a cavern, calling my name and then bad names, ones I wouldna dare tae utter, and then I felt as if slime were pouring frae their mouths and running all ower my body, as though my body were naked and covered in filthy fleem.

I woke to saft light, very early morn. Voices whispering, my mither saying. "Shush, lassie, shush." My face was pappled in sweat and I was that weak I could bare lift a haund.

"It's turnit," a voice said and, as my een swam shakily intae focus, I saw a Sister standing nearby. "The fever is on its way," said my mither, wiping my face with a damp clout.

"Minnie." My voice cracked like a frog.

"Dinna try to speak, lass. Save your strength. The chill took a haud of you, but, thank God, you will be better soon."

The next twa days my strength returned but slowly. Mither barely left my bedside and when she went to rest, a Sister was there, praying her beads or mending, a white still presence in the room. I was too weak to wonder what would happen, how this would haud us up on our journey, but on the third day my appetite returned and I found myself ravenous for the broth my mither brocht me. She smiled to see me so restored and said, "Can you rise now, lass?"

"Aye, Mither."

"Father Anthony thinks that we may be able to catch up with the ithers if we go on a cart. Do you feel able to leave on the morrow?"

"I dinna ken, Mither." I felt better but I didna wish to leave the safety and peace. "Can we no stay here a few mair days? Can we no travel by oursels?"

"It is safer tae travel wi the group. When we reach the shrine we will receive the blessing of Our Lady and pray for a safe delivery. She is the best protectress of your bairn."

She leant near and whispered, "Trust, my child. Father Anthony is not only a good man, but a wise one."

Father Anthony

Father Anthony's trust in Providence, and confidence in his own part in fulfilling the Lord's purpose, were rarely shaken. Even the arrival of the reply to his letter, the tone of which he had found somewhat surprising, had not discouraged him.

Father Anthony had assumed that the man would be overjoyed at the discovery of his grandson, but the letter merely thanked Father Anthony for the communication he had sent and requested that, if it were not too inconvenient, he would be grateful for whatever knowledge Father Anthony might be able to ascertain about the suitor of his daughter, now believed deceased, and any events which may have occurred during his daughter's visit to Scotland.

A letter, even one sent through the private envoys of such an important man, must necessarily be expressed in a circumspect manner; nevertheless Father Anthony had expected a little more warmth of tone. Apparently the man wished him to find out whether there was any evidence that the suitor had, in fact, seduced his daughter; Father Anthony had assumed that this must be the case, but it was possible that another was responsible, in which case the paternity of the boy could be in question. Father Anthony resolved to carry out the arrangements he had made for Deirdre, but decided to withhold certain information from the grandfather; the details of their liaison and its fruit, the affliction which had befallen Feilamort, were matters which must wait for a more appropriate time.

We travelled the next day in a cartie drawn by twa mules. I dinna ken how Father Anthony managed it, for the Sisters had nae such transport, but I would rather have walked as the road was rough and I felt mysel thrown frae side to side. Next morn the way was less cummersome and by mid-efternoon we had made up time and arrived outside a hamlet. The land was flat and the sky vast, scummled wi cat's-hair cloud. We passed a few ferm-folk working in the surrounding fields as we walked the last hauf-mile to the monastery.

I was exhausted efter the journey and slept fine that nicht. The morn I awoke, feeling clear and clean, hungry and longing for food and drink. We were to spend the day in preparation for the visit to the shrine on the morrow, but the monastery was crowded already and little peace was to be had. Most folk were fasting today but because of my condition and illness I was excused. I ate my fill of the parritch and bannocks and spent time sitting outside with my mither. The river was nearby and we found a gentle spot, sheltered by trees, where we watched the water and recovered frae our travels.

It was the first time I could mind being with her, just the twa of us, and my mither having nae task to haund. At hame she was aye sewing or supervising, attending to duties of one kind or anither; it was strange to sit beside her and watch the licht on the water, the wee insects spin around us. We said little, enjoying the warmth and peace of being thegether. It turned my mind to the times spent with Feilamort. That was what drew me to him in the first place; we could be thegether in silence, only speaking what was needed to be said. I didna mislike folk who talked — I loved Elinor and she rattled awa constantly — but there was something deep and richt about the closeness atween folk who have nae need of unnecessary words.

Then I moved frae the thocht of me and Feilamort as innocent bairns in the woods to the memory of what we had done thegether. My face flushed rid and hot.

It was as if my mither could read my mind. She had ne'er asked aathing about him, but the day, in this quiet and peaceful place, she spake.

"Deirdre, I am curious aboot the lad. Did ye love him? Do ye think on him still? Or was what ye did . . . just a passing madness?"

"I dinna ken, Mither. We were fond of one anither, like friends. He seemed so young, I thocht on him like a brither and then, and then . . . things were different. And they were going to . . . it was the only chance."

She said nothing, but stroked my haund.

"Minnie, how do ye ken that you love a man?"

She laughed. "The feelings that owerset ye when you're young, they dinna last. They're like the sun that comes out atween rainshowers, a brief moment of glory and oh so beautiful, but dinna try tae get in the harvest then or it'll be ruined. You love a man because you decide you will love him, because you promise you will love him, and the promise and the will is what matters, no fleeting feelings."

She stared at the river as it lowped and pirled, glancy in the sun. "It's different wi a bairn. The love of a bairn is a miracle — it starts in the wame and blazes intae glory when it's born and, frae then on, it has ye in its power. Compared tae the love of a bairn, the love of a man is a poor thing indeed, though hard tae dae without. But, if you will, it can be a solid thing that gies you a strong foundation. Jesus tellt us tae build our hooses on a rock, the rock of God, but in this world the rock of a good man can help build a foundation for a family.

"Do I love your faither? Aye. But dae I feel any swooning feelings when he's near me?" She laughed. "Mibbe no."

I had ne'er heard my mither tell of love afore. Like many folk who keep counsel, once she started tae speak, she spake wisely, but I was young and with child, and my body seemed tae have taen ower my mind and heart. I wasna capable of understaunding sich counsel.

We hadna spoken with Father Anthony since our arrival, as he was staying with the priests in a house apart frae the pilgrims. But later that day he sought us out.

"If you wish to be shriven before you visit the shrine tomorrow, I can hear your confessions."

My mither was in the confessional for a langer time than normal and when she cam out she looked grave. I went in after her.

"Bless me, Father, for I have sinned."

I didna ken how to go on. I felt the wecht of my sin but couldna express it.

"My child?" he said. "Speak what is in your heart. It is the Lord who is listening. And He forgives even before you speak."

"Does the Lord truly forgive even the worst sins?"

"His mercy knows no bounds."

"But I must first repent of my sin. And how can I repent when I am glad I will have my child, who resulted frae it?"

"These are different things. You have repented of the sin you committed and God has forgiven you. You must not think of it again. Trust the Lord. He loves you as a father. The child is a gift of the Lord and so you should be glad and thankful. Do not be afeared."

He absolved me.

"My child, listen well to your mother and do whatever she tells you. God bless you."

Fog covered the trees next morn, a floating silver-grey flim that saftened the shapes of the branches and melted the distance. Mither and I were haufway alang the line of pilgrims and could see neither the start nor the end of it. There was a difference the day, a dindle of excitement flauchtered through us all. The singing was louder, the praying mair fervent and the yatter quieted. The haar began tae lift as the morn wore on, and sunlicht straiked the sky. We picked our way through a forest track then the path opened out and the folk at the front of the line gied a shout. When we reached the open country I could see why. Across the girsing, schintilled the blue sea.

We walked, singing as we went. The procession was sae lang that the hymn echoed through the line. "Salve Regina, mater misericordiae."

The chapel was a bonny wee building, decorated wi carvings of angels and saints, umbrate agin the glistering sea. When we got closer I could see that the entrance to the shrine was narrow and low. Folk were jossing and dushing each ither out the road and I was feart for the bairn and held back, but eventually our turn came. A priest stood at the door and made folk enter in single file; I let go of my mither's airm with reluctance. She gently pushed me forward, stood behind me in the doorway.

Inside it was dark but for the candles on the altar, and it took a moment for my een tae see the statue of Mary, stars circling her heid, hauding the baby Jesus. I felt unworthy and dirty afore the stainless woman who had borne Christ. I wanted that much frae the Blessed Virgin, I wanted her intercession — tae be cleansed of sin, tae be safe and ken that my bairn would be safe. The fear that had been with me all alang, the fear I didna dare speak, that my bairn would be taken awa, owercame me and I started tae weep, tears pouring out as I knelt afore her.

The priest took my haund and laid it on the cauld marble. I said a Hail Mary and blessed mysel. My mither helped me up and knelt doon hersel as I went through to the outer room. A priest was selling badges and holy relics tae pilgrims. Moidert, I waited for my mither as she haunded ower siller, received badges in return. We came out intae the daylight and I rubbed my een for it was that bricht efter the darkness of the crypt lit by caundles.

I felt weary and owerset. It had been that quick efter the lang, lang days of journeying. I wanted tae feel peace with the Virgin. I wanted tae be with her and pray to her quiet, no be rushed through in minutes, with the jabble of others weeping and wailing and praying around us.

At the pilgrim house that nicht there was singing and dancing and playing of cards. I was shocked. I thocht that efter sich a holy experience folk would be quiet and prayerful but it seemed tae have made many of them ready for pranks and madderam. Maist pilgrims spent twa-three days there. Mass and Benediction were celebrated each day, and there was much to eat and drink. Folk seemed filled with a joy and certainty that their visit to the shrine had given them an indulgence and their sins were washed awa.

The auld wife we had met on the journey was close by us in the lodging.

"That's me all cleaned out noo. I've been cleaned out afore and then I've gone and sinned again. But this time I shall not sin again. You see, lass, I canna."

"You canna sin, auldwife?" said my mither.

She laid a wrinklit finger on my mither's airm. "Each of us has a special temptation. This yin is too inclined tae eat, that tae drink, this tae steal and that tae loss his temper. I hae nae inclination to any of these sins. I have aye been temperate in my meat and drink, kind tae all and honest as the day's lang." She leaned in closer and lowered her voice. "My sin was aye the lads, and even as a wife I couldna lee them alane. But noo," she laughed, and her face lined like a ragged auld tree-trunk. "Noo the lads leave me alane — even the auld blind men dinna want me, so I am safe frae sin. And the good Lord can tak me any time for my life here isna worth living." She giggled awa tae hersel.

Her words stayed with me. Was each of us inclined tae one sin only? Which was mine, then? I didna steal but then I had ne'er been tempted as I had aye had enough. I worked and prayed and had as little temper of any I kenned. I had sinned with Feilamort, been carried awa by lust, but I didna ken if I would e'er feel that way again, for the weariness of the journey and the heaviness of the bairn inside me wiped it out. But I never felt, like the auld dame, that I wouldna sin again; I didna feel close tae the Lord, I felt feart.

We walked that efternoon. I wished to sleep, for the heaviness was upon me, but Mither took me awa frae the house and towards the shining sea. Frae a rise we could see the beach below; ower tae the right was the harbour where tall masts stood proud. We descended tae the quayside, stood near one of the ships, which was being loaded for its journey. Around it sat boxes and kists filled with wool and all sorts, bound for far lands, while the men unloaded the fabric and spices we needed in Scotland.

"Here, lass," said my mither. "Tak this for protection."

She took out the medal she had bocht. On one side was an image of Our Lady and on the other, St Christopher, patron saint of travellers. She kissed it and placed it round my neck. "You maun be brave, lass. You maun cross the sea."

"How do you mean? Are we gaun on a boat?"

"You must go."

"But, Minnie, will you no gang wi me?"

"I canna, lass. I wish I could but I maun return hame to your faither and the bairns."

I felt my blood run ice in my veins. I had ne'er been parted frae my mither in my life, except for those few months in the convent, and even then I kenned she wasna far awa.

"I ken that the bairns and Faither need you, but now, Mither, when I am to have my babe, far frae hame, I need you mair."

She pit her airms round me and said, "Deirdre, I ken fine you need me, but it isna possible. Oh lass, you dinna ken the hauf of it."

Looking back, I see that her words hinted that there was something mair at stake than an unwed maid who was with bairn. Why was I being sent so far awa? But at the time I was that hurt and feart that I didna think.

"Where am I to go?"

"I canna say. Deirdre, I ken this is hard. And for me too. Other than the loss of my bairns, it is the worst thing I have had tae endure — it is a kind of death to let ye gang." She stroked my hair, fiercely so it almost hurt. "But we must trust in the Lord."

All around, folk thronged, saying fareweel tae loved ones, cairrying boxes aboard. Father Anthony came towards us, carrying a small pack. "Keep this safe; it contains a few things you will need for the journey. There is a small kist already on board. You must come now, Deirdre, the tide is right."

I looked out to sea. Near the shore it was calm, just a few jaups as it reached land, but further out it was grumlie and looked to presage a storm. Close up the boat was much bigger than it seemed frae the hilltop, but compared tae the vastness of the ocean it looked a poor thing. How could a few timbers and ropes keep us safe frae the jasch of the wave in a gowstie sea?

"But, Father, where am I bound? What about my bairn? Will you gang with me if my mither canna?"

"No, Deirdre, but you will be accompanied."

Mither said, "I wouldna let you leave if I didna trust you would be weel looked efter."

I hadna noticed the figure who had appeared next us till Father Anthony said, "Here is your companion." I turned round and there, happed up in a thick black cloak, was Sister Agnes.

Father Anthony took my airm. "Come, Deirdre, you must board. Make your farewell to your mother."

I pulled my airm awa, took a step back. "I will not gang," I said. "I will not leave my mither."

My minnie pit her airm on my shoulder. "Be brave, lass. It is for the best."

In the clear licht of the sea, her white skin was bluachie and lined; I had ne'er seen her so haggit wi care. I flung mysel intae her airms, wanting tae greet but that owerful wi feeling the tears wouldna come.

Efter a minute that seemed an age, she let go of me and I was led, trist and taivert, on to the boat.

III

Sister Agnes

I do my duty, I ask nae questions. Obedience is the cornerstone of my life: obedience to the Lord and to those in authority over me, in the Lord's name. Some tasks please me and ithers do not, but pleasure is immaterial. Obedience to God's will brings me closer to Him and that is all I desire.

I ken folk think I have achieved self-control through lang hours of prayer and fasting, through habits of denial learned in the convent. They are wrang. As a child I already possessed an unusual degree of discipline and lacked the desire for material things. Of course I enjoyed sweetmeats and playthings when they were given me but I ne'er longed for them as ither bairns did, never quarrelled or clamoured for them. Frequently I gied them to younger ones because I couldna endure their whinging. I soon realised that what I received in return far outweighed brief moments of gratification. My mither and nurse would commend me, saying, "See what a good girl she is, look how she shares with the others, how she forfeits her pleasures for them." Thus I found my reward in virtue rather than indulgence.

Of course there is a kind of self-indulgence in seeking to be valued, though I was too young to understand that. But as I grew older I realised that abstinence was a way to a deeper

133

knowledge of the Lord. His path is easy. Some novices cried that their lovely hair would be cut, their fine claes taen frae them, but I embraced these things for I kent it would make me even mair pleasing in the eyes of God. Each moment of privation was blessed as it meant I was closer to Him.

What is harder for me is the subjection of my will, not to that of God but to those unworthy of esteem: the drunken priest, the idle Mother Superior, the rich nobleman who wishes his daughter kept out of harm's way in the convent. I subject mysel happily and without question to the will of God and the orders of the superiors whom I respect, but at times my marble exterior is cracked inside, riven with a fury I find difficult to rein.

The task on which I am engaged is neither here nor there. I am prepared to protect the lass frae all dangers, baith spiritual and physical. Though my habit commands some protection, I dinna rely on it for sich a mission. I am weel prepared for foul play; I was brocht up tae look efter mysel and ithers and have ne'er feared danger.

The lassie is, like so many, foolish, ignorant and allows hersel to be overcome by the flesh; no just the flesh of the lust which has brocht her to this position, but the love of earthly things: the fabrics, the sewing, the sea and sky on which she gazes so constantly. She has fallen into the trap of those who see nature, which is the work of God's hand, as something to be loved in itsel. She thinks she is seeing God in nature perhaps, but in truth she worships false gods.

It isna worth discussing this with her, of course, for it is an intellectual idea beyond her limited understanding. Like a cow or a cat, she is happy in kindness and sad when someone is unkind. She is passionately attached to her mither but she is a woman of very different making: a fine and subtle mind, though untrained. Ah, that woman would have made an excellent Sister, perhaps even a Mother Superior. Of course there is still time. Many a marriet woman has entered the convent after being widowed and with children grown. I hope so. And it is for her sake and the sake of Father Anthony, who kens mair about this strange business, that I tak charge of this lass.

I watched frae the deck as the land grew smaller and smaller in the distance and the friendly wee houses on shore disappeared. Bricht and dancing were the waves atween us and the land; the breeze cooled my cheeks and made my een sting but there was warmth behind the sun. To the east the sky was lowering, dark grey lined wi siller licht. The sea birds cawed and skraiked around us. My heart was as stone.

Sister Agnes said little. She showed me where we were tae sleep and arranged our few belongings neatly. The cabin held five women, all nuns except me, and we had box beds set intae the timbers. I kenned we were fortunate as maist folk on board had tae mak do with rough and ready sleeping places. This boat went back and fore, trading, and passengers were taken as space permitted. Maist of them were merchants but some were pilgrims. I still didna ken what our story was and was feart I might say the wrang thing so I said naught. Always the easiest thing for me in any case, but easier still noo, for efter the first hauf-hour of our journey, the sickness cam upon me. I didna boke much but I wammbled and was that owercome wi fauchliness I could barely lift my heid.

I had dreaded the cauldness of Sister Agnes, but her icy haunds were welcome as she held my heid tae be sick and efterwards soothed my brow with a white clout wrung out in cool watter. There was a slight scent to it, shilp and snell. Sister Teresa, who was skilled in herbs and healing, had given it to Sister Agnes. "This will soothe the lass and is safe for her bairn. Is she to join her husband?"

"Dinna speak of him for she may become hysterical," said Sister Agnes.

"Ah, how sad. I will pray for his soul."

Hauf deleerit wi the sickness I clutched Sister Agnes' airm. "Is he . . .?"

"Ssh, lassie," she said and, as the other nun drew further awa, she put her face close and whispered, "Say nothing. Ships have een and ears too."

I hadna thocht of Feilamort for lang, so bumbazed was I wi all the things that had been happening. I still didna understaund why they were taking me on this ship. Why could they no find a quiet place where I could have the bairn with my mither close by?

Efter the first day I felt better and spent my time on deck as much as I could. I ne'er tired of the sea and wondered at how I had lived all my life awa frae it. The birds that followed the boat were unlike the birds on land, though I kenned many birds crossed the sea in autumn and winter. Was it as strange for them the first time as it was for me? They would be with their mithers and faithers, brothers and sisters though.

I took little comfort frae the presence of Sister Agnes, though she was kind enough in her way. Kind like the statue that lets you to shelter under its owerhang when the rain comes. Sister Agnes ensured that I ate, that I was neither too cauld or too hot, that I didna stay out too lang in the sun or rain; she took care of me as she would a package which must be delivered safely to its destination.

I had discovered frae one of the wee cabin lads that the boat was bound for Bruges, a fine trading place according to the lad, filled with beautiful shops and fine linens and silks. The merchants on board would ply their trade there and the pilgrims would go onward tae one of the shrines. "Some even go as far as Rome," he said, his een shiny at the thocht of it.

I sat on the deck watching the clouds birl and skite across the blue sky. My mind was filled with naught but clouds.

Father Anthony

It was the custom in Scotland that the royal entourage travelled round the castles of the realm, dispensing justice and making its presence known to the nobility and poorer classes alike. After a period of residence it moved on, leaving the debris of its visit to be cleared. It was during such a quiet period that Father Anthony arrived at a monastery adjacent to one of the royal castles. The Franciscans acted as confessors to the royal family of Scotland and here lived several priests with whom Father Anthony was well acquainted. There were letters to be delivered to the Abbot and certain matters, concerning only the order, to be discussed. When these were settled, Father Anthony deemed it fitting to confide in Father Dauvit, as they walked the pathway of the garden in the quiet hour of the afternoon.

"The grandfather wishes to know the paternity of the child. While the person we have discussed is most likely, it is possible someone else is responsible. If so, the child's father may be alive."

"After so many years, such a thing would be impossible tae prove," said Father Dauvit. "Tis a sad story, though hardly uncommon. The temptations of the flesh are oft yielded to, and nobles, even those with royal blood, yield just as easily as aabody else."

"The child was born shortly after word arrived of the father's death."

"The name ye mention, a kinsman of the King — it would be possible tae verify the date of his death. If that should fit with the date of the child's birth . . ." Father Dauvit shrugged. "It seems plausible enough. I dinna see how we could be mair definite than that."

Father Anthony shook his head. "I am troubled by this business. From what I know of the young woman, she was as virtuous as St Catherine."

Father Dauvit gave a wry smile. "Sometimes it is the maist innocent who are easiest seduced."

"But could there have been a marriage? A secret one? That would explain matters."

"I doubt it. These lads have ne'er needed tae marry a lass tae have their way with her."

"But she might have believed herself to be married? By a secret ceremony perhaps?"

"It is possible that, to salve her conscience, they may have entered intae such an arrangement," said Father Dauvit. "But it is of little import."

Father Dauvit looked intently at Father Anthony, scrutinising his face as if to see through the external reality, calculate the true measure of the man. When he had satisfied himself, he spoke slowly.

"When I came here at first, filled with ideals about holy matrimony and the evils of fornication, I was shocked by the behaviour of the nobility. Nowadays, while I still disapprove, I am no longer shocked. To them, marriage is important for the

140

creation of a legitimate heir. But they do not deny their bastard children, far frae it. They are given houses, titles, high positions, some even in the Church. This child isna legitimate but there is nae reason why he canna inherit his grandfather's estate. His mother wasna of royal birth, was she?"

"The situation is a strange one. Her father, a nobleman, owns a piece of land which, by means of an ancient charter, lies outwith the jurisdiction of any of the surrounding dynasties. Genova, Provence, Savoy and Aquitaine have all attempted to lay claim to it with no success. But through marriage, one could acquire territory of great beauty and strategic importance."

Father Dauvit laid his hand on Father Anthony's arm. "This seems to me mair a temporal matter than a spiritual one. Are you certain that, by attending to it, you are carrying out God's will?"

Father Anthony looked up at the shoots just beginning to spring from the trees, savouring their fresh hopefulness.

"I understand your fears. I have prayed and prayed. It is not the temporal matters of power and land-ownership which concern me. Each of us is placed on this earth to fulfil a task, and earthly power is granted in order to do God's will. If this tale is true, power was misused: a young woman was deceived and a child deprived of his birthright."

Father Anthony resumed his journey, feeling that little had been resolved. The name of the young woman's seducer was unknown, would in all probability remain unknown, so the boy was without a father. That the suitor, a kinsman of the King, had had his way with an innocent young lass was, sadly, only to be expected. And perhaps, for the sake of the

141

boy, it was better that his paternity should be unknown. In troubled times such as these, who could tell when the bastard child of a distant cousin might become of use to those who sought power through him. If his grandfather acknowledged him, he would be heir to his considerable estate, but Father Anthony knew little of the man, other than that his daughter had been afraid of revealing her situation to him.

He recalled the words of Father Dauvit. Perhaps he had begun to concentrate overmuch on attempting to contrive the future of this child; he should trust in the Lord and his mercy and love. In spite of his rationalisation, however, Father Anthony could not rest content.

Bruges was a bustling place, a guddle of folk and boxes and cries in all languages. It was strange tae sail through the smooth flat calm of the canal efter the rough watters of the sea, tae float towards the tall buildings wi their craw-stepped roofs. A jummle of kists and boxes covered the quayside; I stared at the goods piled up, ne'er having seen sich things afore. Lemons and oranges, fruits I couldna name that were shiny, or specklit or knurlie-skinned. Merchants were examining silks and brocades in emerald and ruby and curale. I wanted tae stop and watch the sailors unload the cargo, the women in their big white headdresses, the gentry in their fine velvet robes and fur collars, but Sister Agnes hurried me awa tae our lodgings. I had hoped that we would be staying in one of the tall hooses that ringed the harbour; they were painted up bricht colours and had wooden carvings on them. But we were bound for the convent, just out of the city. A cart had been sent tae meet us at the harbour and, alang with the ither nuns, we clambered in and rattled our way through the crowds; I could catch only glimpses of the fancy churches and gold statues as we passed.

The convent was a tall narrow hoose wi a walled gairden. Some of the nuns were working there, tending tae the vegetables. We entered a quiet hallway where a youngish woman, wi skin like milk, greeted us and showed us into the room of the Mother Superior, who embraced Sister Agnes, kissing her on baith cheeks. I was surprised as I had ne'er seen sich affection atween Sisters afore. Then she held out her haunds and grasped mines firmly. Though her face was practically unlined, her haunds were gnarled and the joints swollen. She kissed me on baith cheeks, grazing my face with her dry lips.

She spoke with Sister Agnes in what sounded like French but wi an accent different frae My Lady. I was bone-weary and paid little heed to their conversation, just stood there longing for my bed. Mother Superior patted me on the shoulder and we were shown upstair by the lassie who'd greeted us in the hall. I thocht I wouldna mak it up the stair, it was that tall and winding.

Sister Agnes said, "Rest here, Deirdre. Sleep weel efter the journey." I stood at the door for a moment, taking it in; I'd ne'er seen aathing so bonny as that wee wooden bed with its snaw-white cover, starched and smelling of the fresh air. The room was high up and there was a tall narrow windae, owerlooking the gairden. Below I could see the nuns working, one pulling weeds, the ither picking leaves. The sun was bricht and barely a cloud skiffed the sky, the smell was the freshness of the sea. The lassie came in with a bowl of watter, a piece of soap and a white towel.

144

Everything the nuns used here seemed tae be white and plain and, though I'd always loved the colours of our bricht clouts at hame, there was a peace and tranquillity in the plainness.

The lassie waited for me tae wash in the bowl. I felt embarrassed, sae clarty I was frae the journey. The soap smelled of lavender and the towel was saft on my skin. When she left, I lay on the bed and closed my een. Almost immediately I sank intae a deep sleep, only the sound of the birds in the gairden fleeing through my mind.

We stayed at the convent three days and I thocht I had went tae Heaven. I was permitted tae sit outside or rest in the room as I pleased. I didna have to rise early or follow the services of the Sisters. Much of my time was spent in the gairden where I sat on a wooden seat and watched the bees bizzing slowly frae flooer tae flooer, herb tae herb. The nuns grew many vegetables but also flooers, some of which were used for medicines. One of the Sisters, a big rough-looking wumman wi muckle rid haunds, tended to these plants and she would sometimes jabber awa tae me if I was nearby. I tellt her I didna ken whit she was saying but it never seemed tae bother her, she just continued. The Sisters here were unlike those in the convent at hame. They didna seem tae keep the silence; I heard them blethering thegether inside the building and sometimes peals of laughter and giggles would sing out frae the kitchen or the hallway. I barely saw Sister Agnes while I was there. When she wasna praying with the other nuns, she spent much time with the Mother Superior. I saw them talking in the gairden thegether, heids bent. Sister Agnes seemed lichter here too, though she ne'er lost her air of mortfundyit.

Three days of rest and fresh air, with the soups and stews which built up my strength; I kenned I was being made ready for the next stage of the journey, whatever that would be, but I couldna help praying each nicht that they would let me hae my bairn here in this safe and douce place. I ken that the good Lord will grant us our prayers and give us what is good for us and pleasing to Him, but I still dinna feel richt about asking Him for anything, nae matter how much I want it, or how good it may seem to be. I can pray hard for someone who is sick or tae keep my family safe frae harm but if I beg something for mysel, I canna really believe He will gie it to me. But I knelt beside my bed each nicht, praying that the Lord would let me stay in the convent.

"Even just till my bairn is born, Lord, till it is auld enough tae travel, keep me here where I will be safe and looked after by the good Sisters." I gazed at the crucifix on the wall and the sufferings of Jesus came intae my mind — the nails in his flesh, the crown of thorns — it seemed that what I asked was so insignificant. He died to save everyone. What was my life worth, what did the life of my bairn mean tae anyone bar a handful of folk in the world? I thocht of my mither, far awa, and I wept, tears falling ontae the starched white coverlet.

Signor Carlo

Our plans have been changed. Though I have attempted to find out what has caused this, all I can glean is a general rumour of plague. Since this type of talk forms an almost ceaseless undercurrent to life in this part of the country, I have no way of knowing the truth of the matter, nor whether Monsieur Garnet is, in fact, behind the arrangements.

My Lady has taken her daughter and her retinue and gone to visit some relatives a little distance from here. The boy and I have been left to make our preparations for another journey, to the home of her kinsman, who is referred to as the Master. She granted me an interview before she left and, in her usual way, made it seem as if I were doing her a great favour, though, of course, she knows as well as I do that I have little choice but to accede to her wishes.

"Signor Carlo, as you know I am taking my daughter to visit some relations."

"Indeed, My Lady."

"I wish to leave Feilamort in your charge. Do you not feel it would be beneficial to him to have some peace and quiet to study and practise without the demands of singing for guests? The late hours and excitement may be detrimental to his wellbeing, while in the house of the Master you will be able to concentrate on music."

"There would certainly be advantages to such a plan, My Lady."

"And the travel, too — my little bird is delicate and needs tender care."

"The Master is agreeable to our visit?"

"Of course — it is at his special request that you go. Word of Feilamort's voice has reached him and he begs that you pay him a visit. Everything will be arranged for your comfort."

The boy entered, looking like a dog who was about to be kicked by an irate master. Of late he is ill at ease with Her Ladyship, even more so than with everyone else. Only when he is singing does he ever seem to achieve peace of mind.

"Mon petit," said My Lady, stroking his hair. "I have just been speaking to Signor Carlo about you. We are delighted at your progress. Lady Alicia and I are going on a short journey to visit some relatives and we think you would be better staying with Signor Carlo in a lovely house, to continue your studies."

"Thank you," he muttered, barely lifting his eyes from his feet.

"I will miss you, but I feel it is for the best. In due course we shall join you at the house of the Master."

"Oui, My Lady."

"Now, give me a kiss, and wish us well."

Feilamort bowed to Her Ladyship and submitted to being kissed with good enough grace. He is not a fool, the boy. I sensed his relief was as great as mine at the thought of a tranquil life, even if such tranquillity should prove to be only a temporary state.

148

My prayers werena answered. On the fourth morn, Sister Agnes and I, happed up in cloaks with a basket of food at our feet, set aff frae the convent in the same cartie that had brocht us here. Pierre, our driver, spake rarely, usually to mutter under his breath at the mule. Sister Agnes prayed her beads; at first she tried tae get me tae join in with her, but the motion of the cartie was too much for me and I lapsed intae silence. Sister Agnes seemed unaffected by travelling, bore the easy and the rough paths as if there were nae difference atween tham. The countryside was flatter than any I'd ever seen, streetching yella and green for miles as far as you could see. We spent the nichts in monasteries which had guesthouses for pilgrims. We saw naught of these places; arrived at nicht, supped a bowl of soup and slept, rising early tae be on the road next morn. At the second stop I tried tae ask Sister Agnes about where we were bound but she shushed me speedily.

"Silence, remember your vow."

By the third day I had given up thinking. The world had shrunk tae the space within me: my belly full of child who kicked and streetched, the boke rising in my craw, the weariness aching through my limbs. I couldna imagine the bairn ever being born, it seemed that much a part of me, the thing that anchored me to this world. My mind and spirit were elsewhere, floating in some place above the clouds. I watched the sky, the whisps and puffs of white in its blue; their drift was my drift, their stillness mine. Late in the efternoon, judging by the lang shadows and straggling licht, Sister Agnes began tae speak sharply with the cartie driver. I couldna mak it out, her speaking in French and the mannie in his tongue, which was liken to but no the same as French; he seemed tae be wanting to stop and she urging him onwards. Eventually, something prevailed on him, and we moved forward quicker. I was thrown around the cartie and I cried out tae Sister Agnes, "Can we no slow doon? Please."

"We must reach the next place by nightfall."

The mannie turnt but she gied him a look that would have turnt ye tae stone, and he speeded again.

The track had left the flat land and we were now passing through a forest trail; the licht through the trees was bonny, like tae hame, and I wanted tae weep for the pain and the fear and the longing for my minnie. The driver said something tae Sister Agnes which she ignored and he returned tae his muttering at the mule. Then, as if frae naewhere, a whirl of cloaks and horses and we were surrounded. I screamed and Sister Agnes wheeshed me. When I oped my een I could see that there were only twa of them, hoods shrouding their faces. The driver got doon frae the cart and stood hauding the mule. The men made a sign that we were tae get doon also.

150

Sister Agnes spake with them. I could hear the word "bébé" and she signed that my time was near. She pointed at her habit and rosaries, as if to show that we had nae jewellery. One of them kept arguing with her, his voice rough and demanding; the ither was silent. Then she oped her scrip and removed a coin. I thocht she was going tae gie it him but at the sight of it, the quieter man nodded and pit his haund on the airm of his companion. They rode awa afore I had time tae mak any sense of it.

The driver turnt tae Sister Agnes and mouthed a comment, then he climbed up and we set aff. Efter a few yards I started tae shake. I didna ken what had happened but I kenned that we might have been killed far frae hame. My body was tremmling and shivering. Sister Agnes looked upon me as she might have looked on a dug or a cat that was in her road. She reached in the basket and drew out a flask which she held tae my lips. The bitter juice felt fiery in my throat but it calmed me. I curled up in the bottom of the cart and whimpered, eyes shut tight against what was left of the licht.

I awoke, riven by wild beasts tearing my insides apart. A scream rose frae me; it was like the night cry of wolves I had heard in the forest, but they were far across the sea, and this scream was closer than breath. I shook, afeart of my ain body for makking sich a racket, and of the pain that had caused it. Sister Agnes prayed her beads. The pain having subsided, I breathed deeply and tried tae think. Surely the bairn wasna coming yet

— it maun be anither month at least, if no langer. Mibbe it was a sickness brocht on by the journey.

We continued slowly alang a road beribboned by moonlicht, the pains coming and going. I was somewhere atween sleep and waking, a hauf-world where everything was driffled, as if in a fog; voices were muffled and all around me was faded and oothery. When I reached for something solid it slipped awa, and my legs and airms wouldna dae whit I wanted. The cartie arrived at a large gate, all metal work; muckle great horned beasts glistered silver in the moonlicht. This was guarded by armed men but they oped it efter a few words frae the driver and we passed though. The road seemed tae wind upward and upward; the steep angle made me dizzy and my heid spun. Afore lang, however, we arrived at a courtyard.

I could feel airms raising me up and helping me out of the cartie. "Voici," a voice was saying.

"I canna go any further."

"Dinna waste your breath, lass." Sister Agnes' voice was calm.

I started tae moan, "Naw, naw, I canna, dinna mak me, my bairn will die."

My feet and airms shook, I kenned na whether frae cauld or shock. I was hauf-cairried inside and sank intae a seat. Sister Agnes' face swam above me and I could hear her saying, "You will be well looked after, child, rest now." I thocht she was walking awa frae me and I cried out, tried tae streetch my airm towards her, get her tae stay, but a strong airm pushed me back and a voice said, "Hush, you are safe here."

Anither pain near reft me in twa. I looked up as saft haunds were laid upon me, stroking my airm. A coo-like lassie, her headdress severe round her white face and her big een popping out her skull.

"Calm, calm. Sister Grace is coming, all will be well." She wiped my foreheid wi a cool clout.

Sister Grace is coming. I closed my een. In my mind a tall, angelic figure floated intae the room, scented wi lavender and rosewater, soothing and smoothing all in front of her.

The rough-looking wee bauchle who appeared at my side had little grace about her. The haunds that touched mine were rid and horny but she was sure in her movements. She lifted my clothing and felt round the place where the bairn was. "Vite, très vite."

"It is coming fast," said the young woman.

"It's no time yet, it's too early."

Sister Agnes questioned Sister Grace in French then turned to me. "She says the baby is coming very fast."

"It's no time."

"It is time."

She spoke to Sister Grace again. There seemed to be something very important at stake. Sister Grace appeared to be disagreeing, then shrugged.

"Quickly, but gently now. Can you walk a little?"

"I dinna ken."

"Try."

With Sister Agnes on one side and Sister Grace on the ither, I walked slowly alang the corridor. There I was assailed by anither blatter of pain and, winded, I had tae stop. Breathe, breathe, said Sister Grace in an accent so thick I could barely mak out what she was saying, but she panted alang with me tae show me whit she wanted me tae dae, and her calloused haunds were firm and warm on me.

Sister Agnes said coolly, "It is only a few hundred yards."

I wanted tae wail and weep but again I was owercome by the pain. Sister Grace held me till it passed, breathing with me. My mind was full of moonlicht and shadows; the pains, coming and going fast, shook me frae tap tae bottom. I was the pains, naething but pains: shiny silvery pains, white-bone pains, sharp needle pains ripping apart what steeked me thegether. I thocht only of the bairn, how could it be born frae sich pain.

They had me in a room. I was aware of lang slits of licht and a table in the middle and leaning, resting on the table and Sister Grace saying, "Push, push, bien, bien," and she was there under me wi a bolster and all of a sudden I had my bairn as a cow calves in the field.

I now canna mind the things that happened efter that; there were comings and goings and folk blethering in all languages, but somehow I found mysel in a bed, and tucked in the crook of my airm, nestling at my breist and sooking hard on it, was this wee creature, mair like a kitten than a baby. And the feeling of being wrung out and twisted and tossed everywhere left me suddenly, and I was filled with sich a love and tenderness for this being who had made its way out my body. I stroked his heid gently and held him tae me. I wouldna hae kenned if it were laddie or lassie for they had swaddled it frae tap tae toe but Sister Agnes said, "Praise the Lord for a healthy boy."

Sister Grace stood beside me, her face beaming like a big sun. I looked frae her tae Sister Agnes; she watched the bairn as if it were a strange animal she had ne'er seen afore, while Sister Grace couldna keep her een aff him. "Bel fils," she said. Her haunds, which had seemed so rough at first sight, were as gentle as silk on the babe.

My bairn was a wee scrap of a thing but he sooked for all he was worth and his lungs let out lusty yells when he wanted feeding. The days efter his birth were the maist peaceful and joyous of my life — only the absence of my mither cast a shadow. Louise and Sister Grace tended me and the child with sich gentleness and care, as if we were the maist precious things on earth. They washed me and dressed me in clean linen gounies. I didna ken it was normal for a woman tae bleed efter she had had a bairn but Sister Grace shushed my fears and kept all clean and sweet wi fresh clouts and rose-water. The bairn was swaddled tight and when he wasna feeding he was cooried intae me. Sister Grace and Louise took him and stroked and petted him when I got up tae wash or use the chamber pot.

I was ravenous and couldna get enough tae eat. They brocht me broths and saft breids and all manner of dainty dishes. The room was a big one with tall windaes and pale stone walls; there was little furnishing except a kist but fine curtains hung frae the bed, delicate flooers broidered on them. I didna even rise tae eat my meals;

they placed them on a tray and I supped like a lady. The days and nichts were all one tae me, the bairn feeding and waking as he pleased.

Sae addled were my brains with the bairn and the journey and all that had taen place, I ne'er even stopped tae wonder where I was or in whose house I bided. I assumed it was anither of the houses of nuns or monks where we had stayed alang the way, but, on the third day, awaking frae a sleep wi the bairn's greeting in my lugs and turning him tae latch on, I minded the muckle gates as they glowered in the moonlicht and the guards who stood at them; surely nae convent had sich protection. Why had she brocht me to have the child in this place?

On the third day efter the birth Sister Agnes entered the chamber. She stood by the bed and looked at me and the bairn, the same expression on her face as when she examined a piece of embroidery for faults.

"Sister Grace says you are doing well and the child is growing. He is small due to his early arrival, but strong."

"Aye," I said.

"You should rise and take a short walk in the gairden this afternoon. It will be good for you and the bairn. Louise will accompany ye."

When she left the room I was filled wi this owerwhelming wecht of feeling I didna ken how tae explain. No sadness exactly but just a needing tae greet and greet, as if my insides had turnt tae a roaring river of tears. Sister Agnes had said I should prepare tae go a walk but my legs had turnt tae watter too. I laid my

156

heid against the pillow and wept, my wee bairn still asleep beside me. The next moment, Sister Grace was at the bedside and she patted my shoulder. "Le troisième jour. C'est tout."

Efter my weeping I felt cleaned out as if I'd been purged. Louise helped me intae a cloak and wrapped the bairn even tighter than usual. She took my airm though I could walk quite steadily, indeed felt filled with new energy. Outside the room we went through a doorway and up a stair which led tae a cloistered gairden. Louise let go my airm and stood at the tap of the steps as I walked slowly through the beds laid out wi herbs and vegetables and trailing flooers. Some I recognised, like ingins and mint and lavender, but ithers I'd ne'er seen afore. Grassy paths ran atween the plantings and the scent of the herbs and blossoms rose. I watched the fat bees dauner frae flooer tae flooer in the sunlicht gairden. I thocht I was in Heaven, a douce and gentle Heaven filled wi lang shadows and rippling sunlicht and the delicate colours of the herbs and the differing shades of green. It wasna a showy gairden full of rids and gowds and oranges, but a calm and peaceful place, a place of recovery and healing. I walked through the paths, talking tae the bairn as I went. I didna ken how a bairn could see and understaund what flooers were but I thocht that somehow it seeped through him as the warmth of the sun or the cauld of watter penetrates us. I felt he would tak it in and it would become part of him.

Cloistered like a convent, the gairden had stone paths and arches through which the sun slanted; the plants and bushes sheltered us and in full summer this would be a shady spot tae sit or walk. On the side of the cloister furthest frae the stair where we had entered, was a big archway. I walked through, seeing that there was sun and sky at the ither side. I could hear Louise shout, saying I should keep inside, but by then I was haufway through. Insteid of an open park or anither gairden there was a terrace wi a big stone carved balustrade in front of me. And when I looked ower, far far below, the sea sparkled. I gasped. I turned and looked around at the building streetched high above me and far below me. The castle was built out of the rocks.

Louise had followed me and she took my airm, trying tae get me to return. But I kept gazing at the sea below. We were that high, it looked as if ye could jump and loss yersel in the jewelled waves. The castle was built intae the great rock on one side of the hope; the open water was sweeling and sharp beyond its shelter but inside its haven was douce, only spindrift and tricklets of foam splittering the deep azure and green. I couldna see whit was below — whether there was a landing place or beach — without leaning ower the parapet, and I was feart I'd hurt the bairn. But if there was a way of reaching the castle frae the waterside it must be some sicht, rising up frae the deep. The glimpses I could see were of white stone all carved with strange and fantastical beasts and patterned wi foliage. But Louise was guiding me back through; she seemed agitated about our being there and in any case the bairn was needing fed, girning as he woke frae his sleep.

Back in the room I fed him and, sleepy frae the milk, we baith slumbered, him in peaceful rest, me in dreams of wild seas and strange towers.

Signor Carlo

Paradise on earth. The waters dazzle with the light of heaven itself and as for the flowers — how to describe their colour, their scent making one dizzy. One feels drugged by them, especially after days of tedious travelling. Perched on a rocky hillside, the castle stands high above the fishermen's dwellings which cluster the shore. It is a strange building, unlike any I have seen before; flights of fancy and folly adorn its exterior, the white of the stone is carved and curlicued, while ivy and creeping plants traverse its surface. Its owner is, shall we say, an eccentric, but one with sufficient wealth and power to sustain his way of living. His passion is to seek out that which is unusual and, to his eyes, beautiful. Distributed around the rooms are curious treasures, designed to be handled and inspected: sculptures which appear on the outside to represent something in the natural world — a horse or tree perhaps — but when one looks closely, one finds something strange. The horse has eyes which seem to follow you around the room, the tree has demons growing from its leaves.

Our host is not a young man, but impossible to age with any degree of accuracy. He is rarely seen during daylight hours. In spite of having built his castle in one of the most beautiful and temperate places imaginable, he eschews the sun's light. He stays abed till noon, breakfasts sparingly in his chamber, attends to business matters for an hour with his steward. He keeps the light out of his rooms with thick tapestries hung over the windows. For the remainder of the day he works in his library, poring over ancient scrolls and learned texts, for he speaks many languages. He emerges only in the late afternoon when he takes the air in his walled garden, his face wrapped in cloths to shade him from the sun. All this I learned from the servant who attends me; Tomasso is a chatty fellow and his father is our host's trusted retainer.

The Master, as he is known, leaves his guests to their own devices during the day and meets with them at dinner. They are scholars and Church dignitaries who come for a few days at a time, so conversation is generally of an intellectual disposition. The Master presides at table in a most amiable fashion; the only sign of his rather curious habits is the somewhat waxy appearance of his skin, as though the moon, rather than the sun, warmed him.

The boy and I pursue our usual studies; the sun has made him less conscientious than usual, and, I admit, it affects me similarly. However, I spoke with him today and we agreed that if we are to remain here for a number of weeks, we must settle to a way of working. We shall rise earlier and also work at times outside in the fresh air. We can rest in the afternoon when it becomes unbearably hot, as we do in my homeland. This has the advantage that the boy is fresh for the evening; he is required to sing after dinner when there are guests. The Master observes my pupil keenly and appears pleased by his singing, though less touched than most; even at Mass, when

161

the boy's purity of tone can be heard to its greatest advantage, he remains impassive.

His attitude towards my pupil puzzles me somewhat. Over many years I have become familiar with differing reactions to the voice. Since each of us has a voice and almost everyone raises that voice (whether at work in the field, at play or in church), there is no mystery about singing, except to those of us who understand its deeper significance. Of course, much of what passes for singing is mere caterwauling. That is a very different matter: only the ignorance of most listeners permits it to be called music at all.

I speak of the singing of a trained and beautiful voice. When confronted by such, most are awed, filled with admiration, and many are deeply moved. Those who fall outwith this group are generally of two kinds. A few, whether from deafness or lack of refinement, simply have no appreciation of music; that is a rare condition indeed. The others are usually drawn from those of the intellectual elite. They are more censorious; while appearing to recognise the merits of the voice, they criticise detail, affect comparison with other performances they have heard to the detriment of this one. Of course the overall effect of such appraisal is to draw attention to the fine discernment of the speaker and away from the achievement of the singer, a somewhat characteristic fault of our age. But I digress.

The Master neither responds with extreme warmth, nor does he, as one might expect from such an intellectual man, analyse the performance. I sense, beneath the surface pleasure which he seems to take in the boy's singing, a resistance or detachment which prevents him from engaging wholeheartedly with it. But he is too much of a good host not

162

to appreciate the unique talent possessed by the boy, nor its effect on his guests. I do not claim to understand the Master but it seems to me that he seeks to create his own special world, within which he is free to pursue what interests him; we are here to provide both witness to and elements of his creation.

Situated on the south-west corner of the building, our quarters lack no comfort and have access to a beautiful terrazza overlooking the sea. Every need is taken care of, my pupil is satisfying and my life pleasant. But yet, a sense of uneasiness prevents my full enjoyment of this place, like a half-remembered melody which haunts the mind and hinders repose. I know not its provenance; I shall remain vigilant and, in time, hope to hear its notes more clearly.

When Sister Agnes came tae see me that nicht, I felt different towards her — no as feart as usual.

"Where are we?" I asked. "And why have we come here?"

I expected her tae say I must be patient, as she aye did, but this time she looked at me and nodded. "You are in the house of a very important man. He has sheltered and looked after you because he has taken some interest in your situation. He will want to meet you and see the bairn when you are sufficiently recovered efter your lying-in."

"Are we still in France?"

"We are near to France, but this place has its own special climate."

"I want ye tae tell me where this house is. It seems to be built on the rocks."

"You will learn in good time."

I have ne'er had much of a temper, and that I have learned tae keep weel under control, but I began tae feel the birse rise in me. I tried no tae show her but I couldna help but be ramsh when I said, "I would like a straight answer."

"When the time is richt. But there are mair pressing matters — the child must be baptised."

"Is Father Anthony here?"

"We canna wait till he arrives. Anither priest will perform the sacrament on the morrow. Have you considered a name for the bairn?"

"I dinna ken."

I cry him Babbie, or Bairn. The only name in my mind was that of his faither and I didna want tae call him that. Sich a dreich drear name for a babe, sich a wecht of sadness tae pit on his shoulders.

"This is something to be decided soon."

Again, she vexed me with her "to be decided", as if it were anyone else's decision but my ain.

"I will think on it."

"A good Christian name, an apostle's name perhaps."

She left the room and I burned inside, though I wouldna show it.

I did think on it that nicht, lying beside him. I was saddened that Father Anthony wouldna christen him; I wanted tae hear his sweet voice say the name the bairn would cairry, his gentle haunds mak the cross with chrism on that white wee foreheid. But I kenned we couldna wait. Though small he seemed lusty and strong, but any bairn could get sick. With the stain of original sin upon him, an unbaptised babe didna go tae Heaven, but languished in Limbo. Ghostly babbies floating aboot in a dreich grey fog.

"I baptise thee James, in nomine Patris et Filii et Spiritus Sancti, Amen."

A wee bent mannie, the priest — Monsignor Bertrand, who is chaplain to this hoose. Sister Agnes tellt me he would be leaving when Father Anthony came as he was auld and worn oot, nae longer fit for his duties; his haund shook when he blessed the breid and wine. His een were filmed and his fingers crookit like claws. When he drapped the watter on the bairn's heid, the babbie never grat, just took a breath in, as if surprised, then gurgled.

James is my faither's name. Last nicht I had thocht on every name I kenned, imagining crying the bairn by them, but could think on none better. James, Jamie. But to me he was still the babbie.

Sister Agnes

For the duration of her lying-in, Deirdre will be cared for by Sister Grace and I am permitted to retreat intae the cloistered peace of the convent nearby. I am grateful for this time spent in prayer, reflection and fasting. After the rigours of the journey, though my physical strength is undiminished, my spirit hungers for the quiet of chapel and cell; I would prefer to continue there but I shall gain strength from my time of withdrawal and be ready tae meet whatever is required of me.

Though I fulfil my duties as required, my part in this affair becomes ever mair tedious. The lassie, delivered of her bairn, is no longer content to dae whit she's tellt and seeks information which I canna reveal. Father Anthony is persuaded of the necessity of this endeavour and I ken that his mind is fixed on the divine will, no the foolish vanities of human beings. But the Lord said we must enter by the narrow gate, no the elaborate wrought metal ones. And the architectural fantasies of the scholar would be better used tae serve the glory of God than his ain aspirations.

I long for peace and tranquillity, for hours spent on my knees in adoration. I am made for contemplation. But he wishes to use me for action and I must accede to His will. I mak nae judgment; the Lord's ways are mysterious and His knowledge of us far exceeds our ain. The Lord has granted me a clear eye, but it maks me intolerant of those who see with less discernment. I ken this is a fault and vow tae spend ever longer on my knees praying that he scour it out of me.

Forty days. Sister Grace spread her fingers and repeated the action four times. Forty days like Christ in the wilderness. Had I been at hame, forty days would have passed joyously. Cared for by my mither, the bairn safe by my side, tucked intae a blanket and cairried wherever I went. Forty days here passed like an age. Sister Agnes never came near me, gone to the convent. "Father Anthony will be here soon," she had said afore she left. But Father Anthony ne'er came. I resigned mysel tae thole it and enjoy this time. The bairn was my delicht. A bonny, easy, sunny wee thing, bricht een that seemed tae ken everything. Though I am no by nature a talker, I blethered tae him all the time, sang my minnie's lullabies, tickled and stroked his skin, saft as silk. Sister Grace and Louise loved him and took every chance tae haud him but my body ached for him efter even a short time. My milk ran at the thocht of him, at the sound of his cry. They brocht me a basin of watter and I washed every morn, wondering at the breists which used tae be flat but noo are plump and full tae bursting. My body is rounded and saft, created for my bairn's comfort. At first I felt embarrassed; Sister Grace had nae shame, wasna like Sister Agnes, who would avert her een when you washed. And at hame there was little enough washing; in the winter you'd barely undress, and in the summer you washed in the burn.

Not only did Sister Grace watch me, she would touch and point at me. I didna understaund every word she said but you couldna mistake her tone. She smiled and laughed as she pointed tae the roundness of my breists, even cupped one in her haund and let it fall, delighting in the wecht of it. She examined me for cracks and sores, and when she rubbed her sweet ointment intae me she smiled and said "belle" and "bien". Once I had grown accustomed tae her ways I was glad of her; she was the nearest thing tae a mither I had. Though I loved the closeness of the bairn I needed tae be a bairn mysel sometimes, tae be looked efter, no just fed and kept warm.

Louise was kind. She spake a little of my tongue and the rest we managed wi signs and gestures. She accompanied me intae the gairden but begged me no tae go through the archway again, for fear she would get intae trouble and they would move her somewhere else. I didna want that so I kept tae the paths. The flooers were lowping intae full bloom, each day a new colour, a new bud. They grew high on either side of the paths and we walked through a secret world of flooers. Fat bees bizzed frae one tae anither and the chirrup and trill of the birds reminded me of Feilamort. I wished the bairn could hear his voice soaring above the sounds of the gairden. We stayed out on our walks for longer, taking one in the morn and one in the efternoon. Looking at the beautiful flooers, that rich

170

and roarie and variand compared tae hame, I longed tae get at my needlework again, try tae recreate the beauty.

There came a few days when, though it was still warm, blauds of heavy rain came and went, and we couldna gang outside. A bricht fire was lit in the room tae keep the damp out and mak sure the bairn never caught cauld, though he was that swaddled and cooried close by me that nae cauld could e'er have reached him. His sooking had calmed a bit and he was mair contentit, looking round sometimes when he was awake insteid of immediately reaching for the nipple and fixing his gaze on the bit of skin above; I was relieved as the sooking was rough and my nipples had been sair. Sister Grace had placed leaves on them tae cool the heat and it was easier noo. But with the ease came the desire tae get out the room. It was nae longer a safe haven but a place of prisonment, though I kenned I was a fortunate captive.

On the fortieth day Sister Agnes entered and sat by the fire, opposite the stool where I nursed the bairn. He had stopped feeding and slept, contentit, his face turnt intae me. I had observed that she didna like tae be in my presence when the bairn was feeding; even when he was hidden by the shawl she had a look on her face as if she had detected a foul smell and would leave as soon as she could. The day she was as calm as ever; her brow smooth beneath her cap. I wondered if, when she took it aff, her face collapsed under it.

"Tomorrow the Master wishes to see you and the child. He requests your presence in the evening, afore supper time. Louise will take you part of the way, then I mysel will escort you."

I was full of questions but she waved her haund and dismissed them. "I can tell you nae mair," she said. "Father Anthony is the only one who kens and he has been delayed on his journey here. All I can say is that he is a great lord and you are fortunate indeed to be here."

It was hard tae wait till evening time. I felt my stomach in knots and was unable tae eat much in spite of Sister Grace's coaxing. She made the soup for me with her ain haunds, filled it with vegetables and lentils and good herbs. Usually I wolfed it doon but the day I barely supped, and could eat naught else. I hadna slept much the nicht afore and felt bleary and doilt as I waited for Louise tae come.

I followed her alang narrow corridors, just wide enough for one person tae pass. The slap of our feet on the stane flair echoed in the silence. The passages were kept clean and swept; they were lichted frae above, through grilles which oped on tae some upper passageway. I felt as if the flair were sloping up and doon but because it wasna straight it was difficult tae get any bearings. At the end of the winding corridor was a narrow door. Louise chapped the door and it was oped frae the ither side with some scraping and difficulty. Louise stepped aside tae let me by. She said naething and kept her een on the ground but, as I passed, I felt her squeeze my airm.

On the ither side stood a man of middle years, rid-faced and chuffie, dressed in a brown tunic. He muttered some words I didna ken and beckoned me tae follow. We climbed a steep flight of stairs, then turnt richt and left, this way and that; it was a warren of passages, like a rabbit clappard, and I couldna have minded the way if I had tried. For sich a pudgie man, he moved speedily and I was peching when he stopped at a door so low I would have tae bow my heid tae enter. He took out a great jangle of keys frae his pouch and oped it, motioning me through. I heard the latch cleek behind me.

Sister Agnes was waiting, hauding a caundle which lit her face frae below; its lines stood out, rugged as a rock face. She ne'er spoke, and I followed her alang yet anither corridor, this one straight. At the end was a door, servants standing on either side. They were richly dressed but each had a knife at his belt. The door was opened. I waited for Sister Agnes to go afore me but she nodded and said, "Enter. I will await ye."

The chamber was furnished in crimpson and gowd and green, tapestries covered the walls and there was even one on the flair. I didna ken if the room had nae windaes or if they were concealed by the tapestries, but it was dark, lit by flichtering sconces. It wasna gloomy, but cosy like a cave where you'd taken shelter frae the storm. There was a grand oak table in the centre of the room and, seated on a chair so big that it was like a throne, was the Master. A funny-looking cratur he was, and when I seen him I ceased to have fear of him. He was swathed in velvet robes and his collar was made of white fur I kenned was ermine. They were finely broidered wi a pattern of vine-leaves and tiny flooers. On his heid was a cap of wine-coloured velvet, a tassel hinging at its back. The face which keeked frae these claes had a strange waxen appearance, as if the Master was neither young nor old, but preserved frae Time's passing. Tiny een glittered like a magpie's, and his mouth was a slit in the smooth face. His voice was high-pitched and had a singsong quality which minded me of my grandam's speak.

"So you are Deirdre?" he said.

"Aye, Sir." I curtsied, which was difficult while hauding the bairn.

"And you have brought the child."

"Aye, Sir."

"May I be permitted to see him?"

He came round tae my side of the table, moving slowly but gracefully, like a dancer. He was slight under all the big robes; the foot that poked frae the bottom of the gounie was smaller than mines, encased in a velvet slipper wi gold borders. A heavy rich scent hung aboot him, smochie as the warm air in the room.

He stood beside me while I unwrapped the shawl a bittie frae the bairn so he could see his face better. He was sleeping and his lashes curled up like black feathers. His brow was smooth and his mouth like a rosebud.

"You have a beautiful child," he said, nodding. "Very beautful." He examined me. "You will excuse me if I say I do not see much of the mother's face in this child."

"No, Sir."

"He resembles his father?"

"I think so, Sir."

"He is a fine child. You have looked after him well. I hear you are a very good mother."

"Thank you, Sir."

"Please sit down, Deirdre." He nodded towards a chair and returned to his ain seat on the ither side of the table.

The chair looked comfortable but it was too high for me and the great claw airms made it hard to sit wi the bairn on my lap. I was feart he might wake and start greeting. The Master was the only one who might tell me why I was here; I didna want our interview tae be interrupted.

Spread out on the table were scrolls and parchments. A kist stood open in a corner of the room, full of mair papers, all guddled thegether, and next it was an armoire filled wi books. The Master saw me looking at them.

"You are interested in books?"

"I canna read, Sir."

He laughed, a funny high-pitched laugh. "Deirdre, you do not read, but no doubt you like stories?"

"Aye, Sir."

"Some day, I do not know when, I will tell you a story. But this is not the time." He paused. "Now, what can you do, Deirdre? Apart from look after your child."

"I can sew, Sir. I am an embroideress."

"So I have heard from the good Sister."

He rubbed his chin wi his haund, which was encased in a velvet glove. "You may have noticed that I am a lover of fine needlework, as, indeed, I am a lover of beauty in all its forms."

I looked at the tapestries. Even in the dim licht I could see something of the detail and the fineness of them.

"Deirdre, you are young and have, I understand, led a sheltered life. In time you may come to realise that there are those whose vocation is to do: to sew, to spin, to till, to harvest. And there are those, few in number, whose vocation is to appreciate the fruits of that labour — be they fine wine, glorious music or wonderful tapestries — and to surround themselves with beauty in all its forms." He paused, stared at me with his heid tae one side.

"You have seen something of my home?"

"A wee bit. I ken it is a beautiful place."

"It is unique. I have fashioned it out of the rocks which overlook one of the most beautiful coastlines in perhaps the most sweet and delightful climate on earth. If you want to know what the Garden of Eden might have been like, you only have to think of this place."

He looked me full in the face, his wee een sharp as a futret's.

"Would you like to stay here and work for me on some embroidery, Deirdre?"

I was confused. I had thocht I would be tellt why I was here — why did he ask me tae sew for him?

"But the bairn . . ."

"Of course, your child would stay here with you." He waved his haund as if brushing awa a fly. His thin mouth twisted itsel intae a hauf-smile. "There is room here for a child."

I curtsied, no knowing what to say.

"So, you will be happy here with us for a while?"

"Aye, Sir . . ."

I hesitated. I wanted tae ask, "How did I come tae be in this place, so far frae hame? What do you want of me and the bairn?" but somehow the words stuck in my thrapple.

"Is there something which troubles you?"

His een grew even smaller as he stared at me, like glittery specks in a blank face. I looked doon and my een fell on the papers, piled up wi an ornament tae haud them doon. A bonny, shiny thing it was, fashioned in gowd; at first glance I saw a strachle of leaves growing ower a rock. But as I looked closer, admiring the fine workmanship, I saw what it represented. Among the foliage was the clew of a beast, pointy and sharp and cruel, gouging intae the fleesh of a wee mouse.

"No, Sir," I said.

"I think your child is waking."

I could feel the bairn's wriggling, a wee streetch and yawn, and I kenned it wouldna be lang till he wanted fed. I stood up.

"Thank you, Sir," I said.

"Work well at your sewing, Deirdre. You will be rewarded. I am a good master."

Signor Carlo

I am somewhat disturbed. On the surface all appears smooth and delightful but there are undercurrents which suggest that this calm is false. The brightness of the sun on the sea can hide murky and teeming waters.

The castle appears to be divided into several parts. This upper part, where our host resides, is joined to the other through snakelike trails. The complexity of the design, the way in which it has been created out of the rock, is even more intricate than I had realised. There is another way in, to a dwelling on the lower level; due to the topography of the landscape and the coast, the lower part of the castle is invisible from the upper, though it is possible to pass between them. The cellars and storage areas of this building are in fact higher than the building on the other side.

According to Tomasso, that part of the castle is not much used, but occasionally those guests our host would prefer to keep at a distance are housed there. I assume there are some political reasons for this. I have been too long in the service of the nobility to underestimate the machinations which underpin their lives; the fragility of what appears to be built on the solid rock of wealth and status is at times breathtaking. I have seen ancient houses razed to the ground, alliances ended at the caprice of some Lord or Lady, marriages which seemed made in Heaven end in the decimation of a dynasty. While my humble position, living by my wits and talents at the mercy of others, might seem precarious and unenviable compared to that of someone like My Lady or our host, at least I recognise it fully, and remain on my guard for possible difficulties and strategies to circumnavigate them. I doubt not that the Master has built his castle, with its various entrances and exits and circuitous passageways, in order to protect his security in troubled times and to ensure that different factions may be kept without knowledge of each other.

He is a clever man but perhaps he underestimates the capacity of his servants for gossip. I have heard tell of a young girl who has given birth in mysterious circumstances. Of course this may be no more than an unfortunate incident of the kind which frequently befalls noble lords. Their bastard children litter the world, multiplying like weeds.

Given what I have seen of our host, it seems unlikely that it is his progeny. There is a natural asceticism about him, a delicacy of sensibility which seems to belie such an association. Of course it may not be his own, perhaps that of someone he wishes to shield, a relative or associate. Or it may be that he, like many men, has another side to him. I have been for so long an observer of men that nothing they do can now surprise me.

While the activities and proclivities of my host are none of my business, the future of this boy is. I have heard nothing from My Lady and I begin to wonder what is to become of us. While life is pleasant here, it is not the summit of my ambition; much greater possibilities are opened to me by the boy. This is not a purely selfish position; the Lord gives each of us a talent to be used to His greater glory. I know that by using my talent as a teacher I can help the boy to reach his full potential, and, in doing so, further God's glory.

I thocht they would move me to some part of the castle where I would be with ither women, sewing thegether. But when I returned frae my walk in the gairden with Louise, I found a frame set up by the windae, the canvas streetched upon it. A table sat next the frame, and upon it lay silks in the bonniest of colours. I felt the saftness and smoothness of the threids, longed tae work the colours, place one agin anither.

I heard a cough, no a real cough, one designed tae get your attention, and I turned. A man stood at the door. He was lingit and graceful-looking, mair like a lass than a man, though when he stepped forward intae the licht I could see he was aulder than he first appeared. His hair shone like a chestnut colt's mane, and hung tae his shoulders, sleek like a cap. His claes were of velvet and round his neck was a collar, elaborately broidered in heavy gold threids.

"Madame, the Master has asked me to explain what he wishes you to do." He held a rolled up piece of parchment in his haund. "If you will permit me."

I curtsied.

Sister Grace reached for the babbie and he went to her, happy in her strong airms. The man unrolled the parchment and held it out so I could see. On it was a drawing of a unicorn, its heid in a lady's lap.

"I shall transfer this drawing to the canvas for you to embroider. The unicorn, of course, should be white and the lady's gown azure. The Master wishes a background of flowers but you have the freedom to work them as you think fit."

"Thank you, Sir."

I could hardly believe it; I would be permitted tae broider the flooers as I pleased and I had the maist lovely of silks tae choose from.

"It is the Master's wish that you see the original on which this is modelled." He indicated the door. "If you will follow me."

We walked through a maze of corridors. I had nae idea if this was the same route I had gone afore, though I kenned we must be passing through tae the ither part of the castle as there were guards who unlocked doors for us; they nodded at him but ne'er looked in my face. We entered a room where at first I could barely see aathing as it was that dark. But the man, who had ne'er yet said his name, using a pole with a hook on the end of it, pulled aside a heavy drape. The chamber turnt frae nicht tae day; the sun bleezed in a near-white sky.

"The room is kept dark to protect the tapestries. We can see them only for a short time."

I looked round. Huge tapestries in bold colours covered the walls. Hunting scenes, the forests louping wi birds and animals, wee mice and rabbits keeking out frae the undergrowth, sleek hounds trailing at their master's feet. One with a fountain spewing silver water.

Bricht claes. And woven through it all, the story of the unicorn.

At hame my lady had some fine tapestries but naething like these. The eyes of the beasts stared at ye as if they were alive, the fox looked like tae snap your fingers aff, and as for the flooers — the colours and shapes sang frae the stitching. I longed tae run back tae the room and get started on my work.

We walked round in silence, looking at the tapestries.

The final one was the picture the man had shown me; the background was in jewel colours while the unicorn stood out white and stark.

"Are you familiar with the tale of the unicorn?"

"The unicorn can only be captured by a maiden and, when caught, he puts his heid in her lap."

"Indeed, and that is the part of the story which you will illustrate with your needle."

"They say the unicorn is Christ Our Lord."

"The Master has studied the scriptures and the historical documents. He knows much about the unicorn."

"Is that why he wants this picture?"

"I do not know. I only know that he wishes a smaller, portable version of it. The tapestries are very beautiful, and the work exquisitely skilled, but he thinks that the method of embroidery will permit a delicacy of detail which is more suited to the smaller scale. The Master is an expert in art techniques as well as a student of books."

"He tellt me his vocation is to appreciate beauty."

"The Master treasures the many beautiful possessions with which he surrounds himself."

"What work is it you dae for him?" I wondered at his place here. The tapestry workers at hame, though skilled, werena the same class of man as he was.

"I draw, I copy for him, I am occupied on tasks such as this. And when I am not so occupied, I am permitted to make art of my own. I am fortunate. He is a good master — if you do good work for him he will reward you." He looked at me, serious. "Do you think you know what is required of you? Do you have any questions?"

"Only one, Sir."

He waited.

"I dinna ken your name, Monsieur . . ."

"Alberto." He didna smile but his een saftened a bit. "We shall return to your chamber. I will draw the outline for you now so that you can start as soon as possible. If that pleases you."

My fingers itched to get started.

"That will please me greatly, Monsieur Alberto."

With a great swishing sound, he drew the curtains and the room returned to darkness.

The days took shape. Up wi the bairn, feeding him and breaking my fast. A time outside if weather permitted, then, when the bairn slept in the morn, I worked at my frame. Though I longed tae sew, I was feart too. I had ne'er done aathing of this size or importance, and feared I would mak a mistake. The unicorn was in the centre of the picture so I began with its back. It had been lang since I had spent so much time on my work but my fingers hadna forgotten and I was soon takking pleasure in the rhythm of the stitches. It felt fine tae look closely at the threids, deciding on the colours. Monsieur Alberto came during the morn tae see how the work was progressing. He said little but sometimes would explain things about the drawing.

"See, the weight of the haunch, the way the curve suggests the solidity behind."

The unicorn was the maist difficult part of the piece since it was one colour. The flooers, though complicated, would be easier, familiar, but the unicorn had tae be mair than just a big daud of white in the middle, and it was Monsieur Alberto who helped me see this.

"Perhaps this shade?" He picked out a threid the colour of the mushrooms that grew in the forest at hame. "A little worked along this line . . ." He pointed out the place. "If you think it is good, of course."

"Thank you, Monsieur."

He was usually right in his suggestions, guiding me gently. I used ivory and cream for the outline of the unicorn's leg, began tae see the difference atween milk- and snaw-white. I had aye been one for noticing what was around me and oft found mysel gazing at the way licht played on objects, shaped them. By the time I had worked my way frae the back of the unicorn to its heid I could see it tak life.

At dinner time Sister Grace would return wi the bairn. I was that glad tae see him smiling and laughing. After some time thegether I must needs tak up my needle again while the licht was still good. In the efternoons, Sister Grace minded the bairn in the room while I sewed. He loved tae watch the licht dance in the dust. Sister Grace sang and clapped and pulled at his ears and nose and made him laugh.

The days were easy. I wasna required tae spend lang hours at my needle, naething like the time my mither and the women worked at hame. My meals were brocht tae me and I had naught to dae but sew and look after the bairn, which was my pleasure. But it was a strange shut-up existence. Though I enjoyed the sewing and looked forward tae starting my work each morn, though the babe grew round and plump and bonny, though Sister Grace was kind and the place beautiful, as the days went by I felt as though I were only hauf-alive. Mibbe if it hadna been for the bairn I could have tholed it fine. But I began tae wonder what would happen as he grew. Now he slept many hours in the day, and, when awake, was happy tae be bounced and blethered to. But as time passed he would sleep less, would start tae move of his ain volition, wouldna be contentit with one chamber and the walled gairden.

I had nae idea what they planned for me and no one I could ask. Sister Agnes ne'er came tae see me. At nicht I lay thinking on my life here; I was aware that I was fortunate since my yoke was light and I had all I needed. But when I closed my een I saw a caged bird My Lady used tae keep. Some grand visitor had gien it to her as a present; it had beautiful feathers of gowd and green and looked that bonny all the bairns wanted tae pet it. My mither tellt us no tae touch it and I never.

But we crept up to its cage tae look closer, and it turned and looked at us with een that werena alive. A wee bird has nae place in a cage, it must flee and fung and sing.

I thocht of my life at hame, the freedom tae run in the forest, jouk up and doon the stair for a message, blether with Elinor in the kitchen. There was aye racket and bustle, folk coming and going, everyone working and shouting and joking. I had found it all too noisy, been glad tae work in peace and quiet wi the women. But noo there was mair silence than I could bear.

I missed my mither, there was an ache in my heart for her. I wished she was here with me and the bairn. But you canna wish your life, you maun tak it as it is. The good Lord gives us sorrows tae bear and He gives us blessings. And my blessing was cooried next me, breathing his sweet breaths in and out. If there was a price to be paid for him, I would pay it gladly. Even though I wished I kenned mair about why I was here and what would happen efter the picture was finished, my life was easy and pleasant. I prayed tae live each moment as it came.

One efternoon Father Anthony returned. I never heard his footsteps on the path, it was as if he had appeared like an angel beside me.

"So this is the child." He gazed upon him. "Beautiful."

He blessed the babbie, made the sign of the cross on his foreheid, saying words in Latin. Father Anthony's voice was low and singsong, like the humbumming of a bee. His face was mair lined than I minded, though, forfauchlit frae the journey, nae doubt.

"Father, how long will we stay here?"

"A little while. I must see the Master and discuss matters with him first. I gather he has set you a task — how does your picture do?"

"I am close to the end, Father, perhaps another week."

"Good."

"What happens after?"

"You must be patient a while longer. You are safe here, the child is safe."

"I ken. But, Father, I want to see my mither."

"I have come from her. She sends you this."

He reached intae the pouch in his robe and pulled out a piece of cloth. I unfolded it and took out a wee white bonnet for the bairn, broidered with a trellis of birdies and flooers. My minnie's work. I felt the tiny stitches, imagined her working on it at hame, thinking on her grandchild far awa.

"What of Feilamort, Father?"

"He is safe and well in a place not far from here; he continues to study his singing."

"Father, it wasna richt they did that thing to him."

"It is done. And his voice is preserved."

"It was harsh and cruel."

"Sometimes we can change things, and it is our duty to do so. And sometimes, when things cannot be changed, we must make the best of them."

"Where is he? Can he no come and see his son?"

"Deirdre, we must be patient. The owner of this place is an unusual character. He can be a good master but he has strong ideas about things and it is best not to cross him. I will do what I can; I will try to find out whether Feilamort can come to see you here. Trust the Lord. He has a plan for us all. Sometimes we cannot see it and sometimes we do not agree with Him, but He knows best."

Father Anthony

Father Anthony's correspondence with the Master had led him to expect a man of a somewhat forbidding and possibly irascible nature. Consequently, he was reassured by the Master's hospitality and the beauty of his environment. He was eager to see Feilamort and impressed by his modest and gentle demeanour. On hearing the boy for the first time, Father Anthony was entranced by his angelic tones; he had no doubt that God's will had brought them together.

But as the days passed, Father Anthony began to chafe against the slow progress in this matter. He understood that the Master had reservations about Feilamort, but believed that, having observed him more closely, he would appreciate the boy's innate goodness as well as his rare talent, and claim him as his grandson. Father Anthony had assumed that by now he would have presided over a simple wedding ceremony between the lad and Deirdre, thus legitimising their son, and would be on his way to preach the love of God in another part of the countryside.

Yet matters seemed to have barely moved forward. The young people were living in separate parts of this strange structure, neither knowing of the other's presence. Worse still, the boy was apparently unaware of the existence of his child. While Feilamort continued with his singing, Deirdre had been given some sewing task, apparently at the Master's caprice.

Father Anthony felt an uncharacteristic hesitancy about broaching the subject. In the presence of the Master it was difficult to do other than follow; to deliberately take charge of the topic of discourse was impossible. It was a relief to Father Anthony, therefore, when one night, after dinner, the Master raised the issue.

"I am aware that I have spent much time in deliberation of the matter which you so kindly brought to my attention. I trust you will not think that my silence suggests lack of import. On the contrary, had it been other than a matter of the deepest significance, I might have resolved it sooner. However I am expecting some visitors whose presence is pertinent to this matter; I expect that affairs will begin to move towards a conclusion. But now, I would be grateful if you would permit me some time for spiritual discussion."

Father Anthony felt a surge of excitement within his breast. Since childhood he had loved nothing more than prayer; to be on his knees in the presence of the Blessed Sacrament, to raise his voice to Heaven in the company of other priests, was his delight. But following closely behind this love was his love for discussion of faith, of points of doctrine or scripture. This was a love he rarely had the opportunity to express, since his duty involved him in tending to layfolk who could have no understanding of matters of deep spiritual significance. One of the reasons (which he did not admit to himself) that he had remained in the castle for longer than necessary, was the atmosphere of learning and the scholarly talk of the Master, which nurtured a certain need in him.

As was his custom, the Master had his unicorn cup of wine placed next him. Father Anthony accepted a measure, though normally he only drank wine which had been consecrated and turned into the blood of Christ. There was an intimacy about the warm, dark room and the calm presence of the Master which relaxed Father Anthony; he was prepared for a pleasant hour of theological discussion.

"I wish to ask your opinion of punishment, Father," said the Master. "What do you consider to be its role in the temporal sphere?"

Father Anthony felt a tiny shiver of discomfort rush through him. His natural inclination was to comfort, to cast out fear, to demonstrate that the love of a merciful God was all-encompassing. He knew, of course, that punishment was part of the great scheme of things, but did not like to dwell on it overmuch.

"Clearly, where wrongdoing has taken place, then punishment is justifiable. It must, of course, be commensurate with the offence, and carried out by an official instrument of justice."

"This is a point which interests me particularly. What constitutes an official instrument of justice? May a father chastise his child or a master his servant?"

"In the case of a child or servant, the aim of punishment is surely to correct the wrongdoer. My teacher whipped me for not learning my lessons so I would realise the severity of my actions and not repeat them. That, I would contest, differs from the retributive punishment of a criminal, which should be dealt with by a ruler or court of law."

192

"So you would agree that someone who holds an official position of power, such as myself, has the right to punish someone who has committed a crime?"

"If guilt has been established, duty might express it better."

"A duty, yes."

The Master settled back in his seat, as relaxed as a cat.

Silence sat between them. Father Anthony felt a strong desire to keep speaking, to modify his statement in some way.

"The punishment, of course, must be fitting, that is to say neither too harsh nor too lenient."

The Master nodded, but remained silent.

Father Anthony assumed that the Master would explain the situation further, but instead he changed the subject to that of representations of St Job in the altarpiece.

Around the white of the beast's body were tiny flooers. I used all the different stitches I kenned and loved working them in the jewelled threids. Sometimes I chose with care, pondering which colour would look best; at ither times I closed my een and took the first tae haund, but, like the flooers in the grass, nae matter how they were mixed thegether they looked perfect. God's beauty is random. Father Anthony says He has a plan for us all, but when I look at the flooers and the trees I wonder if it maks any difference which way things come out. Scattered hickertie-pickertie on the canvas, greens and purples and pinks and gowds, they are beautiful.

The gairden gave me ideas, my mind filled wi colours and shapes that I wanted tae put on the picture. The days were bricht, so I could spend mair time sewing; the bairn, though he grew well and was alert when awake, still slept a good deal. Sister Grace said it was the heat and also that he was feeding less through the nicht and was mair contentit.

The only thing that remained was the unicorn's face. I had outlined the heid and shaded in the nostrils and mouth. The lang horn, which twisted round and round

194

as it tapered, was done, though I wanted tae add some detail with a silver threid I had kept specially. But his een were blank. I gazed upon the picture: set agin a background of richly coloured flooers, the Virgin was in the centre, calm in blue and gold. The unicorn, white and solid, knelt; her haund stroked his heid as it lay on her lap, defenceless. The horn, so sharp and hard, was harmless.

Blind een, unseeing.

When Monsieur Alberto arrived that morn I was still uncertain how tae proceed. He stood behind me, looked at the work in that way he had; he seemed able tae tak it all in at once, the whole picture and the finest details.

"You are close to the end," he said.

"Aye, Sir, but the hardest task is afore me."

He nodded. "The eyes reflect the soul."

"Does a unicorn have a soul? The priest says that is the difference atween us and the beasts, that they dinna have souls."

"A unicorn is a special kind of beast, I think. And in any case, here he represents more; he is a symbol of Christ Our Lord." He blessed hissel. "There are many tales of the unicorn, many stories as to the meaning. The Master has studied it deeply."

A shiver ran through me. Up till now I had been happy working on the picture, but with mention of the Master I minded what Father Anthony had said about him: he is a good master but it is best no to cross him. Suppose he found fault with my work? The true meaning of the picture rested on the een of the unicorn. If they werena richt it would be a pretty set of colours and shapes, nae mair.

Monsieur Alberto considered the picture. "The eyes could be closed, in reverence."

"That would be easier," I replied. "The een are the hardest thing tae dae. How can I represent something so full of life in threids and stitches?"

"Perhaps you could have them half-closed, maybe gazing down?"

"I want them open, full of life and gazing with love on the maiden. But that would be hard tae achieve."

"But if you do achieve it, how wonderful. What colour will you make them?"

In all the pictures I hae seen the unicorn's een were blue, what Feilamort had called azzurro; that would echo the colour of the lady's dress. But there was only one colour for me: the brown of my bairn's een, the brown of his faither, the brown I had seen thon first day when that feart wee laddie arrived at the castle.

I fingered my threids, picked three and laid them out in front of me.

Monsieur Alberto looked at them and nodded. "Three colours will make for greater subtlety." He hesitated, seeming to consider something important. "If you wish, before you start, I will take you to see a picture in the Master's collection. You may find it helpful."

A skirl of excitement ran through me at the thocht of returning to the Master's part of the castle. Monsieur Alberto led me through the maze of passageways again, but insteid of the big chamber that held the tapestries, he took me intae a smaller room with a high pointy ceiling. It was dark, and when he pulled aside the great curtain that kept out the licht, I gasped at the view frae the windae. All I could see was sea and sky; it was as if there were nae land and we were on some huge ship sailing a neverending ocean. I made towards the windae but Monsieur Alberto gently took my airm and said, "Here, this is what you must see."

Opposite the windae, set in a stone niche, painted directly on the wall, was the maist beautiful face I had e'er seen: oval, the chin pointed and the nose straight, curly hair tummlin tae her shouders. The skin was creamy, and made you want tae pit your haund out and stroke it, but it was the een that drew you in; they were alive, gazed out frae the picture with a longing expression I couldna comprehend, as if she wanted tae speak.

"I've ne'er seen aucht sae bonny." I turned tae Monsieur Alberto. "Did you paint it?"

He smiled. "If I ever painted anything like this I would die a happy man. No, Madame Deirdre. This is the work of one of the greatest artists ever. He stayed in the castle some years ago and painted this for the Master."

"It's the een that mak it so wonderful," I said.

"That is why I wanted to show this to you. I know that you are working in thread, but look how he does this in paint — see how skilfully he blends the different shades to make up the eye, to bring it alive."

"I could ne'er dae aathing like this. It maks all my work as naught."

"Do not be discouraged. The way to create is to see. The flowers in your painting are beautiful because you have always looked closely and you have seen. Many people look but never see. Stand here; study this painting, spend time with it. Observe what the artist does and then absorb it into yourself. When you return to your work it will be part of you."

After a minute I forgot that we were looking at a picture; this face seemed real to me, and familiar, as though I kenned her, but that must have been because we stood there so lang. I was sure if I had met a woman this fair I would ne'er have forgotten her face. It was as if her gentleness and grace were coming out the painting and entering me, granting me a peacefulness, a stillness in my soul. But there was mair, as if she wanted tae tell me something, or ask me something. I didna ken what it was but there was a bond between us.

Monsieur touched my elbow. "Come, we must go now. I ask you not to mention that I have shown you this picture." He drew the curtain again and the room returned tae darkness. Stumbling, I followed him back doon the lang corridors.

198

Signor Carlo

This evening, some light was shed on the Master's attitude towards my pupil's talents. There were no guests present and I was invited to sit with the Master after dinner, along with the new chaplain. Though I have little sympathy with Franciscan views — too much emphasis on abstinence for my liking — he is certainly an improvement on the last priest, who might have benefited from greater abstinence from the Communion wine. Naturally we discussed music and, after pleasant conversation about the role of music in the liturgy and my experiences of different cities in Europe, the Master said, "Would you agree, Signor, that all music, singing in particular, is an inadequate attempt by man to replicate the musica celestis, the constant singing of the nine orders of angels?"

"Indeed, as all our poor efforts in this world are but a dim reflection of the heavenly realm to which we aspire."

"Are you familiar with the work of Ugolino of Orvieto?"

"Alas no, Sir."

"He speaks of the ineffably sweet song of the celestial hierarchy of angels, proclaiming without end, 'Sanctus, sanctus, sanctus'. This is the beginning and origin of all cosmic, human and instrumental music; from it flows the proportions of all melodies, the concord of all notes in which there is no discord. This harmony imitates the celestial music that exists to praise the creator."

"A beautiful thought," I replied. "And one which sustains me in my vocation."

"You will have heard choirs of young boys who are trained to imitate the angelic host?"

"I recall, with greatest fondness, attending Mass in Notre Dame de Reims, where a chorus angelorum of young boys sang from the gallery, 'Gloria, laus et honor', the choir below alternating with the strophes."

"These moments bring us closer to Heaven," said Father Anthony.

"I did, at one time, consider building a gallery in the chapel here, from which such a choir could perform. But I found myself dissatisfied by the idea that human beings, with their propensity to sin, should be the conduits through which we access the divine." The Master shrugged. "There are, of course, some boys who are pure and virtuous, but all too many, even those whose voices show the greatest beauty, are, at best, foolish and vulgar, or, at worst, corrupt."

"I think you will find that my pupil is of an exceptionally virtuous and fine nature."

He looked at me sharply. "Though somewhat defiled, albeit for the sake of a higher purpose, I understand."

I coloured, unsure how to respond to such a comment, but the Master moved swiftly on as though the remark had never been uttered.

"Moreover," he continued, "I am distrustful of the highly emotional response which such a choir evokes in its listeners."

"You feel that the intellect is insufficiently engaged?" asked Father Anthony.

The Master fixed his gaze upon Father Anthony. "In order to penetrate the mysteries of a work of art, scholarship is of the essence. Those musical works with the greatest depth, which are most likely to bring us closer to the divine, may be obscure in their meaning. The use of the symbolism of number, for example, has not yet fully been understood. In order to bring the piece to its fullest expression, years of study as well as sensitivity and intelligence of the highest order is required. Yet the voice is at its greatest in its earlier years. The two demands are irreconcilable."

The Master sat for a moment in silence. Though I had perceived an excitement in his manner, it was kept, as usual, under restraint.

"Have you ever considered, Signor, Father, that the music which comes closest to the divine would be that which is never performed?"

Father Anthony shook his head. "Forgive me, I am unsure of your meaning, Sir."

"Not only never performed, but written with no intention of its being performed by human agency."

We remained silent in the face of this statement.

"Perhaps I may explain this more easily by reference to the visual arts. Some works can lead us to the sacred realms, and I have in my possession such a work, commissioned from one of the greatest artists who ever lived. It holds within itself the elements of the divine, a reflection of the natural world created by God. But, unlike music, it does not need to be transmitted through a human agency in order for us to appreciate it. The artist has done his work already by creating

201

it; the apprehension of the divine which we experience in its presence is unsullied by any other mediator. We contemplate in silence."

"I bow to the Master's much greater knowledge, but I am confused. It is usually thought that the transmission of music, through the voice or instrument, is the means by which we perceive the divine. Indeed many would say that listening to music is the most direct route to God."

"No, Signor. The music of the angels has been heard directly only by the greatest of saints. We do not know how they experienced this music; since no one else heard it, is it not entirely possible that they apprehended it, not through the ears but through the mind? I contend that the greatest music could never be sung by the human voice; the complexity of its scoring, the intricacy and delicacy of its harmonies exceed its capabilities. But they could be perceived and understood by the human eye. It is through the intellect, not the emotion, that we become closer to God; my desire is to have such music commissioned and written out. My gallery is not a place for the singing of boys, but the preservation and contemplation of musical scores."

It was a hot day but in the Master's chamber a great fire was lit. It roared and sputtered, sending sparks up the lum. The Master sat in his big chair, and I stood while Monsieur Alberto placed the picture on an easel. It had been covered by a white clout tae keep it clean as it was carried here.

The Master nodded and Monsieur Alberto revealed it, still on its working frame. "If the Master likes it he will frame it properly but he wishes to see it first," he had tellt me.

I could see only his back as he rose frae his chair and looked closely at the picture. He stood with his heid tae one side like a bird, his velvet robes draped like feathers. He streetched out a finger and touched the threid, stroked the surface of the picture, running his haund doon the unicorn's heid. I was almost hauding my breath; silence hung round us in spite of the roar of the fire.

Efter what seemed an age, he turned round. Unfathomable were his een, as unfathomable as the look in the picture of the lady. Then his crack of a mouth turned up at one corner in a kind of smile.

"Are you pleased with your work, Deirdre?"

I could feel my body relax and my breath escaped frae my mouth in a sigh. I didna ken whit tae answer. Was it a trick?

"I hae done my best, Sir. I hope it pleases you."

He nodded. "It pleases me."

He turned again tae the picture. "There is a subtlety of touch in some parts which I think is admirable. Do you not agree, Monsieur Alberto?"

"I think Madame Deirdre has done a remarkable job." He smiled. "She is very talented and very industrious. And she learns very quickly."

"Monsieur Alberto, please see to the framing of the piece."

Monsieur Alberto bowed.

The Master returned to his seat and looked directly at me. I kept my een on the ground.

"My child, now that you have completed the work, we must find another task for you."

"Thank you, Sir."

I waited for him to tell me what the task was but he said ne'er a word, just stared intae the distance. Then he looked up as if he had forgotten I was there.

"That is all for the present." He waved his haund and dismissed us.

Father Anthony

Having been brought up in a religious order from the age of seven, Father Anthony was used to the society of men, not women. While he idealised the relationship between Jesus and his Blessed Mother, he was unfamiliar with the reality of motherhood. In undertaking the task of finding Feilamort and helping the Master to uncover the circumstances surrounding his birth, he had been sustained by the belief that the best interests of the boy were bound up with those of his grandfather. He had been surprised that the Master did not immediately own the boy and reinstate him to the position which was rightly his, but had ascribed this to a natural shock, as well as the contemplative tendencies of the Master. Now that he was better acquainted with the Master's strange beliefs, he was less sure.

Father Anthony was troubled. Each night he awoke to the vision of the anguished Virgin, pleading for her child. But there was a difference. That lovely face with its creamy skin and luminous blue eyes, which gazed from every holy picture, had been replaced by the homely features of Deirdre: freckled nose, wild curls and tearful brown eyes. Only the plea was the same, heartfelt: please look after the babe.

The summer was a dream time, the walled gairden a world in itsel. Unlike summer at hame, it seemed tae last an age, and everything grew mair lush and lovely. I walked, hauding the bairn in my airms, showing him the beauty around. Great muckle rose bushes climbed up a wooden trellis, taller than me; flooers were everywhere, spilling across the paths, fanklit wi one anither. I crushed the lavender in my haund and smelled its perfume, held it up tae the bairn. The sky was blue above us and the wee birds sang all around: throstle, lairick, whishie.

At times like this I forgot all but the colours and smells and sounds around us and the closeness of the babbie. I sat on a bench, hauding him; his een were drooping, lashes flichtering and his breath deepened. I gazed upon him, a wee miracle among all the ither miracles about me. Here it was easy to pray, to thank the Lord for all his goodness; yet, my mind was still confused, my heart no at rest. In the bairn's features I saw Feilamort. And the longing for him arose in me again.

The strange happenings ower the past year had left me little time tae think on him. But, watching the bairn, I minded Feilamort: the times we were thegether at hame, his quiet presence when he was but a laddie and the way the madness sprung upon us. I flushed, out here in the open, my body afire at the thocht of what had passed between us tae result in this sleeping wee angel. And what could ne'er happen again.

I was angered at what they had done tae him. If he had had a mither she wouldna have let it happen, that I kenned. Feilamort believed he had nae choice, that it was the price tae be paid for his future, but I would fight with every bit of blood in me for this precious bairn, to keep him safe. In the midst of all that loveliness, my tears fell, for Feilamort, for me and for my mither so far awa.

The next twa days I was in limbo. It was fine tae have mair time wi the bairn but I missed my work and my insides felt all afire, as if I was waiting for something tae happen, though I kenned na whit it was. The sun was bleezing hot and in the gairden we sought shade. In a corner ahint the flooer beds was a patch that had been left wild to banwart and blaver starred wi red poppies; they were bricht and bonny and their roughness minded me of hame. I felt hemmed in by the terrace, by the boundaries of the castle, and I longed tae run in the forest as I had done at hame. On the second efternoon I sat while the bairn slept close by me under the shade of a tree. I found the tears plash doon my cheeks and I buried my face in the wildflowers, heedless of the roughness of their stalks or the bees which made this patch their hame.

It was then that Monsieur Alberto came upon me.

I hadna heard his footsteps but I sensed his shadow and looked up. He held out his haund awkwardly and touched my airm.

"Are you unwell?"

His words made me greet all the harder, big shuddering sobs that wracked my body. "I want tae gang hame," I cried, "I want my minnie, I dinna ken why they are keeping me here."

He sat on the bench close by till I calmed.

"I am sorry I cannot help you, Deirdre. It is hard to be far from those you love."

I wiped my een on my sleeve, took a big breath and said, "Never mind me, I ken I am fortunate and I have my bairn. It is just sometimes . . ."

He nodded.

"I have brought the picture for you to see. Shall we go inside? I do not wish to uncover it in the sunlight."

The picture looked weel in its frame. Monsieur Alberto had chosen a silver one which brocht out the richness of the colours. I tried to examine it as if someone else had done the work and I could see that there was much good in it, but it nae longer seemed like mine. When I said this to Monsieur Alberto he smiled. "That is the way of it. When I have finished with a work I rarely want to see it again, I want to make something new. Only once . . ." He stopped.

"What happened?"

"Once I painted something I wished I could keep, but . . ." He shrugged. "The work we do is not for ourselves; our patrons give us commissions, they pay us and the work is theirs to do with as they wish. It is the way of it."

"The Master said it was the vocation of most to make things and the vocation of a few, like hissel, to appreciate them."

Monsieur Alberto laughed. "That is one way of looking at it. But at least our Master has some true appreciation of beauty. I have worked for other masters who wanted something to show off, for others to think well of them. They could not have told good from inferior."

It was the first time I had heard him speak about anything other than art or the work in haund. I longed tae ask him mair about his life as an artist but didna ken where tae start.

"How lang have you worked here?"

"Many years. There were artists here before me, some who were here only for a short time to do a specific work, and others who stayed longer. My main occupation is to make copies of the Master's pictures and occasionally to paint portraits of his guests; he has liked the work I have done for him."

His face seemed aulder and mair lined than afore.

"I am a good artist, Deirdre, though not a great one, not like some I have seen. But I have one advantage, which is that by nature I am calm and slow to show passion. Some artists who have come here, like the one who painted the picture I showed you, are full of temperament, cannot smooth the paths between themselves and the Master; their work is all. I enjoy the advantages of the life I lead here but I know there are compromises. Most of the time I think they are worth making, but sometimes I wake and dream of what might be if I were braver."

He lifted the clout and began tae wrap the picture.

"But I am what I am."

The next day I was on the terrazza with the bairn and Louise. I sat on a grassy verge, dandling the bairn, who kicked his wee legs and waved his airms.

"He wants to walk," said Louise.

"At hame he would still be swaddled."

Louise shook her heid. "I do not understand."

"Wrapped tightly in clouts till he is aulder. I dinna ken why, but it isna deemed good for babes to move owermuch."

He gurgled and waved his wee fist. He was staring at the sky as he oft did. He loved tae follow the birds' flight and was happy tae be set under a tree where he could watch the licht dapple the leaves and branches.

"Whit dae ye see, wee mannie? Whit dae ye see?" I kissed his saft heid and tickled him under the chin and he chuckled. My een followed his and I looked high up in the sky. "That's a strange birdie."

The angle of the rocks made it impossible tae see the outline of the castle; all was sky reaching up like an endless Heaven and the birds, like dots, high above. But one of the birds didna look like a bird; there was an unnatural stiffness in its movement, and it seemed tae drap oot the sky and disappear frae our sight.

Louise was looking too. "Sometimes I have seen such a thing before. I wonder if something has dropped from the roof. The castle is very high and only the Master ever goes up there with a few of his special guests."

At the time I thocht nae mair about it but that nicht I dreamed of birds flying free.

IV

Signor Carlo

The castle is filled with laughter and gaiety after the arrival of My Lady, accompanied by Monsieur Garnet, Lady Alicia and her betrothed, Monsieur Jacques. Though My Lady travelled with a large retinue, the servants have returned to her cousin's chateau, with only her personal maid remaining. Apparently the Master does not permit visitors to bring their own attendants, as is the custom in most places. It is another of his foibles; according to my informant, he believes it leads to disharmony and encourages gossip. In any case his standards of service are so high that no guest could feel his treatment ungenerous.

It seems that My Lady and her group will be in residence for the next few weeks; the Master plans festivities and celebrations in their honour. On the first evening, the guests were received in the large hall to be shown the Master's famed unicorn tapestries; though I know little of such matters, they are considered wonderful examples. Then we dined in fine style; the larks were particularly delicious.

It was a pleasure and a relief to see My Lady again. Whatever shadows and threats lurk, she seems to brush them away. To be seated across from her is indeed a delight. It is difficult to pay attention to anyone else; in the soft light she shimmers gently like a candle flame. When she turns her gaze towards you, it is like being bathed in the warmth of the sun. I find it hard to imagine she will ever return to the dark northern country of her husband.

"Signor Carlo, how does your pupil progress?"

"Very well, My Lady. He is a diligent boy with great talent."

"The air of the castle suits him?"

"Very much, My Lady."

"I look forward to hearing him tonight."

"I believe not. I have been told to prepare him to sing tomorrow but tonight he rests, on the Master's orders."

"The Master has firm ideas," said Monsieur Garnet. "A man of very definite character."

"Indeed, a remarkable man; one who knows his own will and expects it to be done."

"An admirable trait, of course." Monsieur Garnet placed a piece of lamb in his mouth.

"After such a quiet time here it will be very entertaining to have a party of guests," I continued. "The Master has prepared several nights of entertainment."

Monsieur Garnet turned to me. "Of course, Signor, you will be well used to elaborate displays in your own country."

"I remember my time at the court of one of those now dispossessed of power — his name is best left unsaid — and the wondrous shows which were staged. Not only singing and dancing and all the usual entertainments, but magnificent scenery, machines which simulated cloud and wind and fire, hoists which lifted performers so high in the air that one feared for their safety. But I digress. I believe the Master's theatricality is of a less showy nature."

216

"Perhaps. From what I have seen, he does not lack a sense of timing, nor the ability to keep his audience in suspense."

"In days past, the Master's fêtes were famed. He hired players to act out masques and no expense was spared in the matter of costume." My Lady laughed. "I remember, as a child, being afraid of the great machines which moved, apparently by themselves, though my father, may his soul rest in peace, showed me that there were people inside."

"I have heard of such wonders," said Monsieur Jacques.

"There was an artist here at that time whose mind ran in a most fantastical vein. He created many such objects for the Master. But it is many years since the Master has had fêtes. After his daughter died . . ." She lowered her voice, though the Master was engaged in conversation at the far end of the table. "His heart was broken."

Monsieur Garnet snorted, then attempted to turn the snort into a cough.

My Lady continued. "He is a most generous host. My daughter and her future mari are very fortunate. Of course, we are closely related to the Master."

"I understood as much, though the precise relation-ship . . .?"

"The Master's sister, God rest her soul, was married to my cousin, also gone from this earth. Sadly, they had no children. My daughter is to be married to the son of our other cousin. We are all the family he has."

"As one who has had to make his way in the world without such a benefit, I am well aware how valuable are the ties of family."

"Extremely valuable," said Monsieur Garnet.

* * *

As the meal drew to an end, the Master turned his attention to the young people.

"It is a pleasure to welcome those who are to be joined in holy matrimony. I understand that the nuptials will take place soon, My Lady?"

"Within a few months, Sir. At the home of my cousin, Jacques' father."

"Your husband will travel for the wedding?"

"Alas, this may prove too difficile. Mon cher mari is very busy with the affairs of his estate and at the moment there is much upheaval in the country. It is not wise to travel far from home. But I hope we may have the pleasure of your company at the wedding, Sir."

"I never leave my home — one such as I, whose health is delicate and whose nature cannot bear change . . . you understand, my dear lady."

"Bien sûr, Monsieur."

A bell was rung, obtaining everyone's attention. The Master looked round.

"My dear guests, I have organised this little gathering, these small amusements and celebrations, in order to pay my respects to the young couple who are near kin to me. I wish to bestow upon them some recognition of this joyful occasion."

"We are most grateful, Sir." Monsieur Jacques bowed across the table. He has a most unfortunate manner of speech, to which the Master can hardly be oblivious.

My Lady smiled sweetly at the Master; I could sense excitement prickle under her skin. This must be the moment when the Master will announce they are to be his heirs. I was surprised at his being so open; I had thought that he would

218

toy with them a while longer and perhaps make his announcement to My Lady alone, or even to the young man. But, as I have observed, there is a degree of drama in the Master's being; he was clearly enjoying the close attention.

"Earlier this evening you saw the sequence of tapestries depicting the tale of the unicorn, symbol of Christ Our Lord. He heals us and makes poisoned water safe to drink. He is hunted but is impervious to evil. Yet He humbled himself to be born of a virgin, to take the form of man, and, in laying down His life for us, He gives us eternal life."

Murmurs of assent ran round the table. My Lady blessed herself, with the delicacy of one handling a precious string of pearls.

"However," continued the Master, "there is another interpretation of the story of the unicorn, one more concerned with human love: he is the symbol of a young virile man who cannot be defeated by bows and arrows, but who willingly gives himself up to a maiden and accepts the chains of love and of marriage."

He bowed to the young people. Monsieur Jacques smiled, while Lady Alicia maintained her doll-like expression.

"While this may seem to be a simple and joyful interpretation, I ask you to consider that matrimony is a holy sacrament, and that the love which binds husband and wife is pure. Where men and women forget that God is part of their union, trouble, inevitably, will follow.

"I apologise for straying into darker waters than is perhaps appropriate on such a happy occasion." The Master bowed. "But it is as well to know of such perils in order that we may avoid them, and, if we may not avoid them, we may know how to steer them. There are those among you, those of the older rather than the younger generation, who will understand of what I speak."

An air of solemnity had descended on the company — on My Lady's forehead a slight wrinkle had appeared. But perhaps this was simply a way of increasing the drama, of making the endowment even more meaningful.

"So, I counsel the young people to be as faithful and loving and self-sacrificing as the unicorn, that they may be happy together all their lives."

We raised our cups.

"So that they may remember this message, I present them with a small token of my goodwill."

Two servants appeared, carrying a framed picture covered by a velvet cloth. It was placed on an easel and the cloth removed to reveal a representation of a unicorn, its head in a lady's lap. It was a pretty enough thing, in some kind of needlework, clearly a copy of the final tapestry of the sequence belonging to the Master. But it was small, suited for private devotion rather than something to be displayed in a public room. I could see the puzzlement on the young man's face, but he thanked the Master politely, while Lady Alicia nodded and murmured her gratitude.

There was an uneasy silence; clearly the guests were waiting for the Master to announce some bequest to the young people but he merely continued with his wine, smiling benevolently round the table as though he had settled half his estate on them.

After this little scene, I begin to consider what steps I should take to secure my future. The expectations of My Lady have not, as yet, been fulfilled, though this may, of course, be the

Master's humour in toying with them for a little longer; there is no knowing what she will do if the inheritance is not settled on the young people, and how this may affect the boy. And the future of this boy is my future too. Of course I could have another kind of future — I have been granted sufficient graces and talents from the good Lord to create one — but I would certainly prefer the possibilities opened to me by the boy.

This place, with its warmth and charm, its gracious and luxurious atmosphere, has reawakened in me the longing for that city of the utmost beauty and civilisation, where I was at my happiest; the fulfilment of God's wishes coincided perfectly with my own. In addition, while I cannot claim to be a man of warm affections, I do, it must be said, have some feeling for the boy; in Rome, his position can be secured through his talent and not remain dependent on the humours of the gentry.

I think it best to speak to Monsieur Garnet on this matter.

We climbed a narrow twisty stair, higher and higher till my legs felt they would collapse beneath me. I'd nae idea the castle was this tall; I panted as we stopped on a landing.

"This stair leads to a tower set above the rest of the castle," said Monsieur Alberto. "It is little used. I lived here for several years before I knew of its existence. It is another of the Master's foibles that he likes to keep some parts of his realm secret; I do not believe anyone but he knows every part of the building."

I said nothing but thocht to mysel that, though lairds and ladies think they ken everything, their servants aye find out their secrets.

As we ascended we passed slits of windaes through which I glimpsed the sky. Eventually we reached a door which oped on tae an enormous room. Lining its sides were auld kists and armoires, and piled all round were things I'd ne'er seen the like of: contraptions made of wood and metal and ropes. I placed my haund on one and the dust flew intae the air, catching my throat.

"What is this place, Monsieur?"

"Many years ago this room was used for fêtes and pageants. The Master entertained his guests with singing, dancing and spectacles of all kinds." He oped a kist and pulled out a gounie of rich velvet, faded and dusty, which must have been beautiful once.

"And these?" I pointed to the things placed round the walls.

"Jesters and players clambered on them and they were wheeled round to entertain the audience. A party of guests has arrived, relatives of the Master's, and he has plans for their entertainment. The Master wishes you to use your skills to renew and repair some of these artefacts."

Monsieur Alberto lifted a foostit clout and uncovered one of the machines. A wooden platform, supported by four posts, was mounted on wheels so it could be moved; on the top of the platform was a structure made frae twa planks and a curved piece of wood. Monsieur Alberto tested its strength.

"It is still quite sound — only a little attention and cleaning is needed. But there is another part which requires your skills." He lifted what I thocht was a bundle of lang sticks tied with a piece of leather. When it was unfastened and spread out I saw that the wood was jointed thegether, like an enormous fan; raggity bits of sacking and linen clung to the wooden pieces.

"It is like a wing."

"Yes. There is another just like this — it is part of a costume for one of the players." He lifted the tattered fabric. "The Master wishes you to make new these parts."

I was disappointed. When I had seen the gorgeous velvet of the gounies I had thocht I would be working on them.

"It will be a complex construction, not simply a question of stretching some fabric over the skeleton of the wing. The Master wishes it to be as close to the idea of feathers as possible. I have sketched a template for you." He produced a rolled up piece of parchment on which was drawn a diagram of the wooden framework of the wing; owerlapping pieces of fabric were to be sewn thegether and attached to it.

"There are two wings to be made and their frames will be joined. I will bring all the materials you require — do you have your needles?"

"Aye." My sewing bag was e'er on my person. "But, Sir . . ." I looked round the stoury place. "May I no tak the sewing to my chamber?"

"The Master wishes it to be a secret; only you and I, and a few of his most trusted servants, know what he plans. He prefers you do the work here."

"But the licht, Sir . . ."

He walked across the room and pulled aside a curtain. A windae on the sea flooded blinding licht intae the room. "If you sit here you should have enough."

"Aye, Sir."

"Do you have any questions?"

I shook my heid. "But . . . Monsieur . . ."

"Yes?"

"How did they get all they great muckle things up here through thon narrow wee stair?"

He laughed, a richt deep laugh, and I realised that was the first time I had ever heard Monsieur Alberto laugh properly. He smiled a lot in a wistful way, as if it were his duty tae smile but his hert wasna really in it. His laugh was rusty like a gate which was rarely oped.

"I think you will find, Madame Deirdre," he said, pausing in his mirth, "that they were built here." And then he laughed again, and so did I at being such a daft geek, and our voices rang through that dusty room and echoed out towards the sea.

Next morn Monsieur Alberto accompanied me tae the room high up in the tower where I did my work. He came and went as I sat at the windae; sometimes he mended one of the constructions with hammer and nails, or sat outside, sketching a view from one of the wee windaes in the stair.

I had ne'er been alone with a man afore except for a priest. At hame my mither had been strict and here Sister Grace or Louise were aye with me. Monsieur Alberto's presence was unlike a man's; he was gentle and quiet in his movements, like a cat. He rarely spoke other than tae explain something about the work or to examine what I had done. It was a simple enough task once I had understood it — compared to the unicorn embroidery it barely tested my skills — so I was left with much time tae think. As I sewed I came to wonder about him and his life here; it seemed so solitary. He couldna be friends with the Master as he was too far below him, but he couldna be friends with the servants either. He was neither one thing nor another, betwixt and between.

By efternoon I had finished the sewing and Monsieur had attached the pieces to the frames. As we looked at them I felt there was something missing.

"Monsieur, would it no be better if they looked mair like real feathers? I could use wee pieces of fabric and shape them, fray their edges and owerlap them. It would mak it mair like a bird."

He nodded. "Yes, but we must ensure it does not detract from the practical function. It cannot be too heavy." He seemed in a dwam.

"I dinna understaund, Sir. The player could still ope and shut the wings."

He looked, considered, lifted the wing as if weighing it in his haund. "Try a layer of feathers as you suggest, just around the outer edges of the wings; that will give it the appearance of a bird without affecting the delicate balance required of the construction." He stared at it. "When this is finished I shall join these and see that they fit perfectly."

"Do you no mind, Monsieur, daeing such work yourself?"

"How do you mean?"

"Daeing a carpenter's work when you are an artist."

He lifted the frame. "This is not the work of a carpenter, but an artist. The man who designed this was the one who painted the beautiful portrait I showed you."

"I thocht artists only painted pictures."

"There is much more than that. To design, to construct, to understand how things are constructed, is part of what it is to be an artist. When I first began to paint and draw, I tried to recreate the surface of things but now I wish to make something which, though not alive, appears so. I need to understand the solidity of forms and how they are assembled. It does not devalue me to work on such things" — he gestured at the wooden frames — "indeed it is an honour to bring them back to life."

He replaced the frame on the table, then turned to me. "I discovered something that may be of interest to you, Madame Deirdre. The Master's guests, the ones for whom he prepares this fête . . ."

"Yes, Monsieur."

"Some of the party are from your homeland."

My heart thudded.

"There is a lady, very beautiful, whose husband is from your country. She is here with her daughter and her betrothed."

"My Lady and Lady Alicia?"

"Yes."

I could barely bring mysel tae speak the words.

"And is there a music teacher with them, and a young singer with a beautiful voice?"

"Signor Carlo? Feilamort? Yes, yes, they are here. But . . ." He paused, as if wondering whether to continue. "They did not arrive with the party. They have been here some weeks already."

My heart jammered in my breist and my haund let go my work; the wooden frame clattered to the flair, the fabric and threids fanklit.

"I am sorry."

I knelt to retrieve my work and Monsieur Alberto came to help me. My fingers tremmled that much I could be of little use, but his were steady. When he held out the wing to me, we were that close I could smell the faint scent of geranium that clung to his hair and see the flecks of blue in his grey een. As I took the work frae him I felt his haund brush the back of mines, dry and slightly rough, like canvas.

"Can I help you?"

I wanted tae tell him all, to blurt out the truth, but something held me back; mibbe it was fear that harm might come to the bairn, or mibbe the strange events that had befallen me had bred in me a habit of secretiveness I couldna owercome.

"Do you wish me to tell him you are here?"

He looked at me with such gentleness that I trusted him.

I nodded. "Only him, though, naebody else."

"I understand."

228

Signor Carlo

An extraordinary display. Perhaps extraordinary is too strong a word, but unusual, certainly, most unusual. Our host is a manipulative character, I believe, and does not lack a certain sense of drama.

Last night, after dinner, we assembled in the Master's chamber: Father Anthony, My Lady, Monsieur Garnet and myself, with Lady Alicia and her betrothed. Then arrived a nun, of more than usually plain and forbidding appearance, though her skin, I have to say, is rather fine, and breeding is apparent in her bearing. Wine was poured and we sat most comfortably for a while, our host conversing on art and music with My Lady and Monsieur Garnet. Father Anthony and I added an occasional remark, while the Sister remained more or less silent. She followed our conversation with an intelligent look on her face, occasionally nodding or showing some recognition of what was said; her silence appeared to be the result of the observance of her religious vows rather than a lack of understanding or interest. Eventually the time came for Feilamort to sing; though I do not consider it his best performance by any means, it is impossible for the boy to sound less than outstanding. Afterwards Feilamort withdrew and we sat most comfortably while more wine was poured.

The Master drinks from a remarkable cup.

"I see you admire my goblet, Signor," he said.

"Indeed, Sir, it is a beautiful and unusual vessel."

"It is made from the horn of a unicorn. No doubt you are familiar with its qualities?"

"I have heard that it has remarkable properties of healing. I once stayed at the home of a noblewoman who placed a piece in her wine before drinking."

The Master held up the goblet, examined it; the stem consisted of a spiral, black and white in colour.

"The unicorn dips its horn in water and purifies the stream for the other animals to drink. Its horn has preventative, as well as healing, properties: it is a safeguard against poison."

I did not know how to reply. It was surely unlikely that the Master suspected his guests or his servants of poisoning him. But, having travelled around the noble houses of Europe, I was only too familiar with stories of poison used to remove those who proved troublesome or who stood in someone's way.

"The symbolic and mystical nature of the unicorn has long been the subject of my deepest study. It is, you may say, my passion."

"Mais oui, Sir," said My Lady. "The tapestries which you showed us the other day, which tell the story of the unicorn, were exquisite. I have never seen finer."

The Master nodded. "The tapestries were commissioned to celebrate a marriage union."

"Your own marriage, Sir?" asked My Lady, charming as ever.

"No, My Lady. A marriage which never took place."

230

He paused and the servant unobtrusively stepped round and refilled our cups. This is one of the things which marks out our host from almost any other I have known; the service in his house is perfect but almost unnoticeable. I observed that Sister Agnes refused, as did Father Anthony. I took another full glass — our host's wine cellar is second to none. I sat back in the comfortable chair, looking round the faces in the firelight as our host began.

"Let me tell you a story: a tale as old as life itself, as long as there have been men and women. It is the story of a beautiful young woman: elegant, educated and refined, of noble stock, brought up with every advantage. Given her birth and breeding it was expected that she should make a great match, and that her marriage should give rise to a fruitful line.

"This young woman was not only fair, clever and skilled in all the arts which a noblewoman needs possess, she was also good and pure: a maiden who loved to pray, devoted to Our Blessed Lady. When not engaged in her studies or duties at home, nothing pleased her more than to visit the poor families of the neighbourhood, giving alms and succour. The poor loved her because they recognised the simple goodness of her heart under her fine clothing and the elegance of her manners and breeding. Her learning was not a barrier to her communication with the ignorant, rather it made her understand and tolerate their faults better.

"You may think that such a creature could not exist, that she is the heroine of a fable, but I assure you that she did live on this earth. Her mother was a good and lovely woman, virtuous in every way. Sadly she died before the young woman was fully grown and so her care fell solely to her father. It is hard for a father to undertake the supervision of a

231

daughter, especially one who is about to attain the age of betrothal. It is difficult for a father to understand the subtleties and complexities of finding a good husband. A father is more likely to pay heed to exterior matters: whether the man is of suitable birth and breeding, whether he has sufficiency to provide for his bride, what he has to offer. A mother will see into his heart.

"Be that as it may, the father was left to undertake this task. He sought counsel, sent out his advisers. Of all the potential husbands, one person seemed eminently suitable: of noble birth, well educated, of pleasing manner and appearance. None spoke ill of him. The trouble was that to visit his country required a long journey by land and sea. This father had a horror of travel. He entrusted the care of his daughter to a loyal adviser; she was to be accompanied by a substantial retinue of servants and attendants, including two nuns who would alternate the care of her person and ensure that she was never alone. What more could he have done? No one could fault such provision. Indeed, he was a man whom no one could ever fault, since he allowed no possibility of it. His behaviour was, to the letter, exemplary: a model of what good behaviour should be.

"His daughter arrived safely at the home of her suitor. Her letters were filled with joy and happiness. The young man was handsome, charming, intelligent and educated; they were able to converse deeply as well as dance and play music together. The report from the father's adviser was similarly positive. All appeared well. If the father had a niggling doubt in his mind, he brushed it away like a troublesome fly. That doubt was his daughter's enthusiasm. He had always believed that those who married should not be too fond of one another. A measure of rationality, a space into which some degree of calculation could enter, was a desirable factor in his opinion; his deep respect and affection for his own wife had never been sullied by any sweeping passion. But then, he was not a man of strong passions, while his daughter was a young woman of delicate sensibilities. Perhaps her expression was simply warmer than his. In any case everything else was in order so he gave permission for the match to proceed.

"Formal betrothal had not yet taken place. There were a number of matters which required to be negotiated, so his daughter was to return home while lawyers were consulted and plans made. Before she was halfway there, word was received that the young man had died."

"Such a sad story," said My Lady.

"The young woman requested that she stay for a period of time in seclusion at a convent, in order to grieve, to pray for the repose of his soul and reflect on her life. Her father agreed, though reminded his daughter that, after her period of mourning, she must marry and bring an heir to his estate.

"His daughter never returned. The father was informed by the Mother Superior that his daughter had taken ill of a fever and died. For fear of infection, her body had been buried immediately."

My Lady blessed herself.

"From that moment the father became ever more absorbed in his studies, taking solace in the workings of the mind. The world was filled with turmoil and hardship and ugliness, so he created his own little world of beauty and grace and light, secure and safe. The father ignored the outside world for many years until a messenger arrived, bearing a letter from a

Franciscan priest. And there was something about this missive which forced the man to take heed.

"The letter told another story."

The Master paused, took a sip of wine.

"While the young woman stayed at the convent in France, a child was born to her. Her father had been informed of his daughter's death, but not of the child's existence."

I have expertise in the voice: not only can I teach singing, I can comprehend more than is said in words. In the voice I can discern whether one is healthy, whether one has worked out of doors or remained much inside. I can hear age and youthfulness, I even know when one is close to death. But above all I can register emotion which may be so far buried that the person is himself unaware of it. The Master's voice displayed restraint such as I have rarely observed, the control, cultivated over a lifetime, of a man who appears to have little passion, but somewhere, buried deep within, was an emotion which, if unleashed, could erupt like a volcano.

"The father, who thought he had mourned his daughter already, was torn from top to toe with grief. After some days of inconsolable misery came guilt that he had not protected his daughter; then anger, like a poison which is also an antidote, seeped slowly through every part of his flesh. He hated the man who was responsible for his daughter's shame and that of her lost babe, doomed to bastardy. But this man had died in ignorance of what had happened. Had he lived, in all probability they would have married and legitimised the child. The father's wrath turned towards those who had taken charge after the birth.

"His first thought was to claim the child publicly as his heir. But though the priest had made investigations, these

234

events had happened many years previously; it could not be ascertained precisely what had happened. And the child had disappeared."

He paused.

"Further investigations were necessary."

My mind, which had, at the beginning of his recounting, been pleasantly relaxed by the wine and the warmth of the fire, was now confused and uneasy. This was no tale of the fireside. Even though our host was a man of strange humours, quite capable of spinning tales to make us ill at ease for his own entertainment, it was clear even to an idiot that he must be the father and Father Anthony the priest who revealed the truth of the daughter's fate. But the child? How old would the child be now?

We sat in silence waiting for the Master to speak. My Lady's face was sweet with concern, Father Anthony's calm and pious, while the nun appeared unmoved. And Monsieur Garnet, though as difficult to fathom as ever, had the expression I recognised in myself and in all who make their way by their wits and talents in the service of the rich and powerful. We are less free than the servants who can, among themselves, relax and gossip; we must be wary even of each other.

The Master looked round. "In every parish there are orphans who live as part of large households; the circumstances of their birth are of little consequence. It was discovered that, after the death of its mother, the child, a boy, was placed with a noble family in a nearby chateau, and raised among other nameless children. All he possessed of his mother was a holy medal. At the age of ten or so, along with several other lads in the area, he was sent to the household of

235

a relative in order to be trained as a page. The relative was a lady who had married a Scottish lord. And the child was a slip of a boy, fearful and shy, with naught to recommend him but his beautiful voice."

The wine, smooth on my tongue, turned to vinegar. There was a silence in the room, then a confusion of voices, all speaking at once. My Lady hushed us.

"Sir, you are saying that my little songbird . . . is your grandson?"

"Debased, ignorant of all but music, unfit to take up his position, he is, nevertheless, my grandchild, my closest blood relative."

"He is a delightful child." My Lady's voice was honey edged with salt. "I am most happy that you have been reunited."

The Master nodded.

"But the boy . . . he is unaware of his position?"

"He is unaware of his lineage. His position in this household is that of a singer, under the tutelage of Signor Carlo, who is responsible for his fine voice."

He smiled at me, and I felt myself begin to tremble; it was with difficulty that I controlled visible signs of my discomfort. He must, of course, know of my part in preserving the voice. And it is one thing to perform such an act on a poor boy whose only fortune is that voice, and quite another to perform the same action on a child destined to inherit great riches.

My Lady continued. "Of course it will be a great shock to the boy, you will wish to break the news gently to him."

"In time. For the present I assume I have your word that what you have heard within these walls will not be spoken of.

236

He looked round the room and each person, in his or her own way, acquiesced, My Lady in sweet tones, Monsieur Garnet by a deep bow, the nun a simple nod. However, unless I have misjudged the Master, a man of his wisdom well knows that such a secret, told to so many, will not remain secret for long.

"You must excuse me, I am more tired than I appear. This situation is a most intricate one. I bid you goodnight."

Cauld metal moonbeams trickled through the slit in the stone wall. The bairn slept beside me on the bed, but I lay, staring at the licht. A rustle at the door startled me out a hauf-sleep and there he was, familiar but no familiar: taller and thinner, wearing a beautiful velvet tunic and shoon wi roses embroidered on them. His skin was pale, frae being much indoors I guessed, but his hair was unchanged, and his een: deep and fit tae drown in.

I pulled the blanket round me, feart he would see me in my sark; daft efter what had taen place atween us, but that felt faraway, as if it had happened in anither world. He must have felt the same, as he hesitated by the door. I beckoned him tae came closer and he sat on the edge of the bed.

The bairn's chest rose and fell under the coverlet. Feilamort stared at him as if he couldna believe sich a being existed. He streetched his haund ower the babe's heid but didna touch him, feart tae wake him I suppose. I could see the likeness; their mouths, rounded and saft, were identical. The bairn's een were closed but when he was awake they were Feilamort's. It comforted me when I saw how he resembled his

238

faither, I no longer felt alone. Here in this hauf-licht, it seemed a miracle that we had produced this perfect being.

Feilamort put his haund on my airm. "I never knew, all this time, that you were here in this place."

"Nor I. I canna understaund why they brocht me here tae have our bairn, it maks nae sense. I ken that the Master wants you, for your voice."

Feilamort shook his heid. "He is a strange man. He observes me as if seeking something in me and finding me wanting."

"Father Anthony and Monsieur Alberto say he is good." I stopped. "No. They say he is a good master. That is different."

The babe started tae move in his sleep.

"Will he wake? I wish to see him awake."

"He usually wakes for a feed, then he'll sleep again till morn."

As if he had heard us, he oped his een and started a wee greet, like a kitten. My breists were full and longed for the babe.

I lifted him. Sensing the milk, he girned mair.

"May I stay?"

"Of course."

I pit him to the breist. The warmth and relief of the sooking took haud of me as it aye did. He was a strong babe and sometimes it almost hurt at the start, then eased as he began tae get fuller.

It felt strange at first tae have Feilamort there and nae doubt it felt even stranger for him. At first he looked awa then began to steal glances; when I caught his een we smiled, though embarrassed.

I moved the babe tae the ither breist.

"I have seen women feed their babes many times, but somehow it is different with you."

"I ken."

Full noo, the babbie eased his grip and I took him aff the nipple. I stood and held him out to Feilamort.

"He's tired noo, wanting tae sleep. Rock him."

Feilamort stood, rocking the bairn gently; then, almost whispering, he began tae sing, quiet and saft; mibbe it was a lullaby, or mibbe it just sounded like one. I hadna heard his voice for so long, and it was sweet and pure as ever and even mair tender. I stood watching him and the bairn in a moment of pure happiness.

The spell was broken by a quiet tap on the door.

"I must go now," said Feilamort. He placed the bairn carefully on the bed and pulled the cover ower him.

"But I will return when I can. Here . . ."

He removed his holy medal and and placed it in my haund. "Wear this for me. Keep it for the babe."

"You must have mine, then — or you'll no be protected against evil."

I took aff my ain medal and placed it ower his heid. As he bent to help me our cheeks brushed thegether, like moth wings. In a moment we were in each ither's airms. Then he kissed me on the place where my hair meets my foreheid, and was gone.

I shivered. I climbed intae the bed next the bairn, cooried under the blanket, the medal still in my haund.

It felt smooth tae the touch, auld and worn, the face of the Virgin blurred. Afore putting it round my neck, I turnt it ower. On the back, clearly visible in the moonlicht, was the heid of a unicorn.

Father Anthony

Father Anthony was not surprised at the Master's request that he remain behind after the others left. At last matters would finally be settled; the Master would explain his plans, perhaps even seek his advice.

"Now that you have brought this story into the light, I am at your service, Sir, for the next stage of the matter," he said.

The Master's tiny eyes, sharp and bright as the precious gems which decorated his goblet, surveyed Father Anthony.

"I think you may well understand that I am inclined to see justice done over the matter of my daughter."

"I understand, of course, but surely, Sir, the man responsible is dead. Punishment is in God's hands. And of course, while it is clear from the Ten Commandments that such behaviour is sinful, it has always been appreciated by Mother Church that mitigating circumstances may diminish guilt. An action borne out of youthful passion, with no deliberate intent to do wrong, may, perhaps . . . Even some of the great saints have . . ."

The Master had not taken his eyes off Father Anthony, whose words began to feel like ulcers in his mouth.

"Father, I see you are even less a man of the world than I am."

Father Anthony was unsure whether the slight upturn of the Master's mouth indicated amusement or distaste.

"As you say, the child was conceived as the result of sin, which, had his parents lived to marry, could have been absolved. Indeed, some may attribute the action to youthful passion rather than to deliberate wrongdoing, though I myself do not take this view.

"But what of later occurrences? I was not informed of his birth, he was hidden away, not educated in a fitting matter, and then finally subjected to the greatest of degradations. Should the person responsible for these crimes not be punished?"

It had never occurred to Father Anthony that the boy's ignorance of his position had been anything other than the Mother Superior's benevolent attempt to accede to his mother's wishes.

"I am sure the Mother Superior thought she was acting in his best interests by placing him with a good family. What other explanation could there be, Sir? She may have felt that neither his mother's nor his father's family would welcome him. She may have feared your rejection of him, and since his father had died . . ."

"Since his father did not trouble to wait until he had married his mother before begetting him, he is of little consequence, alive or dead."

"Still, she may have believed the boy was safer out of the way. Though his father is not directly in line to the Scottish throne, the instability of that country is such that even the illegitimate son of the kinsman of a monarch might be seen as useful to some parties and an obstacle to others."

"The boy has a lineage. That is important. Each of us has a place on God's earth, a destiny. I am sure you would admit as much, Father."

"Of course."

"I must tell you, Father, that I find the actions of my daughter quite incomprehensible. I know that women are more base in their natures than men — only the Blessed Virgin stands as a shining beacon of purity to which women can aspire — yet I believed my daughter incapable of fornication. I can only assume that she was either forced, which seems unlikely, or that she succumbed to seduction of her mind.

"My little realm is small but I believe I have created a haven of beauty, of learning and of purity. My daughter, by nature, was fitted for the convent. Had she not been my only child she need not have married, but I required an heir. I sought for her a husband who was of noble birth but not so elevated that my land would be subsumed under a large kingdom or made use of for strategic, rather than aesthetic and scholarly, purposes. I sought one who was learned and studious as well as of good character. Perhaps, like the virtuous Heloise, she was more at danger from a pure and clever man than she would have been from a lusty youth. There is a certain irony in that. Whatever the reason, Feilamort is the result and he is stained by the sin of his parents."

"True. As we are all stained by the sin of our first parents, Adam and Eve."

"And we are redeemed by the sacrifice of Christ Our Lord. Sacrifice is required to wash away sin. This is the message and symbolism of the unicorn, to which I am so devoted.

"But to return to the boy. You, Father, in your, some may say, innocence, others generosity of spirit, believe that the boy was removed in a clandestine fashion out of a desire to follow the mother's wishes or do what was thought best for him. Should his paternity be known, he might be at the mercy of those who wished to seize power through him."

"It is a possibility."

"I too think that someone wishes to seize power, not by making use of the boy's paternity but by suppressing the identity of his mother."

"I do not understand, Sir."

"Look at this in another way, Father. If my daughter had died childless, if there were no heir, who would benefit?"

Father Anthony was bewildered. "I suppose that, unless you were to remarry . . ."

"A most unlikely prospect."

"Then your next of kin would benefit. But surely . . ."

"My next of kin. A simple phrase but, in my case, not such a simple concept."

Father Anthony waited, unable to answer.

"Legally, I could leave my estate to anyone I pleased. There is no doubt that such a prospect appeals to me. But I am a man who is not unmoved by the importance of family ties.

"Until the discovery of my grandson, my closest kin were the cousins of my late sister's husband. Since their children, Lady Alicia and young Jacques, are now betrothed, it was presumed that my favour would fall upon them. I have never stated so explicitly. I am, as you know, a man of caution; it is not unknown for those who expect to inherit to attempt to hasten the process. In any case, I did not choose to make my intentions known. However, these young people, and those

245

who advise them, had good cause to expect favour. Now, Father, who do you think would have reason to suppress the existence of my grandson, and to ensure that he had no heir?"

Father Anthony was distressed by the Master's words.

"Surely, Sir, it is more important to promote reconciliation than to seek revenge? I can understand your distress over your daughter, your desire to avenge the wrong done to her . . . "

The Master placed his goblet on the table so sharply that the sound rang through the room. "That, Father, I very much doubt."

The Master's voice, usually emollient, pierced Father Anthony like a sword tip.

"I apologise, Sir, I did not mean . . ." Father Anthony recovered himself. "But while we mourn the past we must also appreciate the present and hope for the future. You have a fitting heir. Feilamort has a sweet nature and rare talent; it is true that he has not had the benefit of the education and upbringing he should have received, but that can be rectified. Let him and Deirdre be married and take their place here with you and their child. Your estate will be safe in their keeping, now and in the future."

"Father Anthony, I did not ask you to advise me on how to settle my estate. I am somewhat surprised that you should consider this boy, defiled and debased as he is, and an unlettered serving girl to be fitting heirs to this." The Master waved his hand, gesturing towards the opulent interior of his room. "Your role here is to give spiritual, not temporal, advice and you have given it. I wished to clarify the justification for punishment in the circumstances and you have confirmed my own understanding: as you said earlier, most explicitly, it is my duty to punish the wrongdoer."

"In order that punishment be justified, you must be certain of guilt — and surely there is no evidence that anyone acted with deliberate malice towards the boy."

"I assure you, Father, I have investigated the matter thoroughly and I am quite certain of the guilty party."

"But your estate . . . ?"

The Master chuckled to himself. "For a man of God, you seem overly interested in the disposal of my property. Though I myself do not consider the temporal and the spiritual to be disparate. God created the world and everything in it; it is my opinion that in the creation and appreciation of beauty, we come closest to the divine."

Father Anthony was about to say that love and kindness were the closest that we come to the divine but, before he could speak, the Master stood up, signalling an end to the conversation.

"It is true that when I discovered the existence of my grandson, I wanted to see him. I did hope that he might possess the potential to become a suitable heir. I realised almost immediately that it was useless. He resembles my daughter somewhat in appearance but in nothing else, and lacks any capacity to learn what would be necessary for him to fit this position. No, Father, any hope lies in the next generation. In a few weeks, when he can leave his mother, I shall set about educating the babe. By starting early it may be that I can counteract any weaknesses which have crept into the line."

"So the estate will be put in trust for him? I am sure that neither Deirdre nor Feilamort would object to that. They would be happy to stay here with him, together as a little family. I can marry them as soon as can be arranged."

The Master looked at Father Anthony as though he were a child who had to be told the simplest things over and over. He spoke wearily. "The babe will be my heir. There is no need for either Feilamort or the girl to remain here much longer; their part is done. All that remains is to ensure that justice is administered to the perpetrator of the crimes against my descendants."

Next morn it seemed like a dream. But frae the ashes of the dream arose the desire tae be with Feilamort again, the three of us thegether — it was wrang for us tae be parted. And I couldna understaund Father Anthony's part in this. How could he have kenned all the time that Feilamort was here, and never tellt me? If I couldna trust him, who was left?

On the terrazza, I sat wi the bairn under a tree, the leaves sheltering us frae the burning sun. He loved tae watch the branches dance, the play of the licht as it flichtered and swayed. By this time the berries on the rowan in our forest would have turnt frae yella tae rid, brichter than the briests of reidrabs. A holy tree, a place of sanctuary, the berries were the blood of Christ Our Lord, my grandam said. The leaves above us were still spring-green but, bonny as they were, they werena like the trees at hame. Their roots didna go deep doon intae the earth like the oak and birkies, made strong by the saft steady rain my grandam named angel tears. This place is founded on solid rock and the trees grow in beds filled wi soil brocht frae elsewhere; it is replenished by gardeners and watered by haund. Their branches droop in symmetry, sway lightly like fine ladies feart tae trip ower their gounies. These trees could be plucked out and replaced at a whim — the whim of the Master of this fantastical place.

Sister Agnes

All my life I have striven for clarity. Clarity of vision, of word, thocht and deed. It seems tae me that the Lord's will is simple; He tells us that the path is straight and the way clear. Simplicity isna the same as ease, of course, or we should all be saints. But mair oft than no, righteousness is a question of clearing the weeds frae the path, rather than performing great deeds. It isna my place, nor is it God's will, that I should judge men's hearts. But in my hours of contemplation I come time and again tae the guddle of what I see around me in this place. Clarity has been replaced by clartiness.

I ken that Father Anthony is a good and holy man, I ken he understands this strange tale better than I. But I am disturbed. We sat by a sickly fire while he explained the Master's plans for the child; I looked intae the scrappy flames, considering. I have done my duty by her but have thocht of Deirdre as nae mair than a douce, simple lass and he, too, seems an innocent. Mibbe that is the secret of his beautiful voice; he has nae guile and his simplicity shines through. But I look on these young folk and their bairn and I think that they are being used as pawns in a game.

"The Master is Feilamort's grandfather. So, on finding him, why is he no filled with joy? Why does he wish tae keep it secret? If the father could prepare a feast for the Prodigal Son who had abused that father's love, surely the Master can rejoice on being united with this lad who has done nothing wrang. Feilamort is his fleesh and blood and should be treated as such."

"Each soul has a special place in God's universe," says Father Anthony.

No one believes that mair firmly than I. Even as a bairn I kenned His plan for me and I have ne'er wavered in my faith, though I have oft fallen short in my deeds.

"The Master believes Feilamort is not suited, by nature or upbringing, to inherit. He wishes to educate the baby, bring him up to be a fitting successor."

"And what of his parents?"

"Feilamort's vocation is to develop his singing. The Master will arrange for him to go to Rome."

Father Anthony's haunds tightened round the girdle of his robe. I kenned fine he doesna think that at all. This Master has him under some kind of spell, has them all blinded by his learning and his power. I mistrust such bewitchment.

"And what is to become of Deirdre?"

"Deirdre will return with you to Scotland. In the convent her skills can be put to the service of the Lord."

"And she should leave her bairn behind in the service of the Master?"

Father Anthony turned to me. His een are a strange colour of brown, a pale gold.

"It will be a sacrifice, but I believe it is for a higher good."

"Father, this canna be richt. The lass has proved hersel a good mother. Theirs is a strange union but I believe that, given the chance, she and the lad would settle in contentment and, God willing, live decent lives thegether as a family."

Father Anthony is a modest man, sees hissel as the humble instrument of God's will. He believes that God led him to that Sister who tellt him her story. But how much of what happens is God's will and how much our ain, or, worse, that of the Devil? It is easy tae justify our actions by thinking they are destined. Father Anthony sought out the Master, arranged for the lass to travel to his castle. He is the one arranging this next stage.

"How can you be so sure this is God's will, Father?"

I must have been thinking aloud. I hadna meant tae frame the question sae boldly. His calm feathers ruffled a little afore he smoothed them and answered in his usual gentle fashion.

"I have prayed and prayed on this matter."

I nodded.

"In order to test whether a thing be God's will or not, it is helpful to consider whether the outcome tends towards good or evil. Clearly, in this case, the outcome is for good."

I am no sae clear, but say nothing as yet. I must arm mysel for whitever may come.

That nicht, though dark had fallen, it was still sweltery, the air seeming ne'er enough tae draw full breath. The bairn was hingy and no hissel, fussed and fretted tae sook, dozed then woke again, discontentit. His cheeks were warm but no overly so; it was the wecht of the air that troubled us. In the months since I had arrived, I had kenned naught but smolt weather; the sun shone daily but the caller sea-breeze eased its heat. This place was designed tae shield ye frae its worst excesses; fountains played in the mid hours of the day, owerhanging ledges created shady corners on the terrazza. But that nicht it was sae roukie I tossed and turnt, dovering ower for brief spells.

A dinnle of thunder started me awake. The air had cooled and the bairn slept sound by me. Maffled and wi bleary een, I watched the skimmer of licht frae the windae, greenish, like weeds in a sluggish burn. Then it came, the crash and blatter, the hale room lit up silver. The bairn slept still, and I gathered him intae the blanket, wrapped the pair of us in it and made my way up to the terrazza.

A howder of wind blastered across frae the sea, hurling itsel sideyways agin the building. I cooried under the archway for protection, hauding the bairn close; still he ne'er woke. The storm was kene and grashloch, the rain blashed doon and I prayed for any poor boatman caught in sich a nicht. Frae where we stood I couldna see the watter, only hear the clash and scud of the waves, imagine the sweel and sway of it. The lightning was above us noo, shooting lang witchy fingers of siller across the sky, a gowstie sky, the green of a sick plant, violet-edged.

My grandam used tae say that a thunderstorm was God showing us his anger while my faither tellt me He was having a guid redd out, cleaning the air. But the storms at hame werena like this. My hert beat fast, my fingers and toes tingled, as if I were part of it; I could feel its power in my very bones. The bairn squirmed and wee fingers poked frae the blanket like starfish; I thocht he would start greeting, but he oped his een and keeked out the blanket, spellbound.

Thunder hurled round the hills, echoing frae nord tae south. A breath of silence and licht shattered the heavens above us. Then, all of a sudden, like a bairn who wears itsel out efter a tirr, the storm souched awa. The air smelled clean and the morning blinked ower the back of the hills across the bay.

The babbie was still staring up at the sky.

"God's had a guid redd out, lambie."

I picked my way across the debris of the storm, flooerheids and loose earth and stanes, walked tae the balustrade and looked ower. The wind had lowdened and the waves saftened; the streek o day brichtened, the grey of the sea straiked wi blue. The babbie streetched, made a wee whimper. I turnt back and started towards the house, then stopped. Afore me, rosie in the dawn, glowered the clump of trees we had lain under only the ither day. All the leaves were gone and they stood, reaching out their branches, like empty airms.

Signor Carlo

After the revelation of my pupil's identity, I kept close to our chambers. Feilamort, though he can surely have no knowledge of what passed, seemed unsettled, vague and dreamy, while I was fearful and anxious. Our practice was less than fruitful: he gazing out of the window, while I started at every sound in the passageway outside. Though I doubted that the Master would attempt any retribution at the present time, that did not prevent me from waking in the night, sweat pouring from my brow, after dreams of unthinkable horror. A man of the Master's unusual character could not be predictable as simpler characters are; furthermore, a man of his learning would have knowledge of strange and secret ways of taking revenge. I recalled his hand upon the unicorn cup, the way he looked at it when he said it had healing powers and could protect against poison. A man who knows how to cure knows how to kill.

But although I might be seen to have played a significant part in the boy's condition, verily I am not responsible, and do not choose to be a scapegoat. Feilamort was under the charge of My Lady and the procedure took place with her agreement. While it is not to be expected that the Master's displeasure should be vented on her, it is clear to me that there is another who is implicated, who, indeed, arranged, if not instigated, the affair.

I feel like a fowl reared for the pot, who sees the serving maids approach to wring its neck, one from each corner of the pen. I do not trust Monsieur Garnet, but I have greater fear of the Master's vengeance; he wields absolute power in his domain, for good or ill. Monsieur Garnet is a man who seeks his own advancement, and will go to great lengths to procure it, but he is also a man who hesitates to use violence. This I do not attribute to any fine feelings or virtue; he is clever and sees that it is safer to use his brains to remove an obstacle from his path rather than smash his way through it. No doubt Feilamort could easily have become the victim of an accident at many stages of his short life, but he has so far remained safe; why risk the retribution of man or God when it is a simple matter to keep him powerless or out of the way?

If I can persuade Monsieur that his best interests would be served by ensuring that the boy were sent to Rome under my protection, all would be well. Of course, the Master might try to pursue him, but I feel, on reflection, that in the absence of the boy he would return to his true love, that of study. Should I be unsuccessful in enlisting the support of Monsieur Garnet, I regret that I shall have to flee this place altogether.

Before I had the opportunity to speak to Monsieur Garnet, I became possessed of some information concerning my pupil. It is my practice to give small trifles of coppers to the young boy who performs the lowliest tasks around my chambers; in return he keeps his eyes and ears open. On the night when the Master revealed his tale to us, Feilamort paid a visit to the lower part of the castle and met with a young woman who resides there with her babe. My little informant was unable to supply me with much information regarding her identity, but claims she is from over the water. Is this another of the Master's plots or is our little songbird less guileless than he appears?

The storm had blawn away the heaviness and the day was bightsom; the big room bleezed wi licht and the lumbering machines looked even stranger than usual on sich a morn. I had finished the wings and Monsieur Alberto was joining them to the frame so I set to mending any torn parts of the ither machines. Though I was tired, my work was simple and my thochts raced free while my fingers brocht order to frayed and ravelled fabric. I longed to speak with Monsieur Alberto, to ask him about Feilamort, but I didna dare. We were never alone as the men were cleaning and arranging things at Monsieur Alberto's bidding. As soon as they left for their dinner, I went to him and, my voice low, whispered, "Merci."

His face saftened, just for a moment, the slightest turning up of the corners of his mouth, a crinkle at the een, then he nodded and turnt to the machine. "The wings fit well, Madame Deirdre, and, thanks to your good work, it resembles a bird. What do you think?"

"Aye, Sir, it looks fine enough. But how will they work it?"

"You will see tomorrow night, when the fête takes place."

"I dinna think so, Sir."

He looked surprised for a moment, as though he had forgotten my position. I thocht he was about to speak, but one of the servants entered.

"The Master requires your presence, Monsieur. He wishes to finalise the arrangements for tomorrow."

"Madame Deirdre will remain for a time; she has a little more to do here before she can return to her room." Monsieur Alberto turned to me and bowed. "I am uncertain how long the Master will keep me. But if there is anything you require, remember I am at your service."

My sewing was done in nae time and I began to move around the room, lifting fabric scraps and threid, tidying remnants. The workers were still at their dinner; only the messenger remained and he lay slumped in a corner, een closed. The men who helped Monsieur Alberto had become used tae my presence; I didna think he slept, or, if he did, it was a light doze, easily broken, but he wasna watching me with any degree of attentiveness.

I went out on the terrazza and keeked ower the edge. It was many flairs higher than the one where I went wi the babbie, and, by the look of the view, faced slightly further south, though the building was that confusing it was hard tae understaund how it all fitted thegether. Frae the little I had observed, and what Monsieur Alberto had said, there were many such terrazzas of varying sizes on different flairs, each attached tae a suite of rooms. The Master used his ain private one and the guests had theirs too. I wondered at the mind which had conjured up sich a construction.

Far, far below, the watter was smooth; though the sea was outganging, I could hear bare a clatch, only the pleep of the fleeing gulls. You could near touch the silence here. At hame, even in the quiet room where we sewed, there was aye the shouts and laughter and blethers echoing frae doon the stair, the yowfing of dugs in the yard. Awa in the distance I thocht I heard the thin whisper of a voice in song, but probably it was my fancy.

When I returned to the room, the man was sound, and great loud sowffing snores shuddered through him. I near giggled out loud, he looked that funny. Elinor and me used tae laugh at Douglas when he fell asleep in the kitchen with his mouth wide open; she tickled his nose wi a feather to wake him. It was that lang since I had laughed and jouked about wi someone my age. Louise was douce and kind but we still didna understaund each ither's tongues weel enough for banter. And she was serious, afeart she'd get intae trouble. Lost in a dwam, it was a minute afore I realised that this was the first time I hadna been watched ower. Without thinking, I crept past the man and intae the passageway.

Like all the rest, it sloped up and doon; there were few doors leading frae it. I thocht I had gone in the opposite direction to the one which led to my chamber but in a short time I recognised a door I had seen afore, with a flaw near the lock where the wood was gouged out; I kenned I had somehow come round in circles. I turnt and heided back again, afeart I would be found afore I had had time tae explore. I didna have any plan in mind, I didna think it would be possible for me tae find where they were keeping Feilamort, but I was daft with the freedom of being in the place by mysel, like a bairn going where it has been forbidden.

Though I stepped lightly, my feet seemed tae whap agin the stane flair. At the end of the passage was a wee twisty stair, so narrow I was presssed tae the wall the whole way. I followed it as it rose and fell — up three steps and doon six, doon five and up seven — till eventually it kept going upward. A single slit of a windae lit the steps. At the top was a door, pointed in an arch; I stood outside it, afeart tae enter. A faint sound drifted upwards; mibbe a bird's cry, but it could have been that the mannie had awakened and was seeking me. I took a deep breath and lifted the latch, expecting the door tae creak or jar but it was smooth as if weel used.

The room was so licht it took my breath awa. It was circular, windaes set at regular intervals in the pale stane. All you could see was the sky, fiteichtie, like winter skin. Sketches of wings and machines were strewn on the table; in a guddle on the flair lay jointed mannikins, airms and legs this way and that, taigled thegether. All my wanderings had brocht me to Monsieur Alberto's workroom. I didna want tae be there, tae trespass on him, but when I turnt to leave I noticed a stack of papers covered ower by a bonny cloth of gold. I kenned it was wrang but I was drawn tae its loveliness and couldna help mysel. As I fingered the fabric, no meaning to pry, it slid awa, revealing a set of drawings. They were of a beautiful lady, the one in the painting he had shown me; there were sketches of her frae differing angles, her heid turnt this way and that, some mair finished than others, some quick rough sketches as if he had captured a fleeting moment. One was of her een, filled with that longing I had seen in the painting. Anither was her haunds, as if in prayer. And in the last one — the finest, I thocht — she was glancing backwards, as if caught without realising she was observed. As I traced my finger just above the drawing, alang the delicate line of her cheekbane, the door oped behind me.

I would it had been anyone but him. My face flushed as reid as a rodden. My haund shook. It would have made me feel better had he been angered with me, but he just stared for a moment, then turnt and closed the door.

"When I returned from the Master I assumed you had been taken back to your own chamber."

"I am sorry, Monsieur, I ken I shouldna be here."

"I do not mind your being here, but it can be unwise to stray from those places the Master permits your presence."

"I am sorry I touched your things but your pictures are so bonny . . ." And I dinna ken why, mibbe it was that he seemed so calm, but I burst intae tears.

I felt like a right dowfie as I gowled like a bairn, snochtering on my sleeve. Monsieur Alberto took a lace handkerchief frae his pouch and haunded it to me; I

264

girned mair than ever. He stood next me, and I felt his haund pat my heid, tentatively, as if I were a wee dug.

My tears stopped and I sank intae the chair, worn out.

Monsieur Alberto smiled, one of his wee hauf-smiles. "Better?"

I near started again, but controlled mysel, took a deep breath and nodded.

"I am glad you like the pictures," he said. "I know that, compared to the painting downstairs, they are nothing, but I put my heart and all my skill into them."

"She is very beautiful."

"She was."

"She is . . . in your work." I lifted the last of them. "I like this one especially."

We looked at the picture thegether. Though I was used tae the still, steady way that Monsieur Alberto observed things, I was struck by the intensity of his gaze and something about the way he looked at the drawing made me want tae ask him, did you love her? Did you look at her in secret when she didna ken you were watching, did she love you back? The words near came out my mouth without thinking. "Did you . . .?" Then something about the line of her neck, the shape of her mouth, the curl falling frae her headdress, made me stop.

"It canna be."

Monsieur Alberto nodded. "I did not realise myself when I first saw him. They are not so very alike, only at certain angles and in certain expressions can the resemblance be noticed. Once you know, you see a quality they share; it is hard to define but can be felt." He lifted the drawing. "But I do not think it can be put into a drawing, other than by one of great genius."

"Feilamort never kenned his mother."

"I am certain the Master did not know of his existence until recently. His daughter went away to be betrothed and never returned. We were in mourning for three years."

"Why did he bring Feilamort here, then no tell him the truth? How could he keep this knowledge frae him?"

"I do not think it is possible to understand the Master's thinking. He has now informed his guests that Feilamort is his lost grandson, with strict instructions that it be kept secret. He must know that instruction is likely to be ignored; one of the men has already spoken of it to me."

I lifted another picture, one where her gaze looked directly out, placed it in front of us. As I looked, it blurred and melted intae the image of my ain minnie, that familiar to me I could conjure it up wi my een shut, and I thocht how awful, ne'er to have seen the face of your mither.

"Feilamort must be tellt. He canna hear of it frae servants' gossip."

"It will be a terrible shock." Monsieur Alberto began to tidy the drawings intae a neat pile. He stopped, looked up at me. "Father Anthony knows more of this than anyone; it was he who brought the boy and the Master together. And he is a gentle man."

"I dinna understaund Father Anthony. I used tae think he was a saint, but how could he ken all these things and ne'er tell us?"

"It is hard to appreciate the influence of the Master."

"Monsieur, would you no tell him yoursel?"

"I?" Monsieur Alberto placed his haund on his breist; his slender white fingers spreading across the dark blue velvet of his tunic.

"You kenned his mither."

"No. I spent many hours in observing her, but she was far above me in everything."

I pointed to the pictures. "You could ne'er have drawn her like this unless you kenned her. Please. You can tell him what she was like, Father Anthony canna."

Monsieur Alberto bowed his heid, placing his haunds thegether, as if in prayer. Then he looked at me, his gaze steady.

"I admire you greatly, Madame Deirdre."

He returned to arranging things on the table, speaking as though to hissel. "All the time I have been here I have accepted the Master's eccentricities, his manipulation of events; it seemed to me they were no worse, and often much better, than those of other masters. Life here is peaceful, his servants are well treated, his guests happy and the environment is one of great beauty. I have been able to pursue art and, at times . . . have been happy."

He covered the drawings with the gold clout.

"However, I am afraid that can no longer be. The Master has given me certain instructions. Matters are coming to a head."

Monsieur Alberto looked me full in the face. "I will do as you ask; if I go now, I may be able to tell him before he hears in another way. But, however he hears, he will need tenderness. I will attempt to bring him to you later." He placed his haund on my shoulder. "You must have courage, Deirdre. I will do all I can to help, but I may not be able to act for you directly. Trust Father Anthony and the good Sister. And hold fast to love."

Sister Agnes

I met Monsieur Garnet in the lobby which leads to Deirdre's chamber. He was speaking to Louise, as charmingly as he is capable of, but she was backed intae a corner, the poor lass. Clearly she didna ken whit tae say; afeart tae gie something awa, by her very innocence, she probably has.

"May I help you, Sir? You seem to have got yoursel lost."

He swung round and, though the smile was still stuck on, the een were cauld.

"A remarkable construction indeed. I had no idea that this part existed."

"You have stumbled intae the women's quarters by mistake, Sir. The Master is most scrupulous in his care of the female servants and they are housed alongside we Sisters. I pray you to return to the main part of the castle, in order to avoid unnecessary trouble."

He bowed. "I should not wish to cause any unnecessary trouble."

"I shall accompany you. In case you should loss yoursel again."

I took him back by the maist confusing route I could, though I suspect that man could be led blindfold through a maze and still mind the way. When I returned I questioned

269

Louise closely, but she could tell me naething. "He seemed to come from nowhere," was all she said. "He asked me who lived in this part of the castle and I did know how to answer. I said only the Sisters. But I think he heard the babe."

"If you ever see this man here again, call for help frae me or one of the trusted servants. He is dangerous — he may hurt the bairn."

Her een filled with tears and she crossed hersel. She is a good lass, with a heart too tender for the life she has been given. She is destined tae become a novice but she would be better suited to a husband and bairns of her ain.

"Dinna fear, lass, just tak great care. And pray to the good Lord to keep them safe."

I couldna settle, waiting for Monsieur Alberto to bring Feilamort. I kenned it probably wouldna be till efter nightfall, but that didna stop me watching out for him. Louise kept finissing about, starting at the least wee noise. I had been playing wi the bairn, lifting him up and birling him round, dancing him on my knees, but he wearied of the game and I made to tak him outside. Louise shook her heid, and stood in front of the door tae stop me.

"Whit's wrang, Louise? I want tae gang out on the terrazza."

"You must wait for Sister Agnes."

I minded the words of Monsieur Alberto; he'd cried her the good Sister. I had ne'er thocht of her as good, merely cauld, one who did her duty wi nae feelings. Father Anthony was good through and through; it was him I had trusted, but he had kept Feilamort and me apart. Everything was twisty and fanklit.

When a knock came at the door, we baith started. Louise didna ope it, but stood, asking who was there. Monsieur Alberto's voice was soft, telling Louise she was wanted by Sister Agnes.

Louise oped the door a crack. "I cannot leave Deirdre, Monsieur."

They spoke thegether in French, he reassuring her. "I will remain here myself. She will be safe."

Eventually Louise agreed. "But you must keep the door locked, Sister Agnes says."

After Louise's steps had faded intae the distance, Monsieur Alberto said, "We do not have long. I will wait outside." A moment later, Feilamort entered.

He reached out his haunds to me, and I took them; strange how they were that much bigger than mine now. Then a smile spread ower his face as he saw the bairn; he sat next him on the flair and Jamie grasped his faither's fingers, tried tae pit them intae his mouth. Feilamort lifted the babbie and sat him on his knees, rubbing their noses thegether, makking him laugh. I knelt beside them, pit my haund on Feilamort's airm, laid my heid on his shoulder.

"You ken."

He nodded. "He told me what he knew. That she went away and never came back, that the Master never knew she had had a babe; he says Father Anthony can tell me more. But he showed me her picture. He said she was good as well as beautiful."

The bairn was pulling at Feilamort's hair. "Watch or he will get it fanklit in his fingers — it will hurt ye."

His wee haunds were ticht round the silky locks; as I tried tae remove them he girned at me for spoiling his play. "He has a strong grip for sich a wee mannie."

Feilamort ne'er winced.

I wanted tae ask him many things, but I kenned it wasna richt. As we sat thegether wi the bairn, I could sense the feelings that rose frae him as they rise frae the trees in the forest; the joyfulness and the wecht of sadness that are part of living.

It seemed but a moment we sat there afore Monsieur Alberto signalled that he maun leave.

Sister Agnes

I sought father Anthony immediately after I had returned Monsieur Garnet to the ither part of the house.

"Father, a word, if you please. The bairn is no longer safe."

Father Anthony was at his prayers, and turned round, shocked at my entering his chamber. In truth I was shocked mysel at my boldness, but I could no longer thole the jiggery-pokery. While he remained on his knees the hale place could fall about our ears.

"Father, I ken this isna seeming, but we maun act. These twa young folk and the bairn must be got awa."

I tellt him about Monsieur Garnet's creeping about and that Louise thocht he had heard the babe.

"He cannot know the child is Feilamort's," said Father Anthony.

"He doesna need to know, only to suspect. If Feilamort and the bairn are got rid of, Lady Alicia and Monsieur Jacques will inherit and he keeps his power. And if My Lady's husband were tae die . . . there may be another place he hopes to take."

Father Anthony looked at me, incredulous. Lord have mercy on me for my lack of charity but even a holy priest can be a holy fool and I begin to think that is the case with Father Anthony. He canna see where the danger lies.

"Father, I have seen the way thon sleekit cratur looks at Feilamort, as a cat looks upon a singing bird in a cage. As if tae say, you may be safe now, but I'll watch and wait. I am sure that man was responsible for whit was done to the boy. His nest is feathered by My Lady and she wants to see her daughter heir to this place. Now she will ne'er dirty her haunds with ill-doing, she'll slip out the road of anything soiled and stained, but him — I wouldna walk in front of him on a dark road."

"The Master has power here. He will not let them be hurt."

"It is only a matter of time. For all the Master's plotting and planning, he's nae match for thon sleekit tod."

"Sister, I intend to speak to the Master as soon as it is possible for me to do so."

"The Master manipulates everyone. You may think he is doing it for the best, but it's no richt."

"I have been praying for help."

Father Anthony looked grey and drawn. He has never had a stalwart appearance but aye looked healthy in a thin, wiry way; noo the flesh was drawn ower his cheekbones and pouched under his een like one who has slept little and worried owermuch. Pity, such as I have rarely felt, flooded through me. Father Anthony, a man douce and pleasing, who seemed tae walk lightly with God's angels surrounding him, was drawn and bent like an auld man.

"Courage, Father. You maun tell me all you ken and thegether we will prevent evil-doing. You are not alone, Father. God is with you.

"And," I muttered under my breath, "He has sent me tae help you."

A quiet knock, barely audible, on the door, then it opened, slowly, an inch or two. My heart beat faster. Monsieur Alberto appeared, looking back intae the passageway as if checking that he was unseen, before entering the room.

He bowed. "I am sorry I disturb you but I must speak with you in confidence."

"Do sit, Sir," said Father Anthony. "You wish confession?"

I made to leave. "I will return when you have finished, Father."

"Please stay, Sister. It is not my sin which concerns me." Monsieur Alberto continued in a quiet tone. "The Master intends the demise of Monsieur Garnet."

Monsieur Alberto is a thoughtful man, and he spoke in serious tones. But when he tellt us the Master's plan, it was all I could dae tae keep a straight face.

"The man has lost his mind."

"Such wickedness," said Father Anthony.

"Such idiocy," I replied. "I never heard of foolishness like this."

Father Anthony shook his heid. "He spoke to me of revenge, though I was not certain of the guilty party."

Though I pitied him, I was fair scunnered by Father Anthony. When he had first involved me in this enterprise, he was decisive, able tae take charge of matters; now he was like an auld grandam, moaning frae her seat by the fireside but unable to haud twa ideas thegether in her addled brain.

"Surely it's all havers — I ne'er heard sich a daft idea."

Monsieur Alberto shook his heid. "It is far-fetched, yes, but not beyond the realms of possibility. I have some experience of the matter and believe it could be achieved; the Master would not attempt it otherwise. It is true the Master hopes for revenge, but he believes that by offering Monsieur Garnet a choice in whether to participate in the experiment, he himself is absolved of responsibility in the affair."

Father Anthony continued. "In the Master's view, whether Monsieur Garnet accepts or rejects the challenge, it is of his own free will and the final outcome is in God's hands. This scheme will give Monsieur Garnet his chances — the Master thinks this way to avoid mortal sin. We must attempt to prevent it."

"It doesna sound much of a choice," I replied. "But I dinna want the fate of the bairn to depend on the Master's daft plan. Monsieur, is there nothing we can do to get them out of this place?"

"That is no easy task. No one goes from here without the express permission of the Master; the servants have the strictest instructions. Even one such as myself, who has worked here for many years and is trusted in almost all parts of the building, would have difficulty leaving without authorisation."

"I bow to your judgement. But since the Master seeks tae bring up the bairn as his heir, he is an obstacle to Monsieur Garnet's plans. If they stay here, they are in grave danger."

Monsieur Alberto leaned forward in his seat. "But can they be taken to a place of safety? It would be ill-advised to remove them from the castle, where the Master provides them with some measure of protection, if they are then prey to dangers which may befall them on the road, perhaps on Monsieur Garnet's instructions."

"There are convents where we may stay, and Father Anthony also has connections at safe houses."

I thocht it fitting no tae mention my ain ability tae protect them frae danger. Even wise men like Monsieur Alberto are prone to underestimate the skills of women. And that underestimation is oft of great usefulness.

Monsieur Alberto continued. "The Master's plan provides the only opportunity for escape. Everyone in the castle will be occupied on the terrazza. If we can remove the guards from the entrances of the castle . . ." He paused. "We would need to have everything in place by tomorrow night."

"There is no difficulty about the girl and her child," I said. "And I trust Louise completely."

"I shall see to the boy," said Monsieur Alberto. "I have an idea, not wholly formed . . . it will take much courage but we may be able to turn the Master's challenge to our advantage. I will know by tonight . . . let us finalise our plans then."

The bairn slept sound in his crib while Sister Agnes and I sat on either side of the hearth. White cloud closed round us frae the sea; in an hour the sun would burn it awa and a bricht blue sky smile on us, but the pale licht muddied Sister Agnes' clear skin and it seemed to me that a faint shadow bruised her een. I took a deep breath and began.

"Sister, naebody tellt me Feilamort was here all the time. He didna ken who his mither was — he didna even ken he had a child. It isna richt."

"My part in this affair has been to ensure your safety and that of the bairn. Until the last few days I didna ken the reasons you were brocht here mysel."

She looked at me in silence for a moment. "Things have changed and we maun act to get you all awa frae here. Till then, for your safety and that of the bairn, keep close to this room. Louise and Sister Grace, of course, will tend ye but they ken naught of the plan. Trust no one but mysel, Father Anthony and Monsieur Alberto."

"You treat me as though I were an idiot," I said. "Am I tae ken nothing?"

"I am protecting you. If you ken nothing ye can say nothing. And if you are safe so is your child."

"I wouldna tell secrets."

She sighed. "Lass, when the time comes ye will ken all. For now, think only of the babe. I dinna want tae fright ye but Monsieur Garnet was outside this room earlier in the day. And mibbe that's just his nosiness, but ye maun mind that this bairn is heir tae the Master and there are those who will seek to manipulate the situation."

At the thocht of harm befalling the bairn, my hert thumped that loud I feared it would burst through my bosie.

"I would fight to the death for him."

Sister Agnes put her cool haund on mine, the closest she came to showing comfort.

"Dinna be feart, lass. Pray to the good Lord who keeps us safe in the hollow of his haund. There is not a breath of this babe He doesna watch ower." She patted my airm. "And now, Louise will help ye prepare for the nicht. All being weel, something will tak place that should have happened a lang time ago."

I looked at her, confused, and she smiled, a rare smile. "Your wedding, lass."

We stood in the moonlicht, in a room close tae mine that served us as a chapel. A crucifix hung on the wall and a plain altar, dressed wi a simple cloth, had been placed in front of it. The crib was brocht intae the room, but efter what Sister Agnes had tellt me I couldna bear tae pit the bairn doon, and held him close in the shawl, sound asleep.

Louise had helped me dress in a clean frock, and pulled my hair back wi ribbons. She had placed flooers on the table, wee white and violet daisies, bonnier than all the showy blooms in the gairden. Feilamort and I stood thegether while Father Anthony performed the ceremony. It wasna like any ither wedding I had seen; there was nae Mass, just the sacrament. Father Anthony looked pale and pikit-like; his voice, gentle as ever, was wauf and tremmling. But Feilamort's voice was sweet and strong when he answered, "I will," and he smiled as he placed his haund on mines, warm like a flichtering birdie. We stood for a moment after Father Anthony had pronounced us wed, the three of us joined thegether, Feilamort and I wi the babe tosie in the shawl. Afore he left, he squeezed my haund and his lips brushed my cheek. Nae words.

Father Anthony

For the first time in his life, there was no succour for Father Anthony in his prayers. He, the comforter of lost souls, of those who suffered grief or doubt, found no relief in the familiar words of his Office, the rhythms of the rosary, nor the silent contemplation of the crucifix. God, who had always been so close to Father Anthony that he felt Him in his every breath, had deserted him. A cold and clammy sensation suffused his flesh, his heart was leaden and his soul in agony. Father Anthony was a modest man, who, in daily examination of his conscience and in the sacrament of confession, recognised his faults and failings and prayed for grace to overcome them. But this was different. With a heavy heart, Father Anthony realised that, like a swimmer tempted out of his depth by the sight of a distant glorious shore, he had succumbed to pride. Believing he was acting in accordance with God's will, he had become entangled in the thorns of the Devil.

Mired in confusion, he desired nothing more than to escape to his spiritual director and be cleansed of his sin. But that must wait. In order to avoid even worse harm, he must act, be part of this plan concocted by Monsieur Alberto and Sister Agnes. Action was not in Father Anthony's nature; he was a craft designed for a gently flowing river on a delightful summer's day, lacking the strength and stamina for storm-tossed waters. Nonetheless, it was upon these waters he was cast, and soon his measure would be tested. Father Anthony threw himself prostrate and prayed.

The bairn was sound, sleeping like the wee angel he is. I wanted tae lift him and haud him close, but couldna bear tae wake him. Sister Grace sat smiling in her rocking chair; her face is like a dod of dough left out tae rise afore being put in the oven, but there's something so loving in her smile that I canna think her aught than beautiful. I drew my chair close tae hers and the baith of us sat, my haunds hauding her thick, lined ones.

Soothed by her presence, I was dozing when Sister Agnes came. I hadna expected her so soon and was aware of a sense of urgency in her movements, though on the surface they seemed as smooth as ever.

"Wrap yoursel and the bairn up warm and come with me. The entertainment is about tae start."

"The bairn is asleep."

"He will stay asleep."

"What must I dae? What is going tae happen?"

"Child, it isna your place to question. Swaddle the bairn tight in your shawl. Keep him there, weel out of sicht, and stay close by Louise."

She was daeing it again, treating me as if I had nae sense. But this time I kept my counsel and said naught, for the sake of the bairn. As we proceeded through the maze of passageways, Sister Agnes fingered her beads, praying.

"Lord look with favour on thy servants, save us frae harm. Holy Mother of God, pray for us."

"Amen," I whispered.

V

The room was that different frae when I had last seen it. In the centre was a lang table, dressed in fine linen, the silver dishes gleaming in the licht frae the big sconces which lined the walls. The Master, in his velvet and ermine robes, sat at its heid, the guests round him. My Lady, as beautiful as ever, was at his richt haund and Monsieur Garnet sat by her side, smirking and sooking up tae her good style, though she is aye too sharp tae favour one ower another. I cooried closer to Louise, held the babe even tighter at the sight of him. The place was crowded; Monsieur Alberto had said ladies and gentlemen frae neighbouring houses would be invited. Apart frae those waiting at table, the servants were permitted tae gather in the corner of the room to await the entertainment. It was unlike the castle at hame, where we all ate in the same hall; the Master preserved mair distinction. Louise and the bairn and I remained out of sight, weel warned by Sister Agnes, lest I should be recognised.

After they had eaten, Feilamort was called upon tae sing for the company.

"You appreciate music, I believe, Monsieur Garnet?" said the Master.

"I do."

"Especially, I am told, the voices of young boys."

"There is nothing purer, Sir," said Monsieur Garnet, inclining his heid towards the Master. "Most fitting for such an occasion."

Feilamort sang "Ave Maria". For a moment, as is usual when he sings, there was silence, then applause.

"We shall have more music later in the evening," said the Master. "But now, something rather special."

The servants cleared the remains of dishes frae the table and moved it out the road. The musicians played as the machines were revealed one by one, to the delicht of the guests. On the first, coloured flags birled round, while jesters capered on top. Another was like a giant horse which moved across the room on wheels, pushed by servants who were covered with dark cloaks so they seemed invisible. A man in armour rode on top and behind him sat a lady, strewing rose petals at the guests. A masked man, in a hooded cloak patterned like an eagle, performed a dance, whurling and spiralling round the guests. There was much merriment and laughter, much admiration at the spectacle. Louise and I huddled thegether in the corner.

"Now," said the Master, "I have a very interesting device to show you." He led the guests to the other side of the room. We followed behind, keeking through the crowd. A red velvet curtain was drawn aside, revealing huge doors, open to the terrazza. The nicht was clear but no yet full black, inky-blue with stars strenkellt across the heavens. On the terrazza, in front of the stone balcony, was the giant birdie, mounted on its wooden scaffolding. Louise and I squeezed through intae a corner where we could have a good view.

I hadna seen it all put thegether afore and it looked enormous, looming above us, silhouetted agin the nicht sky, its feathers jaggy like a droukit craw.

"Come closer," said the Master.

"It is a wonderful construction," said My Lady.

"Ingenious," said Monsieur Garnet, examining the wings.

The Master pointed. "This part here pulls back, rather like a crossbow, but with these levers the tension is greatly increased."

Monsieur Garnet bent his heid to see better.

"When the tension is released, the bird flies. The wings have been calibrated to replicate exactly the mechanism of flight."

"Most impressive, Sir."

"It has long been the dream of man to fly. Icarus, they say, achieved his dream for a brief time but the heat of the sun was too much for him. But to fly at night would present no such problems — do you agree, Monsieur Garnet?"

"An intriguing prospect, but a dangerous one."

"Perhaps. That may depend on how much a man desires flight."

The Master gazed out beyond the terrazza. "In my experience, desire comes in two forms: one is the desire for something new, something unknown. In the Garden of Eden, Adam and Eve ate the fruit which they had been forbidden to taste and satisfied their desire for the unknown. No doubt that is also the desire which motivated Icarus, the desire to be greater and to know more. But there is also a lesser form of desire, that of wishing to escape from something. Of course, in certain circumstances, where a man wishes very much to get away, it may prove as powerful as the other."

He turned to Monsieur Garnet. "I have long wished to know whether my machine works. It was created by a great mind, the greatest I have ever encountered, and I am a learned man, familiar with the achievements of mankind. The device has been tested with mannikins and wax models; improvements have been made in the light of these experiments and it appears to function beautifully. Once launched, on a night such as this, with a suitable wind, one should glide across the bay and land safely on the other side. But I need a man who has the courage, the heart, to attempt flight."

"You have many servants," said Monsieur Garnet. "You will no doubt find one who would risk his life for a price."

"To be the first man to fly successfully is not the task for a servant, surely. This man's name will be remembered throughout history."

"This man may well be remembered as an idiot who drowned in the sea or dashed his brains out on the rocks below."

"Such an endeavour does not interest you, Monsieur? I thought you were a man who embraced challenge."

Monsieur Garnet threw back his heid and laughed. My Lady gave a slight giggle then covered her mouth. The rest of the crowd was silent.

All the players had stopped their cavorting, except for the dancer, who crouched and whiddered, flaucht-braid, pecked and stabbed the air with his neb. He snaked close tae the ground, capering around the construction, then struck out as if attacking a rival bird, stopping short in mid-air. His haunds were fearsome metal clews, sharpened to a point, which could have riven fleesh apart. He turnt tae Monsieur Garnet, his heid cocked tae one side, held out the gruesome clews as though in invitation. Then he gied a cry and danced aff again, pavie and snell.

For a moment Monsieur Garnet and the Master looked at each other, then Monsieur Garnet relaxed, smiled and began to examine the machine. "So one is attached here." He lifted the leather straps which were fixed to the wings. "And positions the feet here." He indicated the place. "I see."

"There is another fastening — it is well thought out."

"And once strapped in, the bow is pulled back — by several strong men, I assume?"

"Three is sufficient, Monsieur."

"And then . . ." He mimed the action of firing an arrow.

"Flight."

"I cannot deny it is an enticing thought."

Monsieur Garnet gazed at the machine, appraising it as though he were considering whether it were worth buying. He turned to the Master with a sneer on his

293

face. I thocht he was about to walk awa, but he shrugged, and said, "Let it be done."

The Master clapped his haunds. Monsieur Garnet was helped up on the machine and the straps attached. Tomasso and twa other men wound the mechanism at the back which worked the bow, hauding it taut in readiness. All was still. You could barely hear a breath as we watched Monsieur Garnet, airms outstretched like a bird of prey; Tomasso and the other men stood tense, hauding ticht till the signal was given.

Then Monsieur Alberto said, "We must check that the straps are secure." He stepped forward, and chaos ensued.

The area round the machine was crowded and there was that much jossing and shoving that it was difficult tae see whit was happening, but Monsieur Garnet was somehow gone from the machine and Feilamort had taen his place, strapped ontae the bird.

"Hold, hold, Tomasso, do not let go," the Master cried out. "Do not let him go!"

Tomasso's face was purple with effort but somehow he lost his balance. With unimaginable force and power the bird flew, high up in an arc, like an arrow, while Feilamort's voice soared ower the castle. For a moment it was like a seabird caught on a current, floating as though held, and then I could see nae mair for someone grabbed me frae behind and said, "Now, lass, we must go, now."

I was pushed out the back and awa doon the stair, Sister Agnes shoving me frae behind, hauf hauding me up. Outside there was a cart waiting for us and she hid

294

me under some blankets in the back, the bairn safely cooried in beside me.

I was sobbing and girning and wailing, but she grabbed my airm and pinched me and said, "Lass, haud your wheest. Ye maun compose yersel if we are tae get awa. God is merciful, God is looking after us all. Ye must do His will. And for the next wee while ye maun do mine or there will be trouble for us all."

Signor Carlo

For three days I dared not leave my chamber. Servants have attended to me, bringing food which I feared to eat. I could not sleep, my mind constantly returning to that dreadful moment. I tried to reconstruct the events leading up to it but all was confusion. When the Master spoke of his flying machine and suggested that Monsieur Garnet should actually go on it, I thought it an elaborate joke they had concocted. I expected that at the last minute some animal would be substituted and we would be treated to the spectacle of a rabbit catapulted into the air. But the boy, the boy, and, worst of all, his pure voice was the last thing I heard, a broken chord echoing across the bay.

My heart races when I think of it; I must try to control myself or I shall become ill.

I thought it politic not to ask the servants anything, but the woman who attended me yesterday was talkative and could speak of nothing else.

"They've been out, searching the water constantly, Sir. Even at night, as long as there is trace of the moon, the Master insists. My son has been helping, every man who is able has been called into service."

"It is dreadful."

"It is, Sir, a fine young lad. But you know how boys are, what foolish pranks they play. I have four sons, and I mind well what they used to get up to when they were younger. Mercifully mine are all grown now. But my sister's boy lost an arm as a result of a dare, playing about with a scythe. They have no sense."

"The guests, are they still here?"

"Oh yes, Sir, they are, but it is as quiet as the grave. The Master keeps to his chamber, paces up and down, only attending to the reports of the searchers. And the guests keep to their place. My daughter, who serves the ladies, says she has heard talk that they wish to leave but do not like to go until the search for the boy is ended."

Three days we journeyed, with bare a stop. The cart took us some way, then we walked through woods, rough sleeping under blankets thegether, the bairn and me with Louise and Sister Agnes. Then onward tae the next place where another cartie picked us up. I hadna time tae think on it then, my body weary and my mind that trauchled and confused; all my life, till this past year, I had ne'er spent a nicht awa frae hame, but since then I have been dragged frae one place tae anither wi nae idea where I was going. Eventually we reached a wee tummled cottage in the woods where a silent auld man and his grim wifie took us in. We were fed and given beds but they barely looked at us.

"It is better for them," said Louise, who was the only one of us who could understaund their tongue. "They are helping us because of Father Anthony but they are afraid of soldiers coming after us."

I had given up asking questions, was glad to rest in a bed and have some hot broth tae sup.

I couldna stop thinking of Feilamort, in dread of whit has become of him. Next morn Sister Agnes was tight-lipped, even mair poker-faced than usual. She tells me no tae speak of him. "Dinna worry, all will be well," she says, but something is afoot. She is preoccupied. Someone may be following us and I dinna understaund why we are spending time here when we should be on the road. I want tae be gone frae this grim place.

"We have tae make further arrangements," is all she will say.

I sat with the bairn outside the cottage. The bare licht that flichtered through the forest was grey and made the trees look deid even though they still bore leaves; a dreich place it was compared tae the castle with its glistering sea and sky. My heart was heavy. Sister Agnes had forbidden me tae speak of Feilamort, had forbidden me tae speak of aathing except what was immediately required, and I lacked the will tae argue wi her. I tried tae enjoy this time wi the bairn, the peace I have craved on the lang miles, but I couldna. But the bairn seemed ne'er tae notice the dreichness of his surroundings. There was a heap of twigs under the tree; I picked them up and haunded them tae him one by one and he threw them back at me. Then he got tired of that and took the whole pile of them, rubbed his wee haunds in them till they were mawkit and held them out, chuckling. The past few weeks he had been hauling hissel up and moving alang, hauding on tae whatever was around him. He pulled hissel up agin the tree and I reached out. He took one step, then anither, towards me. I saw the licht in his een as he realised he had moved by hissel, then he slipped and landed on his bahoukie. As we baith laughed and I pulled him up again, I saw, across

299

his shoulder, a figure appear in the distance through the trees. Fear clutched my hert and I snatched up the babe and rushed intae the house.

Signor Carlo

I know not what I should do. There is no place for me here; though I think it unlikely on the whole that the Master will attempt revenge, he is a man of unpredictable humours and, in any case, has no need of me. I could travel with My Lady's party, since I am still in her employ. Though Lady Alicia will no doubt be married soon, there may be some use for a singing master to help arrange musical events in the chateau. I have proved my loyalty to Monsieur Garnet and he may reward me. In any case I see no other option at the moment, until I can make use of my contacts to find another place.

The prospect, though, is not pleasing. I had always assumed that at some stage in the future, when My Lady had no further need of Feilamort, we might find a place where his voice could be used for its true end. The voice of an angel should praise God; its fitting place is in God's own country, in the seat of Holy Mother Church. If only I could be sure that the boy is truly lost. On the face of it, this seems to be inevitable, but this strange castle shows only part of its structure and hides the rest. Within its walls I sense something unexpressed, unsung.

On the third day, when a knock at my door announced the arrival of breakfast, I was surprised to see Tomasso. The fellow looked drawn and haggard, placed my food on the table with only a brief greeting.

"I am glad to see you back, Tomasso."

"Thank you, Signor."

The warm bread smelled delicious. All I had eaten since that dreadful night was what the little lad had procured for me. I did not trust any of the other servants, but surely good Tomasso would not act as the Master's messenger of death? Still, one cannot be too careful.

As Tomasso tidied the chamber I tried to work out how best to approach the subject.

"It must have been a terrible shock for you, Tomasso."

He looked me full in the face. "I have not been able to shut my eyes but the awful scene returns to me. I am filled with regret that I could not hold the machine back."

"There is no sign of the boy?"

"They have called off the search."

I nodded.

"Tomasso, may I ask you something? I am so confused. I know some terrible mishap occurred and I wonder if you are able to tell me what they intended to happen?"

"I thought it was a joke worked out between them, Signor. I understood that Monsieur Garnet would feign acceptance of the challenge, then they would put a model figure in his place. We had practised the whole day long. Monsieur Alberto made notes on the path of the flight and adjusted the machine, making improvements to it with each trial. He has many models which he attached to the machine and let fly. He said they would dress one up as Monsieur Garnet and, once Monsieur Garnet was got down from the machine, his mannikin would fly in his place. No one could have expected that the boy . . ." He fell silent.

"The servant who attended me yesterday believed that it was a prank, but it seems unlike the boy to play such a trick."

Tomasso's face was open and honest. "What else could it be, Signor? I was concentrating hard on my part in holding the bow, but I saw him climb on to the machine willingly. No one forced him."

Tomasso rearranged a knife which had moved from its place on the table.

"All I know is that I would give anything to know who it was that made me lose my balance and allow the machine to fly."

The man that I saw was a messenger for Sister Agnes, but she still willna tell me what is happening. I dinna ken why I dae as she says, like a sheep wi nae mind of my ain. If we had stayed at the Master's house, surely he would have looked efter us and the bairn, kept us safe frae Monsieur Garnet — after all, Feilamort is his ain fleesh and blood. But mibbe no, who can tell with sich a man. And I am as defenceless as a babe mysel; I dinna ken a soul, I dinna understaund the language. Where could I go? What could I dae? I keep quiet and pray constantly in my heart, for the Lord is good. But it's no my life which is at stake. Though I am helpless without Sister Agnes, the bairn is helpless without me. In bed I toss and turn, my dreams storm-tossed.

It was the middle of the nicht when I woke; at first I was confused then I realised she was beside me, her airm on my shoulder. "Ssh," she said, squeezing hard. "Say nothing. Wrap the bairn warmly but avoid waking him if you can."

"Whit is it?"

"We must leave immediately, we canna delay."

I wrapped my cloak round the pair of us, gathered thegether our few possessions and followed her, feeling our way in the dark, she guarding the way in front of me.

Twa days' travel ower rough ground, keeping out of sight in case we had been followed. The bairn girned when he wasna sleeping; it is hard for a child of his age to be kept still for lang. Mercifully the motion of the cartie kept him asleep longer than usual — would I had been able tae sleep as he did, for I felt the motion sair and they had tae stop for me tae be sick several times. How awful it was, how shamed I felt tae be boking up in front of others. Though they, of course, stood at a distance, my face burned.

She barely spake a word to me. Even efter the first stage of our journey, in the cool dark of the morn, when we had tae be silent, she kept her ain counsel.

"You are a young widow. We have been to the healing shrine to cure the bairn's gripping sickness, and we now return hame."

My heart rose.

"Are we really going hame?"

"The less ye ken, the better," she said.

"I am sick of being kept in the dark."

"I am protecting you. If you ken nothing ye can say nothing. And if you are safe so is your child." She sighed. "I can tell you nae mair at present. When the time comes you will know everything. Mair, even, than you wish. Trust me. I shall take you to a place of safety."

Signor Carlo

I am undone. While I have been skulking in my chamber, My Lady and her company have departed, to return to the home of Monsieur Jacques and his family. Apparently Monsieur Garnet was gone days ago, no one knows where. The garrulous woman arrived to clean and share the gossip of the lower orders.

"Such a palaver. Her Ladyship's carriages away down the hill, with black plumage and ribbons all over them. At least she left in daylight, which is more than can be said for the priest."

"Father Anthony is gone?"

"Yes, Sir, and the Sister too, but not together, I believe. Though it has been known for such things to happen." She laughed, and I smiled and nodded, though I felt nauseous.

I took a coin from my purse and held it in my palm, where it glittered and could not fail to catch her eye.

"There is much talk?"

"Too much, if you ask me. Much of it plain daft."

She glanced at the coin, as if it were a speck of dust, then looked me in the eye. "Some still believe that the boy is not drowned, but reached the other side and escaped."

"There is evidence?"

"Some say they have been seen on the road, a boy and a priest. But you know how people talk."

"Is there mention of a girl too, perhaps?"

"The sewing lass, the one with the bairn? They also left that night. Took advantage of the commotion." She paused. "You're the only one left, Sir."

Finally we stopped at the convent and peace owertook us. A clean bed, a walled gairden where the bairn could run, and an end tae the terrible journeying. I lay with the bairn in a wee room high in the eaves. Though it was efternoon, we were that exhausted we fell asleep, and when I awoke the sun had moved round and lang shadows cast their darkness across the bed. The bairn was awake, gurgling and reaching out tae grasp the medal round my neck. I tickled his wee haunds and he smiled. Thank God he is sich a good babbie; it would be hard indeed if he were girnie and bad tempered. I sat up and lifted the child. I felt hungry and hoped it was near to supper time. All I wanted was to stay here for a wee while, safe.

Sister Agnes watches me continually. I am feart and dinna feel trust in her. I wish I had someone tae talk to; Louise is no longer with us, left behind at the last place we stopped. We wept thegether when we parted but she is gone to her family and will be safe there. But, without her, how I miss my minnie and Elinor.

Yesterday afternoon I saw Sister Agnes frae the windae, in the kitchen gairden ower to the side of the building. She was talking to a man in the corner shaded by trees. Why would she be speaking in such a covert way? I dinna believe I am thinking these things — she is a holy Sister, she canna be daeing aathing bad — but my mind has been so tormented and turnt upside doon by all that has happened. I must keep the bairn close by me, look efter him and pray that all will become richt.

The walled gairden was a place of tranquillity; sheltered frae wind and storm. Fruit grew in abundance: rizzar and pome, hindberry and gowdnap. In the Master's realm it was hard tae ken whit season you were in — an eternal summer hung ower the place — but here the brambles and grosets had ripened and the cherries were past their best. Vegetable beds were laid out neatly by the door that led frae the convent, the curly cabbage leaves and fennel fronds as fair as any flooer. The Sisters grew a wealth of flooers too and I saw many used for medicines: banwart, luffage, witches' paps. I pressed a lavender heid, breathed its scent in deeply.

I hunkered doon to the bairn and held out my haunds; he grabbed them and pulled hissel up frae the ground. Jamie stoated alang, hauding on tae me, and each time he took a step his wee face filled with so much joy at being able tae move. I wished I could tak sich pure pleasure in being alive, but I was pressed doon with thochts of what might be. I lifted him up, birled round, then stopped, my heart pounding. At the entrance to the gairden was a figure, dressed in a grey hooded cloak. I stood still, afeart I was mistaken, then started tae run and in a moment I was in the airms of Feilamort, the babe nestled atween us. And tears came, sudden, as though a dam had burst on a river; I clung to him, feeling my legs wouldna haud me.

"I thocht I would ne'er see you again," I sobbed. "I thocht you were drowned."

"It was all trickery — a plan to get me away."

"Surely they could have smuggled you out the castle?"

He shook his heid. "It was the only chance. So that you and the babe could leave under cover of the commotion."

"You could have died."

"I trusted him."

"Father Anthony?"

Feilamort smiled. "He is a good priest, but has no knowledge of machines. I meant Monsieur Alberto. He persuaded me that it would work safely."

I wiped my face wi my sleeve. "I dinna understaund — when I was sewing the wings, I thocht they were for one of the players."

"The Master planned to punish Monsieur Garnet and assumed he would accept the challenge. If the bird failed, he would face injury or death. But if it succeeded, at least the Master would have the satisfaction of knowing he had been responsible for man's flight. This scheme was kept secret from all except Monsieur Alberto, whose expertise was necessary. The men who were to fire the machine had to know something so they were told it was a jest; at the last minute, Monsieur Garnet would step down and a mannikin substituted and let fly."

"I saw the mannikins in Monsieur Alberto's room."

"They were used to perfect the calculations."

"But how did you come tae fly instead of Monsieur Garnet?"

"Monsieur Alberto told him of the Master's plans in advance, professing to be on Monsieur Garnet's side, to seek favour from him. Monsieur Garnet agreed that he would pretend to accept the Master's challenge, then, at a sign from Monsieur Alberto, he would stand down and the substitution would be made."

"So Monsieur Garnet believed a mannikin would fly in his place."

Feilamort shook his heid. "Monsieur Garnet knew I would be substituted; that was why he agreed. Monsieur Alberto persuaded him that there was virtually no chance of my survival."

My tears started afresh.

He touched my cheek. "You will wet the child's head."

The vision came back to me: the big birdie fleeing out intae the darkness. I shivered.

Feilamort stroked the babe's silken curls. "I was afraid right up until the second before it happened, then the fear seemed to leave me and, as I flew upward, a sensation filled my body such as I have never experienced. First there was speed and wind rushing in my ears like a sea, then a peacefulness, a stillness as though I was held by the air, then I floated, landing in the water like a leaf."

The bairn writhed and wriggled; I placed him on the ground atween us and he pulled hissel up, hauding on tae Feilamort's legs.

"The machine was calibrated so that my flight took me over the hope to land in shallow water. I swam to shore, where Father Anthony was waiting with a boat. We followed you here."

"Where is Father Anthony?"

"He and Sister Agnes are discussing the next part of their plan."

I looked up at the clouds, scuffing across the sky, and I wondered whether Feilamort and I would have any say in these plans for us.

Sister Agnes

The pallor has lessened on Father Anthony's cheek, but his hair has whitened over the past weeks and his een glitter like one who sleeps little. His voice affects a confidence belied by his appearance; he twists and turns the parchment in his hands.

"The matter must be resolved. We have taken them away from the Master, but we cannot guarantee their safety. If the information you have received is correct, then Monsieur Garnet is still in pursuit. I think the child would be safer with the Master. And Feilamort and Deirdre would be safer without the child."

"You speak as if the bairn were a package, to be left here and there at the convenience of others."

"Sister, I am trying to find the best place for him in the circumstances, bearing in mind the new information I have received in this missive."

I looked with disgust at the letter he had shown me. Plotting and planning are unnatural to me. I ken what is richt and what is wrang and I follow the Lord's path. But in this matter I have been forced tae tak up the position of one who negotiates and debates and discusses. Ach, it's all skite, but it maun be done. Father Anthony had lost his way, of that there was nae doubt.

"I needna remind you, Father, that marriage is a sacrament."

"Of course, but this is a special case. Under the circumstances, clearly such a union could bear no further fruit and would be in name only. I myself could accompany the boy and Signor Carlo to Rome. Afterwards I must go to Assisi. I think it best for Deirdre to return to Scotland."

I spake under my breath. "And what of the babe?"

There have been too many conversations in dark corners, too many secret and hurried plots. It is only when things come intae the licht that they are seen in their truth and simplicity. I watched frae the windae as they walked thegether in the sun, the three of them, the picture of innocence; I prayed that their path would be as smooth as those of the convent gairden.

We walked in silence. I felt shy; it was strange tae be with him in this place, so different frae the bonny woods where we had run as bairns.

"It seems an age," he said.

The babbie was cooried ower my shoulder, heavy with sleep.

"In the Master's house I used tae lay him doon in the cradle but I canna bear to be apart frae him here. I cairry him everywhere and when I sleep he lies next me."

"You are a beautiful mother, Deirdre."

I felt my face flush. As we continued alang the path that led through the fruit trees, Feilamort spake.

"All my life I have wondered about my mother. I was told that she had died and no one knew who my father was; in this I was much like many other children. But it was impossible for me to believe it fully. Somewhere in my heart I still hoped she was alive; though I did not expect to be reunited with her, I oft wondered where she was, had she married and borne other children. Sometimes, when I saw a woman look at a babe with love and tenderness, I imagined that perhaps she had looked at me like that." He glanced at me, then looked awa. "As I have seen you look at him."

He paused tae raise a branch that hung doon, haud it up so we could continue. "It was hard when Father Anthony told me that there was no doubt she had passed away not long after I was born. But I know for sure that she did love me."

He turned and pit his airms round me; he was that slight the bones of his chist were sticking through his claes like a baby bird. I rested my heid on his neck and we stood, enfolding the babe, the trees, heavy with fruit, trailing round us.

It all happened that quick. I dinna ken frae where he came but, without sound or warning, Feilamort and I were wrenched apart and the bairn snatched frae between us. A man was racing awa, cairrying him. I started tae follow as fast as I could but it was like a dream when time stands still and, in spite of my efforts, my legs didna seem tae be moving. Feilamort raced ahead of me, shouting at the tap of his voice, a voice so unlike the sweet tones of his singing, as harsh as the cracked pitch of an auld wifie.

The man sped towards the high wall where, leaning ower, his accomplice was waiting to take the babe. I kept on, my heart thudding, the boke rising in me, unable to take my een aff the babbie, willing that Feilamort would be able tae reach him in time to wrest the bairn frae his grasp. Suddenly the man on the wall let out a cry, slumped, then slithered and fell backwards to the far side, felled by an arrow which had come frae the direction of the convent. The ither looked back in panic. He tried vainly to climb the wall with the babe in his airms, then placed him on the ground and made his escape just as Feilamort reached the wall and scooped our babbie intae his airms.

My legs could bare haud me, my mind was in sich a lather. Wee Jamie was gowling and roaring at the tap of his lungs and I shushed him, examining his body tae see nae harm had come to him.

"Is he all right?" asked Feilamort.

"I don't think he's hurted," I said. "Are you, wee mannie?"

"I doubt a bairn who maks that racket has much wrang wi him." Sister Agnes emerged frae the door of the convent. "We will ask Sister Adele, who is skilled in nursing, to check him for injuries, but I think he is fine."

"What of the men who tried to take him?" asked Feilamort. "They will escape."

"Servants are looking for them, but I think there is little chance they will be caught. They will be hired men who came frae naewhere and will disappear intae naewhere."

"But the one who was wounded?"

"Merely a flesh wound, in his shoulder. To disable, nae mair."

It was then that I noticed what Sister Agnes carried. "But it was you . . ."

She patted my airm. "A good Sister must be skilled in mair than prayers and embroidery. Some have proficiency in cooking or gardening, others in healing.

317

As a lass I was taught the art of archery by my faither and I am thankful it has been of use on occasion."

It was the way she spake, in sich a matter of fact tone, that affected me; I realised how close we had been to peril, here in this place of peace and sanctuary. Suddenly waumish and dizzy, I felt my legs crumple beneath me.

Sister Agnes

It was nae surprise that the lass should have fainted; efter the danger is ower, that is when the mind and body succumb to panic. It has been a harsh time for her, certainly, but she is made of strong stuff. Sister Adele gied her a draught, then she slept for a while, the bairn next her.

Feilamort waited outside the room like a wee dug; he is a strange lad, ghostlike in his silent presence. But there is a bond between him and the lass — they are alike in their faithfulness to one anither and the bairn. I sat in the room, unwilling to leave my charges; though I was unsurprised at the events of this morn, I was disturbed by them. However, this may at last persuade Father Anthony of the need for urgency.

Between them, Father Anthony and Sister Agnes explained the wild and wondrous story. And though Feilamort kenned mair of it than I, he sat as though listening to some spinner of tales on a cauld winter nicht.

"So now, it must be decided what is to become of you." Father Anthony's voice was flat, unlike hissel. "The Master wants the child for his heir."

I held him even tighter, so he girned and I wheeshed him.

"He will not have the bairn."

Sister Agnes nodded.

Father Anthony continued. "I have received a letter from My Lady. She suggests that Feilamort goes to Rome, where Signor Carlo has important connections. A voice such as Feilamort's is a talent which must be used for the Lord's purposes. Feilamort could sing for the Lord in the choir — the greatest choir on earth. Think what that would mean, how this wonderful gift, for which he has sacrificed so much, could be used in the service of God."

I was dumb, unable tae comprehend whit he was saying. Did he mean we should all go tae Rome or that Feilamort should go away again, just when we had found each ither? I looked at Feilamort and, though he remained silent, his look gave me courage to speak.

"But, Father, we are marriet now."

Father Anthony rose and stood with his back tae the windae, his heid haloed in the licht. How weary he was and how much aulder he looked; his hair was lyart and his skin like plumblede.

"Though your marriage legitimises the child, given the particular circumstances such a marriage would be in name only and could be annulled; for you there could be a husband, other babes, a family."

He looked intae the distance. "And, of course, there is Monsieur Garnet. The events of this afternoooon make matters even more pressing. I think there is little doubt that the men who attempted to seize the babe were under his orders. And if he tries again, we cannot rely on Sister Agnes being nearby." Father Anthony gied a hauf-smile, then his face became serious. "The child would be safer with the Master, who has an interest in keeping him alive and the power to protect him. And if you did take such a course, My Lady has suggested that she would take a special interest in the babe."

"I am sure that she would." Sister Agnes looked as if she had trod on keech. "But I dinna think her interest is of any interest tae aabody but hersel."

Fear, like a damp dark cloak, started tae furl around me. "How can the bairn ever be safe if they all want him for their ain ends?"

"Dinna be troubled, child," said Sister Agnes. "We do not tell you these things tae make you afeared, only to mak you aware of the danger. We wish you to know what the possible consequences are, and tae mak your decision in the light of all that is known."

Father Anthony spake earnestly. "If you give the babe to the Master, he would be well looked after, and safe as is possible. The Master's method of upbringing might be unusual but, as you know, he is not a cruel man and is capable of love. Sister Grace would look after him. The child, when he grows, will be heir to the wonderful realm of the Master and will be a fine and learned young man."

The memory of the sun shining on the water frae the balcony, the bricht flooers in the gairden, the tenderness of Sister Grace. It couldna be; I would haud him tight, keep him close tae my bosie for as long as I could.

My minnie, my minnie, if only she were here.

Father Anthony returned to his seat. "Of course, you could go back to Scotland together. It is likely that Feilamort could find a place; the music of the liturgy is flourishing, the court has fine musicians and the King is fond of music. The Master is unlikely to follow you there and in any case would have little claim on the child, though he might try to make a case that the boy would be better off with him." He paused. "But Monsieur Garnet — there is no telling what he might attempt. Are you prepared to live each day in fear, watching for any stranger at the gate, any servant who may be looking to better his position by a little spying?"

"I canna be separated from my babe."

"Even if his life might be better without you?"

The dagger was sharp in my soul.

"I dinna believe he can be better off without me."

"That is sentiment, child." His words were harsh, but there was a trace of gentleness behind them. "There are many babes who have been better off without the mother who birthed them."

Feilamort had been silent till now, but he put his haund on my airm, and said, "He will never be better off than when he is with Deirdre. And, if she wishes, we shall stay together, whatever the troubles and dangers."

He was that slight, Feilamort, looked as though the wind would blaw him ower, but as he spake I felt as safe as I ever had. God had joined us thegether and God would look efter us and our babe, our joy.

Sister Agnes

The lass thinks I have been harsh on them, and mibbe she is right. But if I hadna, wha kens how things might have turned out. The Lord creates us all in His likeness, but no all alike. We maun each take what he has gien us and make best use of it, as in the Parable of the Talents. Father Anthony, his sweetness restored tae him, sets aff for Assisi, there tae shrive sinners and, by his presence, make the love of God felt among them. I ken I have judged him wanting in many ways, but I have ne'er doubted his gifts or his sincerity.

Signor Carlo has already left for Rome, where his mair worldly gifts will nae doubt prove useful. Though who can say that one gift is spiritual and another less so. All gifts are frae the Lord; the question is whether we use them for His ends or our ain. And sometimes, though our purpose may be selfish or merely muddled, the ends of the Lord are served in any case. After all, thon mannie used his talent as a teacher to train and discipline the lad so that his voice came to its fruition. And sich a voice has but one end: to praise and honour its creator.

I pray that he and the lass will find peace thegether wi their bairn and that those who may seek tae harm them will content theirsels with what they already have. Once we arrive, they will no longer be my responsibility; I am bound for the convent. Already the Master's realm seems like a dream, or a state of befuddlement brocht on by a fever. The freshness of the sea air blasts awa its staleness and I long for the cauld clean skies of hame. I am fitted for northern climes and yearn for the blatter of hail on an oaken door, the icy draught through a chapel windae.

We stood on deck as the boat approached the land. A day of contrasts it had been; sometimes the rain and lashing wind had forced us under, then it buffed itsel awa tae this: blue, heavenly blue, and dancing white waves. The wind was cauld but I was happed up wi a big blanket round me and the bairn. He is that big now and when he drops aff tae sleep is even heavier; I shifted him frae one airm to the ither. Feilamort standing by my side, smiled and shared the wecht. Naething could be mair different frae the journey that brocht me awa frae my mither. For we are heided hame thegether.

This morn Sister Agnes haunded me whit looked like a scroll inside a cloth.

"Monsieur Alberto gave me something for you, to be kept safe till ye returned tae Scottish soil. He says it is rightly yours and sends it with his good wishes for your futures."

I unwrapped it carefully; it was the unicorn embroidery I had made. I spread it on the table, so we could look at it, me and Feilamort. Though I could see my errors and places where I could have done better, the colours were bricht and bonny, and the unicorn watched, gazing lovingly at us, een wide open, deep brown like the een of Feilmort and the babbie.

Fog, black as nicht. Sound muffled and dull. Grey and dreich the day we returned tae Scottish soil. I feared the boat wouldna succeed; we stayed motionless for a while, seemingly suspended in time and space. Then white licht crept round the grey of the haar and the blurred outline became the shore. All was damp, the wool of my cloak wrapped round me and the bairn, Feilamort's haund on my airm. Then I saw her, standing on the pier, engulfed in her shawl, hair escaping, whirled all ways by the wind.

I could barely wait till they anchored the boat and laid doon the plank for us tae walk across. Tears blinded me as I ran intae her airms. She enwrapped me and the bairn, then pulled awa, turned doon the shawl a bittie tae see his wee face. Beaming, she turned tae Feilamort standing beside me.

"This is the happiest of days."

She touched my face, stroking my skin, feeling the line of my cheekbanes and jaw, looking intae my een all the while. "There are lines here where there used tae be nane. It has been a lang journey you have made, my lassie."

She clasped me close inside her shawl like a babbie; the familiar scent of her skin surrounded me. I minded the last time we had been thegether, that melancholy day we were parted. It seemed years had passed since then; so much had befallen me, for good and ill. And I kenned there would still be danger and troubles, but I couldna feel them then, in her airms.

Hame.

A Word About The Scots Words

I use scots words to suggest character and place as they are often more specific than the English equivalents. But perhaps more than anything I love the wonderful sound quality of the language, which is both beautiful and evocative. I hope that, in context, the meaning is often self-explanatory; "a hushle of wind" suggests its definition and you can hear the birds "cheetle and chirm and chirple".

But some readers may like to know the dictionary definitions in a wee bit more detail, and there are a few words which might be hard to guess. Here is a selection.

Colours
fiteichtie: whitish

purpoir: purple (cloth) (Like other words, such as *trist*, suggest Scots-French links.)

vermeloun: vermilion

wald: yellow dye obtained from weld, the plant

Animals and Birds
corbie: raven

lintie: linnet
speug: sparrow
tod: fox
wullcat: wild cat

Plants and Trees
clow: clove pink
sauch: willow

Sewing and Embroidery
baissing: basting
brusery: embroidery
ranter: rough, hasty stitching, darning
steek: to stitch (also means to close)
surfle: to gather, ruck a hem; overcast an edge of
   cloth; trim with lace

General
bightsom: easy, relaxed
cranreuch: hoar-frost
fauchliness: lack of strength, weariness
forfauchlit: worn out, exhausted
freck: active, eager, bold
grummle: to make muddy
lachter: a tuft of grass (also a lock of hair)
lyart: (of hair) streaked with white
madderam: boisterous fun, wild pranks, hilarity
mizzles: disappears, melts away
moonbroch: a halo round the moon, believed to be a
   sign of an approaching storm
taivert: muddled, bewildered

ISO 9001:2000 for Small Businesses

To Lalita with love